BURNING
DOWN
GEORGE
ORWELL'S
HOUSE

Also by Andrew Ervin
Extraordinary Renditions

BURNING DOWN GEORGE ORWELL'S HOUSE

ANDREW ERVIN

SOHO

Excerpt from *The Collected Essays, Journalism and Letters of George Orwell, Volume I: An Age Like This, 1920–1940*. Copyright © 1968 by Sonia Brownell Orwell and renewed 1996 by Mark Hamilton. Reprinted by permission of Houghton Mifflin Harcourt Publishing Company and Penguin Books, 1993. All rights reserved.

Excerpt from *Pack My Bag* by Henry Green. First published by Chatto & Windus and reproduced by permission of The Random House Group Ltd. Copyright © 1940 by The Estate of Henry Yorke. Reprinted by permission of New Directions Publishing Corp. All rights reserved.

Published by
Soho Press, Inc.
853 Broadway
New York, NY 10003

Library of Congress Cataloging-in-Publication Data
Ervin, Andrew.
Burning down George Orwell's house / Andrew Ervin.

ISBN 978-1-61695-494-9
PB ISBN 978-1-61695-652-3
eISBN 978-1-61695-495-6
1. Orwell, George, 1903–1950—Homes and haunts—Scotland—Jura—Fiction.
I. Title.
PS3605.R855B87 2015
2014042466

Interior design by Janine Agro, Soho Press, Inc.

Printed in the United States of America

10 9 8 7 6 5 4 3 2 1

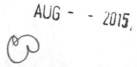

To Elivi

"A shop near here sells mandrakes, but I'm afraid they won't have been procured in the correct manner. Remind me sometime to tell you an interesting thing about werwolves."

—Eric A. Blair, letter to Dennis Collings (1931)

BURNING
DOWN
GEORGE
ORWELL'S
HOUSE

I.

Even standing still, finally, Ray Welter's body remained in motion and subject to inner tidal forces beyond his control. The rain felt more like the idea of wetness than anything resembling drops and it made its way inside his coat and new boots. Everything ached. He struggled to recall with any certainty what the word *dry* referred to. The rain fell upward. He wanted to cry.

The journey had been a thirty-six-hour nightmare spent suffocating in an airplane seat, riding in a bus on the wrong side of the road, sailing, and hitchhiking—and he still had to wait for what looked like a five-minute ride over to the Isle of Jura. A talkative, red-faced woman had dropped him off at the ferry terminal. "You might as well give me that fancy wristwatch of yours," she had said. "You certainly won't be needing it out here." At least that was what he thought she said. The accent would take some getting used to. "And you just wait till you get ahold of these paps."

Ray could discern two of Jura's three mountains through the fog and rain and from the eastern side of Islay, the Paps of Jura looked exactly like a woman's breasts. There was no mistaking it. The entire island resembled a naked girl lying on her back.

He stood at the very precipice of the wired world. The air tasted fresher than anything he had ever sucked into his Chicago-polluted lungs. His pores worked to rid themselves of the poisons of his previous life and he shivered from the sweaty underclothes, yet some source of heat rose to his face. Across the sound, a ferryman attended to his duties on the deck of a blue-green boat big enough to tote maybe a dozen cars. Jura was *so* close. Overheated and shivering at the same time, Ray now understood why that island was among the least populated of Scotland's Inner Hebrides. No direct, public connection existed from the mainland. He carried with him only an elaborate backpack and a suitcase that contained the sum of his worldly possessions.

He wandered along the waterfront and awaited the next-to-last leg of the journey. One of Islay's six whisky distilleries loomed over the ferry port, but he couldn't discern the presence inside of bodies or spirits. It looked deserted, without as much as a gift shop where he could buy a carryout bottle. A sip of scotch would have tasted so fucking perfect. Over on the inert boat, the ferryman moved slowly and without demonstrable purpose or motivation, oblivious to the weather.

A row of squat houses boasted the greenest lawns on the

gods' green earth. Swing sets and seesaws of molded plastic punctuated the grass with happy colors. All of Scotland was green, even greener than the springtime prairie back home. Back at his former home. Out here, Ray discovered a new shade of green. Not quite celadon or vert or even snotgreen, it was the color to which he would forever compare every other green. He already thought of it as Jura green. The acrid smell of burning peat from the chimneys taunted him with the promise of warmth. The hardened mud substitute they used for heat on the islands gave off a strange scent, almost like wood smoke, but more earthy and bitter.

He sat against the empty whisky casks stacked on the stone embankment. The seat of his jeans was already soaked through. He unpeeled the last of his bananas and found it impossible to believe that he had purchased the bunch just that morning. The fluorescence of the supermarket in Oban and the colors of the brightly packaged goods in endless rows glowed in his memory as if from a distant universe.

Ray dropped the peel into the outer pocket of his pack and took a long drink of mineral water that tasted like sidewalk chalk. A blue van approached, its windows clouded inside, and pulled to a stop a few yards from where he sat. The driver flashed his high beams and in reply the ferryman brought the motor to life. A sad-looking girl emerged from the van. She opened an umbrella and buried her face in a paperback, the title of which he couldn't make out. The vehicle reversed course and retreated toward Bowmore. The rear lights glistened red in the wet pavement and only then, and with some regret, did Ray realize how quiet it had been.

Other than the wind and rain, he hadn't heard a sound. No cars, no airplanes, no loud cell phone conversations. It had never before occurred to him that real silence might be possible. He hadn't even recognized it until it disappeared, the victim of the ferry's mechanical roar ricocheting between those Paps. They really did look like breasts. His mind wasn't right.

Man-made noise was one of many new absences that he hoped would define his stay out here. There would be no more bullshit, no more alienation from his own thought processes. He was now officially in absentia from his previous life and ready to begin a new one. The freedom was daunting, but he was up to it. He had to be.

He stood and the ground rolled beneath him like a choppy, concrete sea. Exhaustion had crept into his thighs and lower back. His throat remained parched from the dry airplane and the miles of hiking. That first whisky was going to taste so goddamn good. The girl hiding inside the hood of her raincoat didn't hear him approach, so when he asked, "What are you reading?" she flinched and her book landed in a puddle.

"Don't fucking do that," she said. It was difficult to get a look at her through the layers of rain gear and wool, but she had round cheeks that accentuated her frown. She might have been fifteen or sixteen. "It's none of your business, is it?" She held the book by the spine and shook the water from its pages, then wiped the cover on her skirt, smearing it with dirt.

"I'm so sorry—I didn't mean to scare you."

"Then perhaps stalking up on people isn't your best plan of action."

"I said I was sorry. I'll be happy to buy you a new copy."

"Where do you plan to do that, then?"

"I don't know. How about in Bowmore?"

She mocked his American accent: "How about you leave me alone?"

"Fine, sure. Sorry."

What a hideous child. The ferry pulled to a stop long enough for Ray to follow her aboard. Up close, the ferryman looked older than time itself. "How was school today?" he yelled over the motor.

"*Great*," she whined.

"I should make you swim home. That'd get you some exercise. You must be our Mr. Welter. Right on time too, I'd say." He pointed to the back of his wrist, but he wasn't wearing a watch.

The girl looked up from her book—it was Freud on the cover—long enough to flash Ray the evil eye.

He gave the ferryman the fare and regretted that he had not brought an obol to pay him with. "Call me Ray," he said and shook the man's hand. No cars or other passengers climbed aboard.

"The name's Singer. We get a lot of people out here looking for Orwell. Sounds like you're serious though."

"I don't know about that. I hope so."

"I understand you're staying at the hotel this evening."

"In Craigshouse?"

"Craighouse. No *s* in there. It's the only hotel we have, so I suppose that would be the one. Let me take care of business here if you're going to make it in time for supper."

The boat coughed black smoke into the mist. The motors surged and the ferry—powered by some combination of crowbars, buzz saws, and garbage can lids—backed away from Islay. The motion mimicked Ray's vertiginous balance and the volume of the engines dislodged some bile from the back of his throat. A slave driver down in the galley kept time with a pair of monkey wrenches he banged on a kettledrum full of rusty screws. The vibration found its way to Ray's backbone. The stink of diesel fuel filled his sinus cavity. He would never be still, or dry, ever again. Only motion existed now.

O Argo!

O Pequod!

O Eilean Dhiura!

The boat moved, and Ray was carried by a series of systemic forces: he paced in circles, port to starboard, starboard to port while the boat defied the sound's pull, itself directed by the moon; gravity held him and the ferry and the captain and the sea fast to the spinning earth, which carried all of them around a sun, the existence of which was now speculative; a rivulet of mineral water curled its way through his digestive tract and into his circulatory and respiratory processes, while the pouring rain sought every millimeter of exposed flesh.

Even with the ferry nearing the shore, or the shore near-ing the ferry, Ray still felt like he might never make it to Jura. Zeno's paradox would take over. He would continue to travel half the distance, and then half of that, and half of that, and . . . The closer he got, the more he felt his body shutting down. Famine, dehydration, and fatigue nipped at his heels. Marsh-mallow-like mucus colonized his chest and bits of it escaped up his throat every time he coughed. The Paps loomed larger. He held on to the railing to maintain what remained of his balance. The motion of the boat felt too familiar now, as did the wind, which reminded him of Chicago. The brat school-girl kept her eyes buried in her wet copy of *Civilization and Its Discontents*.

The ferry stopped and *there* became *here*. He had made it. Singer lowered the plank and Ray stepped foot upon the Isle of Jura.

"I'll be seeing you at the hotel just as soon as I've tightened her down here," the ferryman said. "You've come at a good time."

"Great," Ray told him.

"Great," the girl said, making fun of his American accent again.

"Don't mind her," Singer said. "She's not a bad kid once you get to know her. Too smart for her own good, that's her problem."

The air was rich and clean, but he still had to hoof it several miles. He had received the directions via email: from the ferry port, Jura's only paved road curled around the southern butt of the island and then ran two-thirds of the way up the eastern coastline to Craighouse, which sat in the mouth of a bay and faced the Scottish mainland. The caretaker of the hotel there, Mrs. Campbell, was expecting him. He had a reservation for one night.

After a good night of sleep he would pick some supplies up at the Jura Stores, which was owned by the same couple who would serve as his landlords for the next six months. Then he would hitchhike twenty-five miles up toward the northern tip to Barnhill, the estate where George Orwell wrote *Nineteen Eighty-Four*. That was where Ray would begin his new life. It was still difficult to believe.

Before donating his laptop to a Buddhist temple on the North Side, he had searched online for rental properties on Jura, but never imagined that Orwell's very own house would be available. The rental agent he reached in Glasgow said he was very lucky that he phoned when he did. Just that morning a young couple from London had made serious inquiries about buying the property or perhaps renting it as a summer cottage. Barnhill was fully furnished, she had said, and would comfortably sleep eight. The rental had cost him every last dollar that remained in his own name, but getting off the grid for half a year would be worth any expense and hassle from Helen and her junta of divorce attorneys, even with the knowledge that when the lease expired he would be flat broke and have no place to live.

The girl pushed past Ray and climbed into the cab of an old flatbed truck. Bagpipe music blared from the radio and he couldn't figure out if the effect was meant to be ironic. The driver leaned toward the passenger-side door and rolled down the window. He had a perfectly round head with a bulbous nose and slack double chin, his hair buzzed down to a military-style flattop. "You Welter?" he yelled.

"Yeah?"

"Then get the fuck in here."

His legs would not have made it to Craighouse. "Great, I'd love a ride, thank you. I'm going to—"

"To the hotel, aye."

"Look what he did to my book," the girl said.

"You don't need to be reading that shite anyway. You may have noticed that it's raining, Chappie, so would you please get the fuck in here?"

The girl squeezed over so Ray could climb inside. The bagpipes might have been used for interrogational purposes. "Ray Welter," he said, holding out his hand. The cab smelled of rancid meat and whisky—*exceptional* whisky.

The man wiped his fingers on his oily pants before shaking his hand. "I can see you met my Molly."

"Charming girl."

"She's a little bitch. Aren't you, Molly? Smartest person on Jura is why. Or she was before *you* graced us with your presence." He laughed until spittle landed on the inside of the windshield. "Hey close the fucking door, Chappie."

"And your name is?"

"You can call me Mr. Pitcairn."

"It sounds like the whole island was expecting me, Mr. Pitcairn."

"The whole island? Who do you think you are, the king? Did you think we're one big happy family? That we were going to throw you a parade?"

"Dysfunctional family is more like it," Molly said.

"Dysfunctional, eh. How do you like that? That's my Molly for you. Do you think maybe I could be the famous advertising executive and you could drive my truck?"

"How do you know about that?"

Pitcairn made typing motions with his fingers. "We have the Internet here too, you know."

"I'm far from famous, in fact," Ray said, "but I'll give the proposal some thought."

"I'll give the proposal some thought," Pitcairn said, making fun of his American accent just like his daughter had done.

He couldn't believe that this guy had looked him up online. It felt so . . . *intrusive*. One night in Craighouse, then he would be on his own and free—free from all the bullshit and hassle, from the meaningless social rituals and phony smiles, from the technological gadgets that had ruined his attention span and fucked up his very thinking.

"Okay, I've thought about it," he said. "No way in hell."

Pitcairn stepped on the accelerator. Ray rubbed his elbow on the window in order to see out, but that was a mistake.

The narrow road adhered to the coastline and snaked its way between a series of cliffs and the shoreline. The slightest skid on the wet pavement would send them hurtling into the icy water. Pitcairn fumbled with a pack of cigarettes and took every treacherous bend at full speed. Ray bounced in his seat. The tires squealed with each blind turn.

They crossed a small bridge, and the road bent away from Islay and up a hill. Jura appeared to be little more than a collection of craggy mountains protruding from the sea. The shade of green was something else. The terrain was covered in patchy grass and weeds and exposed stone surfaces. Innumerous valleys housed depthless lakes. Blue-white boulders had been strewn everywhere and organized by forces beyond human understanding. The island looked desolate and windswept and raw—in other words, ideal.

The road—now too narrow for more than one car—climbed to a peak but the mist made it difficult to get much of a view.

"There's a standing stone coming up," Molly said. "One of the best preserved examples in the Inner Hebrides."

"If you can fight past the fucking tourists to get at it."

"You can't miss it from the road, and we only get a couple of hundred fucking tourists a year."

"Aye, and it's a couple of hundred too many! Mind your fucking mouth."

They drove through an area of farmland and past a few old houses, then ascended to another bend in the road, which

Pitcairn again took at full speed. Ray had read about the enormity of the island's sheep population, but the statistics did little justice to the reality. They were everywhere. Jura belonged to the sheep, not to the humans.

The road curled to the left to put them parallel with Jura's eastern seaboard. They approached a small forest with a shag carpet of brown and green moss. Clusters of small pines and what appeared to be gnarly beech or birch or something like that sprouted up all over the place. The fog moving in looked like spools of insulation covering the ground as if to protect it from the rain.

Here he was. This was his life now. He could already feel his—

"Look out!" Molly screamed and Pitcairn pressed the brake pedal hard enough to send the truck sliding to a halt. The left side of Ray's head banged into the dashboard. A family of deer scampered off unawares toward the shore.

"Fucking red deer," Pitcairn said. "We need to do something about them."

"They were here before we were," Molly said.

"They're a fucking menace all the same is what they are."

Pitcairn stepped on the gas again. An ugly warehouse provided the first indication that they were approaching Craighouse. The truck gained more speed down the steep hill leading to the town—but perhaps the word *town* was too generous. Craighouse appeared to be a tranquil little village overlooking the sea and dedicated to the fine art of making single-malt scotch. The hills and open water made the huge distillery buildings and the hotel look like parts of a fortress built at the edge of paradise to keep the unwashed heathens at bay.

Ray was still rubbing the pain from his face when Pitcairn jerked the truck to a stop in the gravel parking lot of the Jura Hotel and switched off the ignition to euthanize the bagpiper. The hotel resembled a small palace surrounded by—of all things—palm trees. He could not at that moment articulate what he had expected to find on the Isle of Jura, but a restored nineteenth-century mansion and thriving palm trees never appeared within the realm of possibility. The burning peat and salty air soothed Ray's frazzled, travel-achy bones. The distillery stood directly across the street. He could almost taste it.

"Here you are, Chappie. Once you get settled in I'll see you in the lounge for that whisky."

"Sounds good," he said. "What whisky is that?"

"The one you owe me for driving your Yank arse here. What did you think—that I'm some kind of taxi service?"

"Sure," he said. That sounded fair enough and he couldn't wait for a drink. "I'll meet you at the lounge after I check in. Where is it?"

"Where is it? It's in the fucking hotel, where do you think?"

Pitcairn went inside and Molly moped after him. Ray lifted his suitcase off the back of the truck. It had grown heavier throughout the day and fell to the ground with a thud. His face still hurt and he was coming down with a cold, if not something worse. The sun had set and a mean chill settled into the atmosphere, but it felt good somehow. In the corner of the parking lot stood a red telephone booth and next to it was a port-a-potty painted to look like a second telephone booth.

Six or seven pairs of tall rubber wellingtons, all coated in mud, stood sentry on the porch. Ray sat on the wooden bench to unlace his own boots, the exorbitant price of which still embarrassed him; they were the kind of boots that millionaires wore on guided package tours of Kilimanjaro or Everest. They had seemed like a good idea at the time. The interior of the hotel wasn't much warmer than the exterior. His socks squeegeed water onto the wooden floor and left a trail to the vacant reception desk. The antique floor lamps did their best to rid the lobby of its dusty gloom. A seating area of overstuffed chairs looked like it had been recently occupied: a teapot and some cups and saucers remained scattered on the side tables and armrests. A whiff of cigarette smoke lingered with the scent of peat burning in an enormous stone fireplace. A chorus of drunken laughter called from deeper inside the hotel.

He tapped his fingers on the counter to draw someone's attention. No luck. He cleared his throat and tapped louder. Somebody had to be on duty—they were expecting him, right? He rang the service bell and a woman emerged from the back room. She might have been sixty years old. Her hair was a hornet's nest held in place with a pulley system of ribbons and ivory chopsticks. She wore multiple layers of long, flapping clothes.

"Welcome to Jura, Mr. Welter," she said. "We trust you had a miserable journey."

"Do I look that tired?"

"Don't let it worry you. It happens to everybody. Your room is ready. We expect that you'll be wanting a bath."

"Actually, yeah, a shower would be right on time."

"We don't have showers, only baths. It'll be straight into the tub with you. There's a kettle in the room. We'll have Mr. Fuller stay on in the kitchen until you're ready. We have venison stew on this evening."

"Stew sounds perfect, but I think I'd like to have a bite first. I'm starving."

"It might be best if you were to get into the bath straight away. Yours is room number eleven. First floor, top of the stairs. On your left. We'll have Mr. Fuller stay on in the kitchen until you're ready."

"Don't I need a key?"

Behind the reception desk, twenty room keys hung suspended from a series of iron nails.

"Oh no," she said, not at all amused. "We don't lock our doors on Jura."

Ray lugged his suitcase up the creaky stairs. The drunken laughter resumed in the lounge.

The austerity of his room came as a welcome surprise. There were no potpourri baskets or reproductions of impressionist gardens. It was a plain, square room with some wooden furniture pushed against the white walls. The chair moaned under his weight. He was scared to look at his feet; the longer he could ignore the blisters the better. Mrs. Campbell had turned up the heat high enough to roast a duck on the iron radiator, which chimed and hissed. He filled the electric kettle in the bathroom even though he despised the entire concept of dunking a bag of weeds into a mug and drinking it, but he was in Scotland now.

A contraption of pipes connected the bathtub's brass faucet to the bathroom wall. The showerhead was attached to a flexible tube and it sat cradled atop the spout like an old-fashioned telephone receiver. He made the mistake of looking at himself in the mirror while the tub filled and his entire life came crashing down. His face attested to the crushing weight of the past few weeks, months, years. The already tenuous grasp on his well-being grew even looser. Tears he couldn't feel covered his face. What he needed was so goddamn simple: Ray wanted to *know* again, to be able to delineate right and wrong in an un-deconstructed world of certainty. He wanted to feel the security of binary opposition. Good and bad. He needed to get out of the watchful eye of Big Brother. His time at Barnhill would be his last chance to put himself back together. Failing that, there would be little incentive to care about his continued existence on such a rapidly self-destructing planet.

The water rose around him. He scrubbed at himself with a bar of gritty soap until his hunger and the pruning of his extremities chased him from the tub and into the water that now covered the floor of the bathroom. Every step sent ripples skirting along the tiles. He hoped the water wasn't leaking through to the lobby. There was only one small and rough towel, which he used to dry himself and then soak up what little he could from the floor. He wrung it out several times into the tub, which now boasted a ring of filth that if chemically tested would reveal traces of his exact route from Chicago to Craighouse.

He took the quilt from the foot of the bed and used it to blot the remaining moisture from his body. It didn't feel right to dry his bare ass on someone's hand-sewn blanket, but there was no avoiding it. A musty odor escaped from his suitcase. All of Ray's clothes were wet, as were his books. Even if he could eventually get the paperbacks dry they might never be readable again. The only dry thing he owned was, thankfully, his first edition of *Nineteen Eighty-Four*. He had quadruple-wrapped it in plastic.

He hung some clothes over the radiator and despite his hunger felt an overwhelming desire to sleep, if only for a minute, but they were waiting for him downstairs. He pulled a damp T-shirt over his grumbling belly. The clammy boxer shorts made his entire body shiver all over again. He climbed back inside his new sweater, some tube socks, and a pair of not-entirely-soaked blue jeans. The clothes felt eel-like against his skin.

The hollering and cigarette stink assaulted Ray before he

got downstairs. Pitcairn was the loudest of the bunch by far: "So I says to him, 'What do I look like? Some kind of taxi service?' For a so-called *genius* he sure is a simple fucker."

"Actually, you *are* a taxi service," someone else said, and that sent the others into convulsions of breathless laughter, which mutated into the kind of coughing made possible by lifelong smoking habits.

"Aye, but he doesn't know that, does he?"

"Here he is now, then," said a man of impossible hairiness. He was the hairiest person Ray had ever seen. It was unreal. Five people occupied the lounge, six including Molly, who sat behind the bar reading. The crinkled book resembled his own paperbacks upstairs. The lounge had another fire that roared but gave off little heat. A pile of peat bricks sat on a browning newspaper next to the hearth and a cirrocumulus cloud of cigarette smoke clung to the ceiling.

"So nice of you to join us, Chappie."

"Hello, gentlemen, I'm Ray."

The hairy man stood up and shook his hand. Everyone else remained seated. "The name's Farkas," he said. "This here's Pete, Sponge, Fuller, and you've met Gavin and Molly Pitcairn."

"Watch out for Farkas, eh?" Pete said. "He bites."

That drew a big laugh.

"And that Pete's a real salt of the earth type."

"We've got some stew on for you," Fuller said. "I hope you're hungry?"

"You have no idea. I'm so hungry I could eat a horse."

"Well I'm afraid the menu's limited to venison this evening, Mr. Welter."

"I suppose that'll work. Now who do I have to talk to in order to get a whisky around here?"

"Salt of the earth? Peat? Get it?"

Dozens of bottles—brands Ray had never heard of—covered the three-tiered counter behind the bar. They twinkled in gold and bronze in the firelight. The sight made him feel a little better about his life.

"You like your malts, do you?" Pete asked.

"Maybe a bit too much."

"What'll it be, then, Chappie?" Pitcairn asked. "A dram of the local?"

"That sounds perfect, in fact."

"You heard the man, Molly. Six of the local."

She put her book down with a sigh and slid from her stool. After pulling the cork from the cello-shaped bottle, she poured six healthy drams of the scotch distilled here in Craighouse. Ray wondered if it would taste different so close to the source. He couldn't wait to find out.

"Should I charge these to your room?" she asked.

"Sure, I'll pick up this round. Room—"

"Room eleven, I know."

Molly distributed the whiskies. The men diluted them with water poured from small pitchers the way some people put milk in their coffee.

"Thank you, Welter, eh?" Pete said. He looked to be about fifty with prematurely wrinkled skin and thinning hair. If Ray didn't know better, he would've thought the man possessed a deep and permanent sunburn.

"Please call me Ray."

"Or Chappie!"

The first sip tasted like the sweet ambrosia of the gods. It came as a revelation, a divine benediction, and it immediately washed away the hunger and exhaustion of his journey. Ray had drunk from the River Lethe. The second swallow tasted even better. The world began to feel stable. The voices around him grew vague and indistinct. Some moments later, Pitcairn's coughing fit shook him from his swoon. "Goddamn that's good," Ray said.

"A man who likes his malt, now there's a good sign, eh?" Pete said. He wore a tracksuit so out of fashion that were it dry cleaned and disinfected it would fetch hundreds of dollars at one of the boutiques back in Ray's old neighborhood.

Two of them—Pitcairn and Fuller—were approximately his age, maybe four or five years older. It was hard to get a good look at Farkas beneath all that hair. Sponge appeared to be in his eighties. He sported a wool jacket and a stained tartan tie and sat silently at the head of the table, content to listen to the others. "What kind of name is Sponge?" Ray asked.

"One word of advice," Fuller said, placing an enormous bowl of stew and a basket of bread in front of him. "Don't take your eye off your whisky for one instant whilst that man is present. Good appetite."

"Thank you. This smells . . . interesting."

When Fuller retook his seat he found that his dram had been drained. Only an empty glass remained. "Oh for fuck's sake, Sponge."

"Please excuse me," Ray said and moved his bowl and the bread to a table next to the fire. He wondered how many fireplaces the hotel possessed. "All my clothes are wet, I'm freezing."

"That stew will warm you right up," Fuller said.

"Not to mention the malt, eh? Best thing for you on an evening such as this."

Upon closer inspection in the firelight, the chunks of animal material—*meat* would've been a generous exaggeration—appeared half cooked at best. The severed white tendons gaped open and one of them winked at him from amid the gristly pool. A blue oil spill floated atop the broth. His hiking boots might have been added to the pot for additional flavor, but Ray had an audience and so he forced himself to lift the spoon to his mouth. The texture resisted his attempts at mastication. He ground every tooth he owned against it, but the chunk of meat would not disintegrate. Fortunately, the eye-watering amount of salt came close to masking the rotten meat flavor. If he wasn't being watched, and if he had possessed a napkin, he would've spat the chunk out. Swallowing the meat proved to be a separate ordeal. The whisky chaser helped. He finished his dram and asked for another, and then another, which Molly brought over, each time complaining the entire way. The men watched him with obvious amusement. He hoped they didn't see how repulsed he felt.

"Not bad, is it?" Fuller wanted to know.

"No—not *bad*. But I'm stuffed."

"I bet you are," Pitcairn said and the other men laughed.

He tried to soak up some of the salt and gasoline in his gut with a slice of bread, but it was so stale that he thought it might be toasted. He snapped off a piece, dipped it in the broth, and tried not to wince when he put it in his mouth. "Well, that was great," Ray said. He pushed the bowl away from his body. "But I need to get some sleep, gentlemen."

"How about one more wee dram?"

His mouth filled with rancid saliva, which he forced back down his gullet with an audible gulp. "Next time. It's been a long day."

"Aye, you must be exhausted," Farkas said. His hairiness was remarkable. His eyes blinked from within a forest of bristly beard and eyebrow.

"One word of advice," Fuller said. "However hot Mrs. Campbell has your room, keep your windows closed tonight. The birds down at the beach make a terrible racket in the morning."

"Not to mention the festivities this evening," Molly said.

The adults shot her nasty looks.

"Festivities?" Ray asked.

"It's nothing," Pitcairn told him. "Some old Jura superstition. That's all it is."

"That's all it is, eh?" Pete said.

Any other night, Ray might have pressed the issue.

"Tonight's the equinox," Molly said. "Not that you seem like the kind of guy who'd enjoy watching fat men dance naked around a fire and shoot off guns."

"Dance around a fire?"

"Naked men?" Fuller asked.

"Where *do* you get these ideas, eh? Where does she get these ideas, Pitcairn?"

"It's that fucking school over there putting ideas in her head."

"Fuckin' Islay," Sponge said: the first words he had spoken all evening.

Ray stood and tried to put as much distance between himself and that stew as possible, but he felt drunker than he had realized and had to grip the table for support. The men chuckled at his clumsiness. Molly rolled her eyes in embarrassment.

"Not much of a drinker, are you, Chappie?"

"I do all right. It's just been a long day. Enjoy your nude fire dance or whatever it is you have planned."

"Just a little expedition, that's all, eh?"

"Thanks for the dram," Farkas said. He was by far the friendliest of the bunch.

"What time will you be needing a ride up to Barnhill, then?" Pitcairn asked.

"A ride?"

"It's over twenty miles, isn't it? And there are your supplies from The Stores. What are you going to do, carry them on your back?"

"I—"

The other men were laughing at him now.

"I'll come pick you up after breakfast, how does that sound?"

"Nine o'clock?"

"Six o'clock, seven o'clock, eight o'clock. I don't know. Jesus. After breakfast."

"One word of advice," Fuller said, "you won't be needing your watch any longer, not here."

"Not unless you're hoping to catch old Singer down at the ferry," Farkas said.

"Fuckin' Islay," Sponge said.

"Where is Singer? That codger said he'd be here."

"Doing some preparations, I imagine, eh?"

"Trying to shoot a nonexistent animal, I imagine," Molly said.

Pitcairn slapped the table with both palms. "Would you kindly shut the fuck up, girlie?" he yelled.

"Be a good girl now," Farkas said.

"Okay, I'll see you after breakfast," Ray said. He needed to lie down. "Good night."

"Good night," Farkas said.

Pitcairn's angry whispers followed him to the lobby and

up the stairs. Ray stopped at the landing to eavesdrop but couldn't make out what the men were saying. He was curious about what they had planned but felt way too exhausted to care.

Then it hit him. He raced his legs back up the stairs, pushed through the unlocked door, and tore off his damp pants just in time to relieve his bowels of that stew. It poured out of him in torrents. He expelled what felt like a lifetime's accumulation of poison, then crawled naked under the damp quilt and closed his eyes. Sleep—that was all he required now. Eight uninterrupted, unmoving hours.

They did not arrive.

Sleep and Ray Welter had never learned to play well together. Every night, as long as he could remember, he had always looked forward to morning. He hoped things would be different here, where he wouldn't need to wake up at any certain time to get to a job he hated. He no longer had to do anything. Yet he remained awake for hours with his eyes propped open by excitement, alcohol, jet lag, anxiety.

The hands of the bedside clock didn't budge and Ray realized that the batteries had gone dead or the cord had come unplugged. The bed grew less comfortable by the minute. Hard lumps in the mattress familiarized themselves with the tenderest parts of his back. He heard noises—not necessarily in the room, but not necessarily outside either. Then there was some commotion down in the parking lot. Car doors slamming. Something that sounded like a gunshot followed by a lot of laughter. There might have been a party going on. The noise got to be too much. He threw the covers off and crept to the window. It looked as if the entire population of the island had gathered. They formed a rowdy convoy of rusted trucks with squeaky axles and drove off into the night. Ray put a pillow over his head.

After another hour, or maybe two or three, he threw the blanket off and got up. The noise outside had stopped. He found the driest of his clothes and slipped down the stairs, which creaked enough to wake the other hotel guests, if there were any.

A voice asked from the lounge, "Is that you, Ray?"

It took a moment to discern the hirsute shape sitting next to the dying fire. Spilt or drooled whisky glimmered in Farkas's beard. Only a few small embers remained in the fireplace.

"What are you doing up?"

"Oh just enjoying a wee dram. Pour yourself one."

Ray went to the bar and grabbed the first bottle within reach. It opened with a corky pop. He picked up two glasses that smelled mostly clean.

"Just a wee bit for me. Do you see that slip of paper that says 'Wolfman' on it?"

"Not really."

"That's my tab. Put two tick marks on it."

"Is that your nickname?"

"Gavin's idea of a joke," he said, "not that I find it all that humorous. You might have noticed that he's what you might call unhinged, especially when it comes to outsiders. I'll ask you to stay on his good side, if you can find it."

"That's good to know—I'll stay out of his way."

"Aye, please do. I once watched him pummel a tourist senseless in the hotel parking lot for no reason anyone could see. They had to airlift the poor sod to a hospital." Ray took the chair next to Farkas's and handed him the glass, which he held to his nose. "A bit of the cask strength, then? A good choice."

"Cask strength?"

"Not watered down, like we do. This is the pure thing Slàinte."

"Is that Gaelic?"

"Aye. 'To your health.'"

"Slàinte."

The whisky was stronger than anything Ray had ever tasted. It felt like molten lead in his windpipe. The pain felt great

"I don't mean to pry," Farkas said, "but I would be remiss if I didn't ask what you're doing here. You're obviously a clever man—we've all read about your advertising awards."

"Thanks," Ray said, but heard more sarcasm in his voice than he might have preferred. "It's hard to explain. I knew I needed to get out of Chicago. I considered Nova Scotia, but that didn't feel authentic or something. I'm kind of obsessed with George Orwell, so I decided I wanted to see—I *needed* to see—where he wrote *Nineteen Eighty-Four*."

"I can respect that, I suppose. But most sensible people

might have come for a short holiday, a couple of days at most, but six months?"

"For starters. Maybe I'll stay longer. Who knows?"

"Who knows? 'Nobody knows,'" Farkas sang. "'No-body knows.' Cheers, Ray."

"Cheers, Farkas."

"So how do you find the local malt?" Farkas asked.

"Delicious. I drink quite a bit of it back in Chicago. I *drank* quite a bit, I should say."

"And you know that we keep the best of it for ourselves, don't you?"

"That would make sense."

"Sense, aye—that's precisely what it makes! We make scents at the distillery. You'll have to let me show you around one day."

"You work at the distillery? I'd love to see it," Ray said, and meant it. "I'm going to pour one more of these and call it a day."

"Jet lag is it?"

"Among other things. One more for you too?"

"I wouldn't say no."

Ray poured two more drams and with his eyes now fully adjusted to the low light was able to find his own tab. It said "Chappie" at the top and had more tick marks on it than he could count.

"Cheers, Farkas."

"Cheers, Ray. Down the hatch!"

Farkas drank the entire glass in one long gulp and against his better judgment Ray did the same.

"Okay, I'm going to get some sleep. Or try to."

"You're in the right part of the world for counting sheep, I'll tell you that much. And if I don't see you at breakfast I'll pop up to Barnhill one of these days to say hello."

"I'd like that."

Farkas pulled on his coat. "Now let me see what kind of havoc those boys have wrought this time. Good night, Ray."

"Good night, Farkas."

Back in bed, if sleep ever arrived Ray didn't recognize it as such. Rain pounded against the glass. He stayed under the covers, more than a little drunk, eventually watching the hazy morning light creep across the ceiling to signal the start of his first day on Jura.

THE BANGING AT THE door came as a relief. Ray leapt from bed fully naked and, he soon realized, with his penis more or less erect. He bent over for his pants just as Molly stuck her face into the room. She screamed, and then she laughed. He tried to cover himself, but with one foot wedged halfway into a pant leg he fell over and landed on his sore back. His dick stood up like a half-inflated balloon animal. Molly didn't move or even avert her eyes. "Up and at 'em, Mr. Welter," she said. "So to speak."

It wasn't funny. "Would you please close the door?" he asked.

Molly did just that, though with herself inside the room. She delighted in his embarrassment. Her smile made her look like a different person.

"What are you doing? Turn around!"

"You act like I've never seen a naked man before," she said.

He pulled his pants up under the blanket. They were still wet. "*Have* you?"

"Well . . . no. But you didn't know that!"

He buttoned his jeans. "What do you want?"

"Mrs. Campbell told me to knock you up and fetch you for breakfast."

"Breakfast? What time is it?"

"It's nearly half past six. I can't help it if you're going to sleep all day. What's it going to be?"

"What's what going to be?"

"*Breakfast.* Jesus."

He needed to urinate.

"What do you have?"

"Eggs, bacon, potatoes—"

"That sounds perfect." He would've agreed to anything at that moment so long as it meant getting rid of her. "Now, if you'll please excuse me, I really need to—"

"The full Scottish then?"

"Great, I'll be right down, I promise."

"I'm supposed to wait for you."

"Wait for me?"

"That's what Mrs. Campbell said. 'Wait for him.'"

He pushed past Molly to get to the bathroom, where, without closing the door or lifting the seat, he found just enough time to get his dick out again before unleashing a flash flood. She watched him from the doorway without any sense of shame. "That's it—take your sweet time," she said. "It's not like I have a ferry to catch."

There was no rushing him. He stood there for what felt like ten minutes, until the muscles in his shoulders slackened. He washed his hands and tried to dry them with the damp towel. Deep black lines had formed beneath his eyes. Soreness had taken charge of every muscle.

Molly sat next to him on the end of the bed while he pulled on a pair of socks. "Do you have school today or something?" he asked.

She rolled her eyes. "I've finished every class the school offers. Now I tutor some of the other kids, if you must know. Hurry up."

She marched him down the steps like a prison guard escorting him to his execution. The lounge was empty except for Pitcairn, who sat next to the fireplace slurping at his tea. "You up at last, Chappie?"

"No."

Pitcairn looked like a man who slept even less than Ray did, someone beset on all sides by trouble. Some of it by his own design, to be sure. Given what Farkas had said about Pitcairn's temper, Ray really hoped that Molly wouldn't tell him what had transpired upstairs, that she had been sexually harassed—however inadvertently—by a hungover American.

"He wants the full Scottish," she yelled into the swinging kitchen doors. "How do you take your tea?" she asked.

"Do you have any coffee?"

Pitcairn snorted into his newspaper. "You won't like the coffee," he said.

"Why's that?"

"Because you're a fucking Yank," he said. "Because you come here and you expect everything to be precisely like you have it back home. Only you're not back home, are you? So why do you bother traveling in the first place? Save us both the trouble."

"Actually, Jura is my home now," he said. "I don't have any place else to go, so you're just going to have to deal with having me around."

"You listen to me, Chappie. There's no dealing with seeing our ancestral land taken over by foreigners, do you hear? Making too much noise and disrupting the natural order of things. Nobody invited you here—you remember that!"

"That's enough, Gavin," Fuller said. He stood in the kitchen's doorway and brandished an iron skillet. He had a rag wrapped around the handle, like it was hot from the oven.

"Enough fucking foreigners, I say."

"Get used to it," Ray told him. Not exactly his wittiest retort of all time, but he didn't know what else to say.

"I won't be getting used to any such thing," Pitcairn said.

"Any coffee you have will be great," Ray told Molly.

"Coming right up," Fuller said. "One word of advice: don't let Gavin bother you. He's a little bit of an arsehole to everybody at first."

"Later he becomes a complete arsehole," Molly said.

"Mind your language, Molly," Fuller said, and retreated to the kitchen.

"Aye, mind your fucking language, girlie," Pitcairn said, and returned to his newspaper.

Molly went into the kitchen and returned with a cup of lukewarm tar into which someone had spooned four packets of artificial sugar. Ray did everything in his power to swallow a sip. Determined to enjoy every drop, he steeled himself, but the second taste brought the previous night's nausea out for an encore. "You know something?" he asked Pitcairn.

"What's that?"

"You were right—I don't like the coffee. In fact, it tastes like shit."

Molly, who was busy packing her school bag, released a laugh.

"I told you so, Chappie," Pitcairn said. "But in all fairness, there's not a man, woman, or child who can finish an entire cup of Fuller's coffee. In the future, however, I would appreciate it if you'd watch your language around my Molly."

"How old are you anyway, Molly?"

"Almost eighteen, why?"

He had exposed himself to a seventeen-year-old.

"Seventeen and sharp as a whip," Pitcairn said. "She's got her mother's brains, God bless her."

"She's got your looks though," Fuller said, "the poor thing. Full Scottish breakfast, Mr. Welter." He placed an enormous plate of food in front of Ray, along with a cup of tea.

"Thank you. But please call me Ray. There's absolutely no reason to—what the hell is *that*?" On his plate sat a possum that had puked up its own guts.

"That," Pitcairn said, standing up, "is haggis. You ask for the full Scottish, that's what you get. Come on, girlie. Old Singer doesn't like to wait, you know that."

Ray had thought of haggis—the heart, lungs, and liver of a sheep cooked inside its own stomach—as a national myth, like the Loch Ness monster or the tradition of not wearing underwear beneath a kilt. He waited for Pitcairn and Molly to leave, picked at his food, then pushed the plate away and headed back to his room to catch a few more hours of sleep. Mrs. Campbell caught him before he got to the stairs. She wore the same assortment of black dresses she had on yesterday.

"I suppose you'll be checking out, then, Mr. Welter?" she asked.

"Checking out? Already?"

"They're expecting you over at The Stores and Mr. Pitcairn is to meet you there after he's dropped Molly at the ferry."

"Now?"

"After he's dropped Molly at the ferry. Have you packed your things?"

"I was still hoping to take a shower—a bath, I mean."

"At this time of the day? You took one last night if we're not mistaken. We hear everything that goes on in this hotel." If not on the entire island. "Now you collect your things and don't worry yourself over that mess on the floor. We'll tally up your bill. It looks like you had yourself quite a bit of whisky last night."

Ray had forgotten about all the tick marks added to his bar tab after he went to bed the first time, but he wasn't prepared to argue with her about that. He would get Pitcairn and the rest of those deadbeats to pay him back another time. What on earth had happened to the world-famous Highlands hospitality? "I'll pack my bag and be right down, Mrs. Campbell," he said.

Ray folded his damp clothes back into the suitcase and resigned himself to spending his first two weeks at Barnhill catching up on lost sleep. The jet lag had hit harder than he thought possible. Maybe that's all it was—the constant shaking, the nausea—maybe it was all just the stress of travelling. Mrs. Campbell stood waiting for him behind the reception desk. No evidence suggested the presence of other guests. "We trust you had a pleasant stay, Mr. Welter," she said.

He didn't know how to respond. He had only just arrived and she was expelling him into the cold and rainy morning. Ray did what anyone would do in his position: he lied. "Great, thank you. The room was very comfortable."

"We are glad to hear it. That's one night, plus supper and

breakfast and your lounge bill. One hundred sixty pounds, fifty pence please." She slid a slip of paper across the dusty counter.

Given the state of the US dollar, the bill came to something like two hundred and fifty dollars for a bed and two meals he didn't eat. The homeless people back in Chicago were accustomed to better cuisine. "A hundred and sixty pounds?" he asked.

"And fifty pence, please. It looks to us like you had yourself quite a bit of whisky last night," she said again. "Perhaps that's why you look so peaky this morning."

That was when he snapped.

"I looked peaked because I didn't get any goddamn sleep. That . . . that so-called stew kept me up half the night on the shitter. I didn't even drink that whisky. Okay, maybe four or five of them, but Pitcairn and Pete and Sponge, or whatever his name is, they put them on my tab after I went to bed."

"Mr. Welter!" she said. "We are appalled. We are terribly sorry if our food does not conform to your standards, but we will not stand here and listen to your abusive language. Perhaps that's appropriate in your America, but not here and certainly not in our hotel. As for the bill, if you are so distraught by our service we will tear it up."

And she did. She snatched the paper from the counter and tore it into tiny pieces, which she placed into the pocket of her outermost dress.

"Good day, Mr. Welter," she said and turned to fiddle with the unused keys hanging behind the counter.

"I'm terribly sorry, Mrs. Campbell," Ray said. "I was out of line." She faced him, and he struggled to come up with something to say, some way to explain his outburst, but nothing came to mind. "It's the jet lag. I . . . I . . . no, that's not it. I have no excuse. Take the money and please forgive me. I'm so sorry." Without counting the wad of pound notes, nor returning his change, she slipped them into the same dress pocket. "I haven't slept in days, but it's more than that." He could hear the rain tapping against the windows, the sizzle of peat bricks in the fireplace. "I can't even think straight anymore. I've quit my job. My wife is divorcing me."

"Little wonder too," Mrs. Campbell said. "Given your attitude."

"The tragic part is that I know you're right. My attitude *is* the problem. That's why I'm here. Now the only thing I have left in the world is a rented house I can't totally afford. This island is my final hope. If I don't get myself together I don't know what I'm going to do, and I'm already in the process of sabotaging my stay here too. I'm terribly sorry, Mrs. Campbell. You have a beautiful hotel."

"There, there, Mr. Welter," she said. He didn't know which of them was more embarrassed. "Let's not worry. These misunderstandings happen. We'll see if Mr. Fuller has some tea on. A spot of tea—that's all you need. You just sit next to the

fire and we'll be right back. We'll forget all about this non-
sense, what do you say?"

"Thank you, Mrs. Campbell. I'm so sorry."

"Not at all. You take a seat and try to dry those wet clothes.
You'll catch your death on Jura dressed like that."

For one of the few times in his life, Ray did what he was
told. The leather chair felt like an enormous, broken-in base-
ball mitt. Mrs. Campbell hadn't deserved that kind of abuse.
He had made the worst possible first impression and now
word would spread across the island about what an asshole
that Ray Welter was. He vowed to make himself inconspicu-
ous. He would blend into the scenery, go native. "Fuck are
you doing, Chappie?" Pitcairn demanded and Ray snapped
awake. "Sitting on your arse?"

"I'm not feeling so good. Mrs. Campbell went to—"

"Oh, I'm not feeling so good. Is that a reason to keep me
waiting outside? I got better things to do than look after the
likes of you. Get your twee little boots on. They're expecting
you over at The Stores. I'm in a fucking hurry."

"Just one minute. I'll tell Mrs. Campbell I'm leaving."

"You haven't even paid your bill yet?"

"In fact, I meant to speak to you about that bar tab."

"Oh, right. That was just a bit of fun, Chappie. An initia-
tion, if you please. Welcome to Jura and all that. Come on
now, let's go. I have a suspicion that Mrs. Campbell will realize you've left when she comes out here and sees that you're
gone. She's sharp that way."

"She's making me some tea."

"Well why didn't you say so? I could do with a cup myself. Didn't get much sleep last night."

"Did Mrs. Pitcairn have you up late?"

Pitcairn seemed like the kind of man who would appreciate some lascivious humor.

"I was out on the hunt all bloody night. Besides, I'll have you know that Mrs. Pitcairn is dead."

"I'm sorry," Ray said for the twentieth time that day.

Pitcairn tracked mud across the lobby and took the chair next to Ray's. "Here she is now."

Mrs. Campbell had reappeared from the kitchen carrying a wooden tray on which she balanced a large teapot, milk, sugar, and two dainty, ceramic mugs. "We weren't expecting you, Mr. Pitcairn. We'll fetch another cup."

"*He* was expecting me," Pitcairn said, tilting his head in Ray's direction. "You sit down, Mrs. Campbell. I got feet on my legs same as you." Pitcairn stood with an exaggerated groan and went into the lounge.

She put the tray on a side table and sat on a footstool, sweeping her dresses beneath herself. "We'll have you clean up this mud," she called after Pitcairn.

"Mrs. Campbell," Ray said. "I'd like to apologize again. I feel terrible."

"We won't hear another word of it. How do you take your tea?"

"Milk and sugar, please."

She poured two cups. "This will chase away the chill from your bones," she said.

"Thank you. About that bar tab—"

"Uh oh," Pitcairn said, sitting down. Mrs. Campbell filled his cup.

"What did you do, Mr. Pitcairn?"

"We were just having a little fun at Chappie's expense."

"Quite literally, as it turns out."

"You did no such thing," Mrs. Campbell said. "Were those your beverages on Mr. Welter's bill?"

"I'd prefer not to think about whisky at this moment," Pitcairn said, holding his head.

"You didn't drink that whisky at all, did you, Mr. Welter?"

"Well, I had a few drams," he admitted.

"My head!"

"A few drams?"

"Five or six."

"Can we discuss this later?" Pitcairn pleaded, slurping at his tea.

"Five or six? Why you're as bad as the rest of those boys!"

"Could we *please*—"

"Yet I believe I paid for upwards of twenty. Didn't I?"

"—talk about something else? Anything."

"Mr. Pitcairn! We are appalled that you—"

"We were just having a bit of fun with ole Chappie, weren't we? I'll make it up to you. It all comes out in the wash. Besides, you owe me for driving your arse up and down the island."

"Let's just forget about it," Ray said, "and move on with our lives."

"You hear that, Mrs. Campbell? We're to move on with our lives. Believe me, I'd love to." He slurped at his tea some more. "Drink up and we'll get you over to The Stores. Mrs. Bennett's already got your things packed up."

"What things?"

"The supplies you'll be needing at Barnhill. There isn't exactly a convenience store up there. Is there, Mrs. Campbell?"

"No, there very well is not."

"Now hurry the fuck up, Chappie—excuse me, Mrs. Campbell. She doesn't care for that kind of language."

"We'll expect you back to clean up this mud," Mrs. Campbell said.

Ray gulped down his tea and closed his eyes for a moment. The fire radiated orange and red through his eyelids and he began to drift into the weight of the seat cushions. "Now hurry the fuck up," Pitcairn said. "Let's get you out of here."

HIS LAST STOP BEFORE going to Barnhill involved a tactical, tail-between-his-legs retreat to the role of passive consumer. According to the website of the Jura Stores, the proprietors had arrived from the mainland a decade earlier to sell organic vegetables, fairly traded and shade-grown coffee, and free-range meat no doubt slaughtered with the utmost humanity and compassion. All at obscene prices.

The Bennetts struck Ray as that breed of idealistic entrepreneurs eager to make their fortune in some environmentally or spiritually sound way, perhaps even according to some sad misunderstanding of *sammā ājīva*, but were greedy as any slumlords.

Mrs. Bennett had a long face and a toothy, equine smile that caused her to whistle as she spoke. It threw Ray off at first. He thought she was summoning an animal, but she said, "You'll be wanting a pair of wellieth, I take it?"

"That won't be necessary. In fact, I just bought these boots."

Her husband was nowhere to be seen, but the distorted noise of a radio came from another room. Pitcairn, having already exhausted the harmonic range of his truck's horn hurrying Ray along, now stood in the doorway smoking a cigarette. "I told him his boots were for shite," he said.

"These are some of the best boots money can buy," Ray said. He planned to do a ton of hiking. "I'm sure they'll be great."

"Just hurry the fuck up, would you? I have places I need to be."

"No you don't," Mrs. Bennett said.

"Maybe I don't, but that doesn't mean I want to be standing around here all day waiting for the likes of him to buy his brie and sweeties. Those American shite kickers won't help you on Jura, Chappie."

"I'm afraid he'th right, Mr. Welter. The mud really ith extraordinary here. I do recommend thome wellieth."

"They're French I'll have you know, not American," Ray said. He heard himself playing along with Pitcairn's games.

"I do hope you've brought a thatellite phone in cathe of an emergenthy."

"No, I didn't. That would've been smart."

"If you do encounter a problem, there'th a thettlement up the road from Barnhill. Thomeone there can help you, I'm thure."

"Aye, Chappie, go see Mr. Harris. He's the real friendly sort and loves company."

"Don't lithen to him, Mr. Welter. Mr. Harrith preferth to keep to himthelf, but Mith Wayward ith quite charming."

"That old witch? Stay well clear of her. I'm sure he'll be fine, Mrs. Bennett. Won't you, Chappie? Now hurry the fuck up."

Hundreds of pounds' worth of food and supplies formed a pyramid in the front of the shop. He went over the countless mental lists, yet knew he was forgetting something. He was always forgetting something. He bought a mixed case of scotch—different ages and strengths—and made arrangements for the distillery to deliver a fresh supply on the first day of every month. His plan was to read Orwell and drink himself silly.

Pitcairn watched from the doorway while Ray carried all the boxes to the truck. The rain fell harder than it had the day before; everything got wet before he could get it onto the flatbed.

"Thank you, Mrs. Bennett."

"Tho long, Mr. Welter."

Pitcairn climbed into the cab and started the engine, which made a horrible grinding noise that the devastating volume of the bagpipe cassette couldn't overpower. Exhaust formed a cloud over Ray's head. He already detested this man in a way he had never detested anyone before, except for maybe that fat piece of shit Walter Pentode. As with Pentode, however, he recognized the need to keep relations cordial, which was to say phony. He climbed into the passenger seat and the truck lunged into gear. "Truck's not sounding so hot," he said.

"And what do you know about it, Chappie? I suppose you include auto mechanic among your infinite talents?"

"I don't know a thing about cars, but I do know that your truck sounds like it's on the brink of death."

"I don't see how it's any concern of yours."

"Only until you get me to Barnhill."

"Only until you get me to Barnhill. I'll get you to your precious Barnhill, Chappie, don't you worry. I want you as far away as possible."

Driving on the wrong side of the road didn't bother Ray this time because there was only one lane. If someone came from the other direction he would have to pull to the shoulder to let Pitcairn pass. It was tough to see much of the scenery through the mist. In his exhaustion, it felt like driving through the world's longest car wash. The road followed the coastline north, over stony hills and glens, through small thickets of dense forest and across bog lands and rickety bridges. The road doglegged through the Ardlussa estate, a holdover from a previous and wealthier era. The manor house looked like the set of an old, black-and-white murder mystery. Now it was advertised online as a bed-and-breakfast.

The truck rocked and creaked like a wooden ship on stormy seas. Pitcairn yanked the wheel back and forth in what appeared to be a deliberate effort to smash into every pothole in the road. He grunted each time he hit one. They crossed vast stretches of desolate moorland and cut through groves of woodland straight out of the grimmest fairy tales. Ray's stomach bounced inside his abdomen. Acid rose in his chest. The unsecured boxes knocked against each other on the back of the truck and after twenty minutes, the road ended. A painted sign indicated that cars weren't permitted any farther, but Pitcairn kept going.

"Is this legal?"

"That's just a warning for the bloody tourists. I'm sick and tired of towing out those ungrateful arseholes."

They continued on what appeared to be a rutted goat track with a median of waist-high weeds that followed on a ridge above the water. Across the Sound of Jura, not quite visible through the rain, the Scottish mainland beckoned with all the conveniences Ray had left behind. His lower back throbbed, his stomach waged war with his nervous system, the pipes—the fucking pipes—screeched at him from the speakers like a state-fair show pig headed to the slaughter, but the little scenery the mist didn't hide was dreamlike. The motion of the truck allowed his hangover to gain momentum in the pit of his roiling belly.

"How much farther is it?"

"Almost there now, Chappie, and I'll be done with you and you'll see what you got your sorry self into. I bet Fuller twenty quid you'll come crawling back to the hotel before the full moon."

"The smart money's on Fuller," Ray said.

Pitcairn hit a hole as wide around as his tires. "Fuck! I know for a fact that some of these are so deep they'll take you all the way down to Australia."

"Stop the car," Ray said. He hoped, one last time, to lighten the mood and improve relations before they got any worse. Maybe he could establish some kind of rapport with Pitcairn. It would be a mistake to make enemies on an island this small, particularly dangerous ones. "I could go for some grilled shrimp on the barbie."

"I bet you could, Chappie. I don't go for all that foreign shite myself. We had some of that Chinese ping-pang ching-chong shite in Glasgow years ago around the time of my boy's wedding. The old lady wanted to try it. I don't know why I agreed. 'Those chinkies will eat dogs,' I told her. It's true."

"It's hard to imagine that you were ever married."

"What did you think, that Molly came in the post? That I bought her from Mrs. Bennett? Fucking hell," he said. The front wheel bounded out of another hole. "They almost caught us that time, Chappie. 'You never know what they're feeding you,' I told the missus. I asked the waiter, 'Is there dog in here?' I did, I tell you. She's dead six years now bless her soul."

"Molly seems like a very bright girl."

"Aye, and that's precisely what worries me, Chappie. She'll want to get off of Jura one of these days. You're to stay well clear of her, you understand?"

"You have my word."

"Your word, huh? And what's that worth coming from a man who tricks people into buying shite they bloody well can't afford. Don't look so surprised. We *can* read on Jura, Chappie. As soon as the rental agent rang up Mrs. Bennett, she and Mrs. Campbell learned everything we needed to know about you and your sport utility vehicles."

"I'm glad to hear I was able to provide you with so much entertainment," he said.

They reached a bend in the track and Barnhill came into view. It was glorious. The size of the house might have justified the rental price. Even painted brilliant white, it did not in any way disrupt the natural splendor of the rolling hills and exposed rock faces, but instead blended in among the curvatures of the ground. It looked cozy.

"I'm glad that you'll be all the way the fuck up here. What were you thinking?"

It would be an eight-hour walk back to The Stores for any additional supplies.

"I'm thinking I'm home," Ray said.

A trail led down a little embankment to the house, which sat nestled in a pocket of lower ground between the ridge and a series of hills along the shoreline. The structure had been built on a protrusion into the Sound of Jura, and water surrounded it on three sides; the property included a two-story house with a long garage and a set of stables extending out back to form a U. The hills protected the house from the direct blast of gales from the coast, and a rustic stone wall at the base of the hills appeared to run the entire length of the island. There were no other dwellings in sight. His only neighbors were the countless sheep whose wet wool floated in puffy clouds over the mud. Jura had more of them than the nighttime sky had stars—there had to be hundreds of them clustering in packs large and small.

The front door was on the south side of the property. Ray carried two boxes of supplies down to the stoop before it occurred to him that he didn't have a key. That was what he had been forgetting. Goddamn it.

Pitcairn's truck sat idling at the road, the bagpiper wheezing away, and Ray had to march up there and ask him for a ride all the way back to Craighouse. How could he have been so stupid? Did Pitcairn know he had forgotten it? He had brought Ray all the way up here just so he could gloat. He could already hear it: *Not so smart now, Chappie, are you?* He closed his eyes, took a deep breath. Pitcairn was watching him, and any second now he would lean on the horn.

Ray stood at the door, on the very threshold, but he had to turn around. That had been the story of his life. Out of desperation, he tried the knob—and it turned. The door pushed open and led to a small mudroom. The smell of mildew and garbage punched him in the gut. He put off touring the premises and instead made several trips back up to the truck, where Pitcairn sat smoking a cigarette and reading his newspaper. The boxes of supplies filled the small mudroom and half of the foyer. The whole house stank. After Ray had carried the last of his things inside, he leaned out the door and waved goodbye to Pitcairn, who rolled down his window and whistled. "What do you think you're doing, Chappie?" he yelled.

Ray walked halfway to the truck. "I'm moving in. Why, what do *you* think I'm doing?"

"You owe me twenty-five quid for the ride, yesterday and today. Do you imagine that I drove all the way the fuck up here for a joyride?"

"Oh of course," Ray said. "I owe you twenty-five pounds and *you* owe *me* a hundred something for the bar tab last night. We'll call it an even hundred. So that's seventy-five pounds you owe me, in fact."

"Now, Chappie, we talked about that."

"We talked about that," Ray said, mimicking Pitcairn's brogue. "Thanks for the ride—let's call it even."

"Even? The next time you need help," Pitcairn said, rolling up the window, "don't come crying to me. I'll expect you tomorrow down at the lounge. 'Oh I miss my soda pop and telly programs, boo hoo.'" He turned the truck around and drove off, kicking up a rainbow of mud. He left a cloud of noxious exhaust behind. The bagpipes died a slow and painful death until, like that, Ray was alone. The wind stirred the trees. The water splashed gently against the rocks down at the water. There existed no human noise whatsoever. Unseen birds welcomed him from the hedges. Wind rippled in waves through the high grasses. The wet peat sucked at the treads of his boots as he fled out of the rain and into George Orwell's house.

HE PAUSED FOR A moment at the threshold and then removed his boots in the mudroom. Ray was actually in George Orwell's house. It was difficult to imagine, but Orwell had lived and had written *Nineteen Eighty-Four* right here. He had paced these very floorboards, watched the sound absorb the rain through these same windows. Going into the sitting room was like stepping back in time. The technological world didn't exist here yet. It was glorious, but Ray had work to do.

Some kids had broken in—or more likely had let themselves in through the unlocked front door—and thrown a vomitive party in the sitting room. The stench was unbearable. The hardwood floor sparkled with broken wine bottles. Candy wrappers, beer cans, and old newspapers were strewn everywhere. The two fireplaces at either end of the house would provide his only heat, but no amount of peat could warm even the downstairs, where he also found a dining room, kitchen, and water closet. More unlocked doors led to the garage and stables.

The physical reality of Barnhill immediately taught Ray something extraordinary about *Nineteen Eighty-Four*. He now understood the psyche of the novel's hero Winston Smith, who would eventually give up his resistance and fall in line with Big Brother. Ray had never before appreciated what a cold and murky world Smith lived in; he was oppressed just as much by his material conditions as by any direct interaction with the authorities. The faulty Victory cigarettes and tear-inducing Victory gin were as destructive to one's well-being as the threat of a visit from the Thought Police. Were Smith's bathroom tiles as devoutly stained as these? Did the toilet tank in his apartment gurgle constantly like this one did?

Eric Arthur Blair—known to the reading public as George Orwell—had moved to Jura in May of 1946 and lived here on and off until January of 1949. He arrived shortly after his wife Eileen and beloved sister Marjorie had both passed away. It was a time of food shortages and strict rationing that required real sacrifice and patience of the British working class. London had been scarred by German bombs; even in peacetime he couldn't walk down the street without reliving the endless nights of hiding underground during the air raids. Rather than fighting for government-handout scraps, Orwell escaped the entire system in order to fend for himself and begin work on what would become the greatest novel in the history of the English language. He caught his own fish and crabs, grew his own vegetables—and Ray would do the same. Only after Orwell finished writing his masterpiece did he agree to seek treatment in Glasgow for the tuberculosis that would kill him just six months after its publication. It had all happened right here.

The upstairs hallway connected three bedrooms and a large bathroom with a claw-foot tub. For his room Ray chose the largest one, over the kitchen, that had windows on three sides and afforded north, east, and south views of the water. The house had come furnished but not very furnished. A few token watercolors hung on the walls. A closet contained sheets and blankets and towels. Coming to live in Orwell's house was supposed to provide Ray with some clarity, with the wherewithal to mend the fault lines that had appeared in his personality. In doing something as simple as rifling through the closets he felt like he might learn more about how Orwell had lived. Ray wasn't superstitious enough to believe that he could feel the presence of Orwell's ghost or anything like that, but there was no mistaking that something intangible remained. The grin on his face felt so foreign.

The initial step toward making Barnhill livable involved trying to get a fire started downstairs. A door from the kitchen led to an uninsulated well room, now used for storage. It contained what appeared to be several metric tons of peat, which someone had gone to the trouble of cutting into bricks and stacking in a crisscross pattern. Depending on how fast it burned, and how cold the house would get at night, it might be enough to warm one room for the duration of his stay. In the corner, a shotgun sat propped up against the wall.

Unlike his former colleagues at Logos, Ray had grown up around guns. He wasn't one of those fringe lunatics sitting at home crocheting the Second Amendment into throw pillows, but guns didn't bother him either. Chasing predators from the crops had been one of his chores as a teenager. Considering that he now lived alone at the end of the grid, miles from civilization, it made sense to have one around. He left it where it was and carried an armful of peat bricks back to the sitting room. He fed the least toxic pieces of the partygoers' leftover garbage to the potbellied stove that filled the fireplace, placed three peat bricks on top, and lit the newspaper with a match—and the room filled with black smoke. It bellowed out from the stove in waves. When his panic subsided, he opened the windows to welcome the fresh air in. He flapped his arms to cajole the smoke outside like an uninvited nun who had come seeking a donation for the local parish. Then he remembered the flue. A metal crank on the side of the stove turned with some reluctance. The smoke rose from the fire and went up the chimney, only to displace a nest of birds that had settled in the stovepipe but were now rendered homeless. Orwell had rubbed his own hands warm by this fireplace. Ray could just picture it.

He swept the swirling dust storms out the door and dumped the contents of his suitcase and backpack onto the sitting-room floor. The clothes smelled like they wanted nothing more than to provide a loving home for some colorful mold.

He threw the shirts he would need right away over some dining-room chairs, which he dragged, scraping across the floor, closer to the dancing fire. The smell of the peat made its way into his sinuses and hair. He ripped the new shirts and shorts from their packages and threw the cardboard inserts into the fire.

Once some warmth returned to his fingers and toes, Ray took a walk outside to inspect the property before it got any darker. The garage contained a number of unusual tools and implements, all neatly arranged. He found pumps, motors, a roll of barbed wire. A sealed oil drum filled with some kind of liquid. Sheets of plastic and canvas tarps. He couldn't even speculate about the purposes of the long poles with angular, medieval blades. A wooden crate contained a length of rope, along with a set of frayed jumper cables and the largest spider outside of an atomic-age monster movie.

On one side of the house sat a small garden suitable for planting vegetables, if he could keep the wandering sheep away from them. The animals had the run of the island. They had bells around their necks and jingled as they walked. There were also fruit and nut trees he couldn't identify—maybe Orwell had planted them! Ray fastened a rope between two of them and draped an armful of wet shirts and pants over it. Then he peeled off everything he had on and hung his sweaty clothes on the line.

He stood there, naked and fully exposed to the wilderness and the weather. The cold air and steady mist no

longer bothered him and he started to laugh and then he
kept laughing until he couldn't breathe. The water in the
distance looked so inviting. Some day soon he would go for
a swim. More water fell from the sky. He stomped his feet
in the mud. Some tense beast inside his belly spotted an
exit and went tear-assing for it; his body felt completely
relaxed and at ease. He jumped up and down in the biggest
puddles he could find, still laughing, splashing, shouting.

For a full hour Ray ran in circles around the garden. He
danced and sang and wiggled his arms in the air above his
head. He ran to the top of a hill and rolled—literally rolled—
back down toward the house, the hair on his chest and groin
picking up burrs along the way. Then he jogged back up
and did it again. He rubbed wet earth into the new cuts and
scrapes that found their way onto his arms and legs and ass
cheeks. The mud soon camouflaged every inch, but he piled
more onto his head, into his hair. He was transformed. The
rain ran down his chest in brown rivers. He stayed outside
until the faintest sunlight reflected on the Paps and then set
over Colonsay, an island north of Islay and due west of Jura.
The wind picked up even further and made gentle sweeping noises in the trees. His clothes flapped like a series of
personal flags. He had declared independence.

When the coldness found his skin, he wiped some of the
filth from around his eyes. He was eager to pour a whisky
and warm up again by the fire. He headed back to the house,
but stopped at the front door. A dead animal sat crumpled

on the stoop where a welcome mat might go. It could have been a squirrel or a small possum. Impossible to say. It was more than dead: it had been eviscerated. Its exposed entrails sat coiled in a greasy pile on the top step, still steaming. Some larger creature had moments ago sliced this thing open, crept up to the house, and left it at the door as a kind of offering or threat.

It was at that moment that Ray felt something watching him. Maybe it was just the exhaustion or whatever, but he felt some *thing*, a palpable, animal presence denser than the bushes in which it stirred. Two glossy eyes flickered at him, close to the ground, and then were gone.

Back in the house, he locked the door behind him. Screw local custom. The fire had died and the interior was pitch black. He couldn't tell if his eyes were open or closed. Navigating to the kitchen would require an understanding of the domestic layout he did not yet possess. He had found a box of matches, but to get them again he needed to traverse a thousand miles through the dining room and then to the windowsill above the sink. He shuffled his feet across the dusty floor, reaching blindly for walls, chairs, tables. That creature was lurking outside. He was naked and blind, cocooned in mud and in a strange house in a foreign nation whose language he understood so well yet which remained incomprehensible. Twenty paces took twenty minutes.

He found a drawer full of candles and had just enough

light to drink a long gulp from a bottle of scotch and get upstairs. He pulled a musty quilt from the closet, and—still muddy and terrified—climbed into bed and slept for fourteen hours.

II.

It must have been autumn the first time Ray ran away from home. The corn had been harvested—he remembered that much—and only the broken shoots remained. It was field mouse season, when the fleet of combine harvesters would send the critters into the house for shelter. The peanut-buttered traps snapped as soon as his mother could reset them. Ray had had no motivation for leaving other than curiosity. He could already sense that so many things existed beyond his limited understanding and wanted to see what else was out there and then what was beyond that. He needed to know everything that the world contained. His sister turned her back for a moment, and he escaped into a wasteland of clear-cut prairie that extended a hundred million miles in every direction.

The newfound expansiveness of the land created a seismic reconfiguring of his four-year-old self. The cornstalks chopped at his bare feet. The dust and debris of the fields filled his nose. He kept walking, but not necessarily *away* from anything.

At that time, the Welter farm occupied seventy acres, which Ray Senior had dedicated to the planting of soybeans and feed corn. Even as the nation's thirst for ethanol fuel grew, the family business was already becoming less viable. Every day, construction trucks ferried particleboard and faux-stone panels to the new housing developments at the remotest reaches of the property, which his dad had been forced to sell off piecemeal. That was where Ray headed, toward the clamor of hammering and sawing and engine noise.

After an hour, he arrived in a vast new kingdom where dozens of steamrollers and cement mixers, backhoes and dump trucks had gathered around the plywood skeletons of the new subdivision castles. The sound was wondrous: a gas-powered symphony of sonic textures and tone colors. Then it all stopped. There was some commotion, and a man in a hardhat lifted Ray into a pickup and drove him back to the house. The ride took two minutes. He had been so close to home the entire time. The stranger carried him under his arm like a sack of feed corn, ascended the porch, and knocked on the door. Ray's mother answered.

He didn't understand the conversation but understood all too well the worry he had caused. His father would hear about this. He was thrown into the tub, from where he heard his mother hollering at poor Becky because of his transgression.

Not long after that, seventy acres became forty and then later twenty. The civilized world metastasized onto the fragrant fields that had been his personal playground. Ray and his new neighborhood friends rode their dirt bikes for hours, pissed on passing freight trains, set up their own hobo camp under the interstate. The houses and cars and people continued to encroach upon his childhood home until only a few acres remained and Ray's father fired his last workers and took a job at the factory two towns over.

Ray, a few years later, got accepted into the big land-grant university further downstate and it was during the second semester of freshman year that he first read *Nineteen Eighty-Four*. He picked it up for the first time while eating lunch, and it had grown dark by the time he finished the appendix. The book came as a revelation.

Orwell had predicted *everything*. It was uncanny. His invention of Big Brother had come to fruition in the form of a vast network of conjoined consumers and Ray now understood that he was one of them. How many times had he caught himself wandering through the mall and spending money as a form of entertainment? He surfed the web and purchased things he didn't need in order to distract himself for a few moments from all the bad shit on the evening news. He had been marketed to so constantly and so effectively that he stopped noticing it—until he read *Nineteen Eighty-Four*. Orwell had revealed how the world really operated. Winston Smith's ordeal at the hands of the totalitarian state stayed with Ray for weeks; he couldn't stop thinking about that terror and about how he might live his own life without becoming equally enslaved by the system. That was when he declared a major in advertising, where his talent for invention—or his "genial wise-assery," as his father called it—could be put to lucrative use. The decision was more than financial, however. Ray knew that some key to his self-preservation sat hidden among the now dog-eared pages of *Nineteen Eighty-Four*.

The book's pseudo-academic appendix "The Principles of Newspeak" served as a detailed linguistic analysis of Big Brother's state-mandated language. By changing the official language to Newspeak, the government of Oceania sought to eliminate unnecessary and redundant words, to make the citizens' vocabulary smaller in order to limit what kinds of thoughts were even possible. The people couldn't revolt if they couldn't even conceive of the word *revolution*. Ray wanted to apply the same concept to advertising. Consumers didn't really want to make choices—they wanted the illusion of choice. By changing the way people thought, he could also alter their behavior, especially their spending habits. It sounded so easy, and it was.

A career in advertising would also allow Ray to escape the growing claustrophobia of small-town life for good. Living away from home in the dorms had rekindled his childhood curiosity. The world intimidated him with its vastness, but he still needed to see all of it. Every inch.

Upon graduation he moved to Chicago and in the fall he started his paid internship with the ad agency Logos. The company was known worldwide—it had been responsible for some of the biggest campaigns in recent advertising history. They had popularized Japanese cars in the American-manufacturing Midwest and convinced vast swaths of the electorate to vote against their own best interests in a presidential election. They had proved that choosing one brand of shitty cola over another was a statement of personal identity. He read articles and highlighted the important info, which he then converted into bullet points. The work was tedious, but easy.

He lived in an otherwise Bosnian enclave on the far North Side. The local community center brought in a wild Balkan orchestra from time to time, and Ray learned how to dance the kolo, albeit with some moves of his own invention mixed in. After he had spent another weekend drinking too much and making out with any number of Yugoslavian girls with lots of *j*'s and *z*'s in their names who pretended not to understand his English, he crawled back into his cubicle one Monday morning to find an email summoning him to his manager's office. Someone in the elevator had no doubt smelled the homemade rakija still seeping from his pores and dimed him out. Was he still drunk? It was certainly possible. His clothes reeked.

His boss Theodore "Bud" Jackson was one of six executive vice presidents. Ray had gone out drinking with him a few times at a dive where a former Miss Ukraine tended bar. They watched her wash beer glasses for hours and that was far more entertaining than another stupid ballgame on TV. Bud's career had been a tumultuous one. He had started out as a specialist on mail-order marketing and on his way up the corporate scaffold impregnated an entry-level data enterer who returned to her native Korea. Once a year she mailed him a portrait of his daughter, who he had never met in person. She had to be nine or ten already.

The US consumer market's evolution from analog to digital technologies had required Bud, like everyone else, to diversify his skill set. By age forty, he had become an early adopter of every new technology and helped Logos transition from a traditional ad house into a "creative communications company." Under Bud's watch, *advertising* had become a bad word. Logos didn't have clients, it established strategic partnerships; it didn't make commercials, it created market-driven branding solutions. It was all very Orwellian—he and Ray thought a lot alike. Along the way, Bud also transformed himself into the industry's foremost snack-food guru. Every obese child in America who reached for a second fistful of chips did so in large part because of Bud's tireless efforts. He was losing a loud argument with the operating system of his computer when Ray poked his head in.

Ray's probationary internship period had apparently come to an end. Bud offered him a permanent and full time position, which he accepted without negotiation. The salary was an abstraction. At twenty-four years old he would make more money than his father did down at the plant—and without the daily exposure to known carcinogens. That afternoon, he moved from his cubicle into a slightly larger one.

The work turned out to be far less exciting than he had

envisioned. He spent months at a time rewriting the same two or three concepts for the same two or three small partners. A half-trained monkey could have done his job, but he kept his head down and churned out copy. Sometimes after work he would hit the bars with some coworkers or go on the occasional date and bring a girl home to make sweat angels in the bed sheets.

To keep himself intellectually stimulated at work, Ray taught himself new graphic design and web development languages. He played with open-source CGI programs like they were real-time strategy video games; from his cubicle, after hours, he built parody sites for real companies that were more effective and easier to use than their official sites. After that, he created a Big Brotheresque widget that could scan ten thousand status updates—chosen according to specific user demographics—and aggregate their keywords into a randomly generated ad for a product that did not exist, but which 0.78 percent of those people attempted to purchase. He received so many orders for a flowerpot full of dried elephant dung that he considered finding a company to produce them.

Sometimes he would attempt to pitch his concepts to Bud and the others, but most of the time he kept his mouth shut and received an annual 5 percent raise for his efforts. After a few years he had saved enough money to finagle a sub-prime mortgage on a small condo he couldn't really afford, but which offered an obscured view of Lake Michigan. He hated to leave the pretty Yugoslav girls behind, but it was an easy move otherwise. Everything he owned fit into his car—by far the shittiest one in his new building's underground lot—and it just took one trip downtown. The only decor was a framed black-light propaganda poster in the living room. It featured a man's white face and the words BIG BROTHER IS WATCHING YOU.

AT THE COMPANY'S ANNUAL Winter Holiday Fiesta, during one of his many sallies for a drink, Ray bumped into some unfortunate woman so hard that she spilled her wine. The red shower floated airborne for an eternity before finding a place to settle amid her décolletage. He wiped at it with a napkin before realizing that he was feeling up a stranger—a stranger he had just doused in her own pinot noir. A nebula of stains darkened the front of her dress. She looked at Ray, her mouth agape, then looked down at her ruined clothes. They appeared to be expensive. The extent of the tragedy made itself apparent, and she pulled her shawl around herself. Her lips pursed into a slow smile and she laughed once, very loudly, and then threw her remaining wine at him. The stain didn't register on his holiday sweater, so she took another glass from the table and tried again. The splash caught him dead in the face. His eyes stung. He cried red tears that he tried to blot with a sleeve. The woman—a few years older than him and lovely despite the hideous stain—was laughing so hard she had to cram her shawl into her mouth. Neither of them could contain their laughter.

"I'm Ray," he said.

"Helen."

"Do you work here, Helen?"

"No, I came with one of your colleagues, but she seems to have disappeared."

"I want to show you something."

They shared a bottle of scotch on the roof and watched the falling snow, then warmed each other up in a cubicle over in Billing. She was an English professor at Chicago's most prestigious public university. Her PhD dissertation, as Ray understood it, had reevaluated Romantic-era conceptions of feminine identity and tied them to poetry's apparent origins in ancient mythology and goddess worship. Something like that. She recited from memory "Lines Written a Few Miles above Tintern Abbey" and by the time she got to:

While here I stand, not only with the sense
Of present pleasure, but with pleasing thoughts
That in this moment there is life and food
For future years. And so I dare to hope

Ray recognized something in himself that he could only think of as love. When, her stained party dress half-zipped and her underpants missing in action, she breathed

To blow against thee: and, in after years,
When these wild ecstasies shall be matured
Into a sober pleasure; when thy mind
Shall be a mansion for all lovely forms

he knew that he wanted to marry her. She moved in a few days later.

Originally from the Virginia side of the Washington, DC, suburbs, Helen Bedford was the warmest, most viscerally kindhearted woman Ray had ever met. She was also the smartest person who had ever been nice to him. Being close to her felt good. She had maintained the lithe figure of her days as a competitive tennis player, but the angles of her face and shoulders and hips had softened ever so slightly over the years. She kept her hair cut short to better show off the premature but, she had said, well-earned grey strands. Ray never wanted to stop looking at her.

Every night after work during the following week Ray drove up to her place in Evanston to help her box all her books up. Her teacups and their attendant saucers matched the plates and bowls and serving dishes. The set had been in her family for two generations. She owned a gravy boat. The two of them sat on her living room floor and wrapped each piece in a pillow of bubble wrap and packing tape. Helen was absolutely gorgeous, but didn't seem to be aware of it. Ray couldn't keep his hands off her. "Stop it—I'm filthy," she said and pulled him to the rug by his belt. He kissed every curve, every plane, every follicle he could find on her body, and he could find them all. The plastic sheets beneath them went *pop pop pop pop*.

They got married the following summer in a small service down at the parish his parents and sister belonged to and Ray had to pretend that the mass was something other than a bald-faced farce masked in medieval superstition. Helen's family flew in to the nearest airport and took over an entire floor of a chain hotel next to the interstate. One of her wedding presents for him was a first edition of *Nineteen Eighty-Four* ordered from a bookseller in London. The gift was made even more remarkable by the fact that she had been secreting away small amounts of money—twenty dollars here, fifty there—since the week they met. Instead of a honeymoon, the happy couple stayed put in Chicago. Ray used some vacation days from Logos and they spent a week building forts out of sofa cushions and watching *The Red Shoes* and *I Know Where I'm Going!*

In the fall, she became the acting chair of the Department of English, where she filled in for a sick colleague. Her new responsibilities often kept her at campus late into the night. She also taught two classes, which involved a great deal of preparation and grading, and sat on a number of different departmental committees. With more time on his hands, Ray sometimes went out drinking with Bud, but he also spent more late nights at the office. That was when he began to tinker in secret on the concept that would define his career in advertising.

His project was, at the beginning, nothing more than a mental exercise, a distraction undertaken for the sake of curiosity and to avoid puttering around the condo and waiting for Helen to get home. Some people played video games or watched sports; Ray invented a new platform from which a company like Logos could interface with its strategic partners and their would-be customers. He sought to utilize the Orwellian nature of social media and invent a profitable new method of corporation-consumer interactivity.

He decided on vandalism.

A TRULY MONUMENTAL ADVERTISING campaign could be a work of public performance art, one that could make an ungodly profit if the advertisers learned to put—or learned to pretend to put—the once-private desires of the proles (that was, the consumers) ahead of those of Big Brother (the corporate overlords who hired them). Ray wanted to exploit the proles' false sense of freedom; he would reach out to consumers' greatest aspirational self-images confident in knowing that people purchased things not for who they were but for who they wanted to be.

The idea behind his secret campaign wasn't all that complicated. Contemporary consumers believed that they wanted to be free of corporate manipulation and free of subservience to Big Brother. The average American consumer spent enormous amounts of money in the effort to appear anticonsumerist. Ray had done the same thing for years.

As an experiment, he crafted an anticorporate message and campaign for a real American corporation. Just for laughs, he chose a particular model of military-grade SUV that had been introduced to the public marketplace a decade prior. After the initial novelty had worn off the sales figures plummeted due to a combination of abysmal gas mileage and skyrocketing petroleum costs. Out of boredom, Ray devised the method that would—on paper—make those trucks the most desirable vehicles on the road even amid a global oil crisis and during an era dedicated to environmental sustainability. It was meant to be theoretical.

As the intellectual property of Logos, his project didn't belong to him. He kept it a secret up until the day that Bud sent a company-wide email announcing that they had formed a strategic partnership with the very same manufacturer of the very same military-grade SUVs. Ray read the email three times: Bud would soon begin building a team to interface with the automaker and better enable it to reposition its brand image amid a global marketplace advancing toward greater ecological awareness. Ray leapt from his cubicle.

Being named the account director for a domestic SUV company was a logical step in Bud's career. He had a cell phone pinched between his face and shoulder while he pecked at a keyboard. "Two fifty a barrel," he told the caller. "Yeah . . . I don't know . . . Either the Persian Gulf or the Gulf of Mexico, I forget which—same difference . . . Our projections have it at three hundred by the end of the decade . . . Yes, *this* decade. That's why the small part of Detroit that isn't already boarded up is shitting itself right now. For our purposes, more expensive is better."

Ray tiptoed in. Every footstep required concentration.

Bud lifted his chin at him as if to say, *What do you want?* Ray thought about turning around and walking out. He could forget about his efforts to sell a shitload of SUVs and go back to hiding in his cubicle and spend the rest of his life rewriting the same three goddamn advertisements . . . or he could find out if his theories would work in real life. He handed Bud an unlabeled DVD.

"Jürgen, I'm telling you we'll take care of it," Bud told the telephone. "You won't regret it . . . Yes . . . *Yes.*" He cupped his palm over the receiver. "What is this? I don't have time for games, Man Ray."

Ray slid the disc into one of the computers on his desk and the TV monitors on the wall went blank. The sound of a truck engine filled the room. A speck appeared at a distant horizon on both screens. The image grew larger until it became one of the SUVs that Logos was now partnered with. The truck, its engine roaring with thirst, sped toward the camera as if to mow the viewer down, then it skidded to a halt and filled the screen. A vandal had carved two words into the door as if with a key: "SUV Hogg."

"Let me call you back," Bud said. He sent his phone skidding across the papers on his desk. "What the fuck is this?"

"It's our campaign."

"Close the door. We don't do campaigns, Ray. We establish strategic partnerships and provide market-driven solutions."

"It's our new strategic partnership. Scroll over the truck. It's all there." Words popped out from the hood, from the roof and trunk, from the tires. Clicking on them led to page after page about the proud tradition of petroleum production in American history. It was all very patriotic. Bud's cell phone rang but he ignored it. Ray had earned himself two minutes to make his pitch. "The environment-friendly angle is a mistake," he said.

Bud looked baffled. "A mistake? The contract it took me nine fucking months to procure is a mistake?" His landline rang. He answered both phones and placed them next to each other on the desk so the callers could talk to each other.

"Nothing we do," Ray said, "will convince women or hippies to buy these trucks. Look at where the market's headed. We need to help the automaker reassess the brand's goals and attack a core audience. Men who buy SUVs don't care about the environment or else they wouldn't buy SUVs in the first place. My campaign—sorry, my market-driven solution—is about defiance."

"Defiance."

"Screw the environment."

"Screw the environment? That's your idea? How long have you been working on this?"

"You're always preaching about interactivity. What's more interactive than vandalizing your own truck?"

Bud hung up the two phones. "How did you know we'd get this account?"

"I didn't."

"So you spent, what, a month putting this together? Even if

it was on your own time, you do understand that it's the exact fucksticking opposite of the direction I agreed upon with the client?"

"Give them the DVD. I have a whole platform developed. You've said it yourself that the thirty-second ad is dead, right? So we'll go post-media with this. We'll go post-post media. I'll put it this way: when's the last time you took the L and someone wasn't having a loud personal conversation on his cell phone? Everyone hates that guy, right? But what I have in mind will use the disintegration of public and private space to our advantage. We're going to get twenty of these things—"

"Twenty of what?"

"These SUVs. We get as many as we can and vandalize them."

"Vandalize them?"

"Yes."

"To say 'SUV Hog'?"

"Two *g*'s. We'll copyright it immediately."

"Are you fucking retarded?"

"Every couple weeks we'll scrape 'SUV Hogg' into a truck and park it at that week's hot place. Or outside a stadium before a playoff game."

"You're suggesting that people will buy SUVs because they're getting keyed? Do you appreciate how stupid you sound?"

"It will work."

"No offense, but you're a fucking asshole."

"Think about it for a sec. People will notice that all these trucks are getting vandalized, right? We'll make it look like an organized grassroots effort by some smelly activists and it will get covered on every blog in the city. Think of the buzz," Ray said. He was getting worked up. "Once some imaginary granola-eating pinkos get blamed, buying one of these things will become an act of defiance. Real men are free to waste as much fossil fuel as they want without big government or some hippies telling them what to do."

"Screw the environment?"

"It's a matter of synchronizing the doublespeak message with the new media at our disposal. We can even arrange it ahead of time for the dealerships to provide free paint touch-ups if the truck owners want them—which they won't."

His two minutes expired.

"SUV Hogg. That's not it exactly, but let me give it some thought. I'll run it upstairs. Have you shown this to anybody else?"

"No, I—"

"Don't. You're a strange motherfucker, Sugar Ray."

Four days later, stacks of fresh nondisclosure forms landed on every chair in the building. Bud got the board's permission to name Ray the assistant account director for what would become the Oil Hogg initiative. It was a huge step up in the world. He even got his very own office. At the end of the day Bud and the rest of the team were waiting for him when he arrived downstairs in the parking garage. His car had disappeared from its usual spot. In its place stood a hulking SUV—a bonus for generating the idea. With some ceremony, the CEO herself handed him the keys, which he used to scrape "Oil Hogg" into the paint.

The team kicked the project off by vandalizing the hood or door or rear panel of twenty-four SUVs and then parking them outside Chicago's most popular restaurants and tourist spots. Over the days that followed, a small cadre of sworn-to-secrecy interns posted grainy camera phone images on every social-media platform. The reaction came instantaneously. Hundreds of people liked and re-posted the images; they crowed with delight about the comeuppance of those arrogant, petroleum-guzzling bullies who clogged the roads with their behemoth machines.

No one expected the copycat vandalism that followed. Through the winter, the defacement of SUVs took on its own momentum when students, housewives, and everyday proles got in on the action and started scraping up strangers' vehicles. A wave of low-stakes eco-terrorism washed over Chicago and unwittingly spread the Oil Hogg branding message.

Then Ray's plan began in earnest. He had the interns launch the counter-initiative. They started on AM radio, calling in to right-wing talk shows to say how proud they were of being decent, law-abiding Americans and hence free to despoil the environment any way they damn well pleased. "Longtime listener, first time caller," an intern said live on the air from Bud's office. "I'm proud to be an Oil Hogg."

Supporters called in to echo his sentiments. The new narrative took shape online and on the airwaves, one extolling the red-meat joy of driving big trucks. The rhetoric of the new blogs and memes equated gasoline usage with being a real American. Hundreds of SUV owners whose vehicles had not been vandalized soon did it themselves. Sales boomed citywide and in the northern half of the state. The auto dealers couldn't keep them on the lot. The earnings reports erased any doubt on the part of the Logos board about Ray's unconventional methods.

The fun couldn't last, however. Someone—most likely an intern—wrote an anonymous, tell-all blog post. Chicago's free weekly ran a cover story about car dealerships promoting fake grassroots environmentalist vandalism as a way to market more trucks, and that led to a local news segment in which a trench-coated correspondent stood in front of the Logos office and scratched the Greek letters of the company sign with a key.

There were lawsuits and counter-suits, governmental fines and complaints from a union claiming to represent automobile detailers. The Justice Department was snooping around. To avoid litigation from the truck buyers stupid enough to key their own goddamn vehicles, the manufacturer confessed to the shenanigans and offered to pay for all the paint touch-ups.

The Logos Print Team designed full-page mea culpa advertisements for the region's largest remaining newspapers. The

final leg of the campaign featured fat actors portraying ste-
reotypical pinstriped, cigar-chomping auto executives from
Detroit getting busted for vandalizing their own trucks. Their
buffoonish antics were detailed in an array of short advertorial
webisodes, gamified apps, and social-network widgets. Pro-
testors on both sides of the debate loved the images of fat, rich
people getting marched off to jail.

One of the interns, a young woman named Flora, repur-
posed some Oil Hogg print ads for a series of street-art stencils
and used them to deface half of the abandoned buildings in
downtown Chicago. Her vandalism wasn't officially approved
by Logos, but it wasn't condemned either. She garnered a
great deal of attention around the office and did brilliant work
despite her moral objections. In a company-wide email, she
had called Ray's new step in the Oil Hogg initiative "morally
reprehensible" and "pure concentrated evil, but ingenious."
Ray saved the email.

By making fun of themselves, the SUV manufacturers
turned the scandal into victory and the advertising awards
poured in. Local sales records were shattered as consumers
rallied around the brand. It was rumored that a Chinese con-
glomerate wanted to import the SUVs and was petitioning
the US government for some revisions to an international
trade agreement. In the fiscal quarter that followed, the SUV
out-performed hybrids three to one in the greater Chicago
market. Dealers presold the trucks months in advance of their
production and they continued to get vandalized as fast as they

could escape the Michigan assembly lines. More shifts were added at the factories and the creation of so many new jobs led to significant press coverage about the pending renewal of Detroit—and it was all thanks to him.

RAY WAS IN HIS office when the factory down near his hometown exploded. His mother called him. "The plant's gone," she said and hung up. He remained at his computer and refreshed a browser window to follow what little news and gossip the downstate TV affiliates and social media users could piece together. The number of reported fatalities climbed all morning. Even before the call from Becky he knew that his father was dead.

The town became a chemical hot zone. Forty-six neighbors and friends were gone as well. Ray stayed in Chicago and managed his mother's medical care from afar, safe from the toxic smog that would soon express itself in every variety of physiological anomaly. He refused to expose himself to the poisonous cloud that mushroomed over his hometown. A boil-water advisory remained in effect for eight weeks, in a twenty-five-mile radius, while the death toll crept higher. Thousands of acres of crops had to be destroyed. Corn too toxic to be fed even to animals was sold for ethanol, where in the bellies of sedans and SUVs it gained an even greater toxicity; it was exhaust-piped into the atmosphere and dispersed across the entire Midwest.

Helen did everything in her power to console him, but Ray

spent his days in a trance of rage and denial. He trudged from the condo to the office, and from the office back to the condo. He didn't bother going home some evenings and that didn't sit very well with her, but he felt better when he was safely bunkered down at work. The tedium of spreadsheets and oil price forecasts, the microtrends of American consumer spending habits, distracted Ray from his own inner life. He felt his thought processes growing jumbled and spaghetti-like. Something unfixable had snapped inside him and the awareness of it made it worse.

With nothing to bury, he felt no compulsion to attend the funeral mass. Becky and her husband soon moved in with their mother and—coincidence maybe—they were unable to conceive a child. He had become the last male Welter. The survival or cessation of the entire family name now rested with him. That was the kind of grown-up burden he had spent his entire life not thinking about.

That he stayed at his desk through personal tragedy brought him to the attention of the Logos corporate honchos, but what the board took for stoic dedication to the craft of strategic branding, Ray knew to be abject fear: of facing his father's absence, of his mother's heartbreak, and of the carcinogens in her water, of the distance he felt expanding between himself and his own good nature. He tried not to let his intense grief affect Helen, but from the look on her face while she slept he could tell that he was failing. He had snapped at her a few times, but had never known why. She continued to do everything in her power to help him march through each day.

The employees who had survived the explosion were offered and accepted work as day laborers, digging holes and filling them again until out-of-state demolition engineers arrived to peel acres of contaminated topsoil from what had been among the earth's most fertile farmland, ground that now contained Ray's cracked genetic code in the form of his father's smithereens. The crew cemented over the accident site while every regulatory oversight organization dragged its feet, which were snared in red tape and a hundred-mile-long fence of glazed razor wire.

The aftermath was even worse: bright yellow lines painted upon the site to delineate countless parking spaces surrounding a mecca of convenient, one-stop shopping where his mother now bought aseasonal produce and the disposable electronics Big Brother used to track her movements and convince her to buy even more junk. Becky implored Ray to visit, but he just couldn't. He had his own problems. For the first time in his life, Ray felt something less than indestructible.

Around that time, Ray also started to have some serious reservations about the whole Oil Hogg endeavor. He kept Flora's email in his inbox, where he looked at it every time he powered on a computer or his phone. His depression grew in direct proportion to the sales figures. When he could no longer avoid the practical realities behind his success, he took to drinking more scotch. What he had done *was* morally reprehensible.

Helen urged him to quit and Ray considered it, but he simply couldn't justify doing so. The money was too good; there was no way he could give those paychecks up. He could imagine what his father would have said. His old man would have been disgusted by the very thought of his only son and heir leaving a high paying job in order to save a few trees. It was unthinkable.

Whether the domestic strife resulted from his growing disillusionment with Logos or vice versa, he couldn't say. Helen still sometimes managed to soothe Ray's anxiety attacks with carefully chosen lines of verse, with CDs of Satie and Chopin, but she grew frustrated with his despondency and rededicated herself to her research, to her tenure portfolio, to the students she conferenced with from a treadmill at the campus rec center.

If she was asleep when he got home he would pour a glass of scotch or three to unwind on the balcony. The weather didn't matter. Late at night, Lake Michigan looked like . . . like nothing. It was an enormous, black expanse and it reminded him that he lived every day at the very end of the world. A short boat ride and he could fall off the edge of the earth, down down down down down through the limitless oblivion of the cosmos, and that comforted him. He wouldn't see his wife for days at a time.

During a particularly vindictive quarrel, Ray used a few words that once spoken aloud could never be revoked. She asked him to move out and for the first time in months there was no reason to argue with her. The next day, he leased a corner apartment on the fifteenth floor of a gutted and renovated 1927 high-rise pictured in every architectural guide to Chicago. The deposit and first month's rent paid for the illusion of antiquity; behind the ornate, brick superstructure a network of coaxial cables and wireless receptors provided every manner of computerized and televisionary convenience. The place did not include a parking spot, however, so he left his SUV at the condo and for the next several months he was glad to not have to look at it.

HELEN CALLED VERY EARLY one Saturday morning, which was a bit odd. She didn't leave a message. The coffee-maker had shut itself off and Ray poured a tepid cup. Bud had also sent a series of texts overnight imploring him out for an afternoon of beer and circus. There would be an important hockey game on TV, but Ray wasn't much of a sports fan. He caught his reflection in the door of the refrigerator while reaching for the half and half: he needed a haircut and his face couldn't decide if it was growing a beard or not. *Don't you own a razor?* his dad would have asked, joking but not really joking.

She picked up after the first ring. "It's me," Ray said.

"I know," Helen said. "Your name comes up on the screen."

Good morning to you too. "What's going on?"

There was some variety of crazy, avant-garde singing in the background. It sounded like an argument among three opera singers.

"I need you to come get your SUV. It's an eyesore. I want it out of here."

"We haven't spoken in, what, three weeks and you call me at seven A.M. to talk about my truck?"

"Listen, would you please get rid of it?"

The singers shouted and chirped and barked. They might have had a broken harpsichord or piano and some kind of rusted horn accompanying them.

"What am I supposed to do, park it on the street?"

"That's not my problem."

It wasn't like Helen to pick a fight for no reason. Everything had become subtext with her. Something was up her ass, but it wasn't the truck. "What's gotten into you?"

"It's just that . . . Listen, let's just forget it."

"What is this about, Helen? Do you want me to come over? I can be there in fifteen minutes."

"No! . . . No, I shouldn't have called. I sent you an email," she said and hung up.

He dumped the coffee onto the dishes piled in the sink and listened to a message from Flora. "Hi, Ray?" Her voice cheered him up. When her internship ended, Flora had, with some reluctance, agreed to accept a permanent position.

Bud had once admitted that his frequent fantasies about Flora involved them running away together to a Hawaiian island and taking with them a lifetime supply of tequila and birth-control pills. Ray thought she was attractive, yes, but that was due more to her considerable intellect than the perfect round butt that Bud wanted to "eat an Italian beef sandwich off of."

"In retrospect," she had told his voice mail, "I was wrong about something I wrote in the market summary I turned in today. I looked at the reports again and they make a lot more sense now. I hope it's okay if I email you some revisions, because I already did. If you prefer I can get you hard copies this weekend. Let me know, okay? Okay. Bye!"

He switched his laptop on and deleted the spam that had accumulated overnight. He and Helen had taken to communicating almost exclusively via email. The situation was ridiculous, but for the short term it was best to abide by her wishes. Her use of his full name and the salutatory colon indicated the things that this email would not be: personal, apologetic, salubrious, tender, forgiving, decent. She wanted him to come to her office for an appointment and proposed a meeting time.

An *appointment*? He now needed a goddamn appointment to see his wife?

He texted Bud back:

See you there.

He opened the dishwasher, removed all the glassware that had sat in there so long that it had become dirty again, and then calculated the dishes' best possible arrangement within the limited and awkwardly arranged rack space. Nothing seemed to fit right. Every angle was terrible. Next, he filled three garbage bags with pizza boxes and beer bottles and carried them down the hall to the chute like a derelict Santa Claus preparing to dump them in some bad girl's chimney. They landed fifteen stories below with a crash of broken glass. He pulled the sheets off the bed and stuffed them in a mesh Kletzski's Kleaners laundry sack and did the same with all the stray clothes.

While scanning the news, he spooned a bowl of cold cereal into his mouth. Every day another columnist or editorial writer made another superficial reference to George Orwell: Big Brother-this and thoughtcrime-that. Orwell hadn't only predicted the current state of affairs, he had also provided innumerable journalists with a series of metaphors vague enough to pass as zodiac horoscopes.

CANCER (June 21–July 22) Constant surveillance by the state will undermine your autonomy as a free-thinking individual. Think for yourself and don't be a copycat. Wear something red today.

Orwell was everywhere.

Ray pulled on a T-shirt and a pair of jeans, then tore a white Oxford out of the dry cleaner's sterile plastic. He owned dozens of similar shirts, each with a different pattern of stains and amount of fraying at the collar. The oldest of them was little more than a rag tied to a wire hanger; it was his favorite shirt. Each Christmas, Easter, and birthday another identical one arrived in the mail courtesy of his mother. She had always been a creature of habit, but after the explosion had progressed toward the genuinely eccentric. Dementia had entered the picture. Exchanging three items every year was easier than attempting to explain to her yet again that he had put on a few pounds over the past fifteen years. It was nice that she still recognized his voice on the phone, but that was just a matter of time.

To get to the dry cleaner's Ray had to face the weekend crowd of bad-art browsers and fake-fur-wearing nannies who zoomed their strollers down the sidewalk like they were racing chariots around ancient Sparta. Off-duty cubicle farmers jostled for sidewalk space with panhandlers and homeless war veterans and proud new parents bubbling over with moneyed angst. The gelato stand and microbrewery crowds spilled onto the sidewalks. Exclusive downtown galleries had opened local branches and brought with them chain coffee shops and national retailers of sweatshop-made clothing. It was all so depressing. He joined in the march-step choreography of the herd and carried his laundry through the crowds and to the mostly blind Polish lady down the street.

The ten-minute walk took him through an area that a decade earlier had tipped over to full-blown gentrification. During the last half century the neighborhood had mutated from a bohunk ghetto cut off from Chicago's downtown by the river's Main Branch into a post–GI Bill slum then into a Reagan Renaissance yuppie heaven of renovated row homes and chain boutiques selling mass-produced expressions of individuality. Considering that he had also contributed to the forced displacement and resettlement of the natives, Ray knew he was in no position to complain about the neighborhood colonialism. The local artistic scene had deteriorated after the painters and sculptors had been priced out of their studios by those, like himself, able and willing to pay exorbitant rent for the privilege of living among painters and sculptors.

A construction crew had razed an entire building since he had come home from work last night. A dirt field remained, now adorned with a billboard promising the imminent grand opening of another organic-foods franchise. He couldn't recall what establishment had occupied the space just fourteen hours earlier. Life continued on. Someone had keyed the words "Oil Hogg" into the hood of an SUV parked in front of a sushi restaurant.

The dry cleaner's door had a string of brass bells hanging from the inside handle. Mrs. Kletzski's portable black-and-white TV was cranked up to its maximum, distorted volume.

"Raymond, where have you been hiding?"

"Hello, Mrs. Kletzski. How are you?"

"I've had some of your shirts ready for six weeks!"

"Right—I completely forgot about those."

"I'm not responsible for garments left over six weeks!"

"How much do I owe you?"

"Do you have your ticket?"

"No, Mrs. Kletzski. I never have my ticket, remember?"

"You never have your ticket! Let me see if I can find your slip."

He never saw other customers in the place, yet behind Mrs. Kletzski hung a serpentine of plastic-sheathed clothes. He wanted to go back there one day, maybe hide from the world for a few hours. There was definitely something wrong with him. He was thirty-three years old and wanted to do nothing more than play amid other people's cleaned clothes.

"Welter! Eighteen dollars and twelve cents."

Mrs. Kletzski's pricing obeyed no specific logic. Identical loads could vary by as much as twenty dollars. He gave her a credit card. "I'm not going home right now. Can I leave these with you and get them later?"

"Sign here. This is your copy. I'm not responsible for garments left over six weeks!"

"I'll get them later today, Mrs. Kletzski, I promise. Just the usual for these." He lifted the laundry sacks onto the counter.

"What is it?"

"Sheets, towels. Clothes."

"When do you need them?"

"No rush."

"Monday?"

"Thank you, Mrs. Kletzski."

The bells jingled when he left to battle the rollerbladers, meter maids, and surly pre-teens whose experiences of the physical world were limited to tiny display screens. The homeless people carried paper cups of gourmet coffee ringed with extra cardboard so they wouldn't scald their fingers.

He was supposed to meet Bud at McCrotchety's, the flagship of what would soon become a national chain of theme bars offering sanitized and smoke-free nostalgia. It was meant to resemble an old-fashioned Chicago day-load dive bar, but the traditional urine-and-burnt-peanut stink was missing, as were any real old-timer drunks, who were forced to huddle in the few real dives that remained. McCrotchety's harkened back to an era brought to a close by bars like McCrotchety's.

The bartendress opened a can of beer for Ray before he sat down.

"Thanks, Lily," he said.

"So has Helen divorced your sorry ass yet?" Bud asked.

"We're not getting divorced!"

"How long have you been separated?"

"Ten months."

"When's the last time you talked to her?"

"In fact, we spoke today. I have an appointment to see her on Wednesday."

"An *appointment*? That doesn't seem strange to you?"

"We're both very busy."

"Busy hiring a lawyer to separate you from what's left of your money."

"You're in rare form today. Who're we playing?"

"Detroit."

"I hate Detroit."

"'Hate' is a very strong word."

"I'm trying to get into the whole stupid spirit of male bonding and watching sports. Detroit sucks."

"Like you mean it."

"*Detroit* sucks!"

"Almost."

"Detroit *sucks!*"

"Never fucking mind."

"*Detroit sucks!*"

Lily came back over. "Hey, guys, I need you to watch the language. There are children at the bar."

"What the fuck are children doing at the bar?"

"I can get by nicely without Detroit."

"Better."

Ray had only drunk one beer and already had to piss. Television screens throughout the bar beckoned to him from every direction; some were hooked up to cable and others to a satellite, and the difference created a time warp in which a slap shot bounced off the goaltender's chest protector and then five seconds later did so again on another television. More screens were mounted on the walls above the urinals. He went back to his seat to find Bud conspiring with Lily. She left to help someone else before he could sit.

"Are you aware that you look terrible?"

"You could at least act surprised."

"Still not sleeping?"

"Not really. I need a vacation."

"That's a great idea. Here's my advice. Since Helen's totally about to divorce your ass, you should—"

"Helen is not about to divorce my ass."

"You're joking, right? Of course she's about to divorce you. Everybody can see it except you. Lily can see it. Instead of sitting around whining and waiting for her to take half your money—hell, she already got your condo—you need to start spending it. Take a vacation. Go on a cruise. Get yourself rocked gently to sleep at night knowing you screwed Helen out of the pleasure of screwing you. Speaking of which, while you were in the bathroom Lily asked me what your deal is."

"No she didn't."

"I'm serious."

"What did you tell her?"

"That you're gay."

"No you didn't."

"I did, actually, and I got us some whiskies."

As if summoned, Lily returned with two glasses of scotch.

"I'm not gay," Ray said.

"Excuse me?"

"Bud said he told you I was gay."

"He said you were in the middle of a 'marital schism.' Is that what you called it? He also said that your wife is about to divorce your mopey ass. Your being gay is news to me. Not that I have any problem with that. Enjoy your whiskies— they're on me."

"I'd like to be on her," Bud said.

Before it occurred to him that perhaps he shouldn't be drinking hard alcohol in the middle of the day, Ray took a long sip. It tasted like a generic highland, ten or twelve years old. He fished a few ice cubes from a rocks glass and dropped them into his whisky with a tiny splash.

The bar filled up as the game progressed. The sports-star millionaires representing Chicago were in the process of losing to those representing Detroit. When Ray was a kid, the heated Detroit versus Chicago rivalry had reached epic proportions in his imagination. The gruesome fascination he once had for the hockey fights was now derived from the commercial interruptions. Those thirty-second spots were relics of a previous era, a halcyon time when the advertisements remained separate from the entertainment. Now, there were ads painted onto the ice and superimposed over the action on the screen.

The programs were the commercials. The programs had always been the commercials.

"Give me one of those napkins," Ray said. He took a pen from the bar and tried to calculate the number of barrels of crude oil he was personally responsible for converting into greenhouse gases. He couldn't do it. The mathematics were beyond him. He drank some more scotch that he did or didn't order and then woke up the next morning on a bed with no sheets.

The smell of re-reheated coffee arose from a machine programmed to begin brewing at six A.M. and it roused him from another disturbing dream. Action movies of his own subconscious invention still flickered on his mind. Details gelled into focus. A foreign army had occupied his hometown. Some faceless regiment had appeared by rail in steaming sixty-foot-tall locomotive behemoths as streamlined and fearsome as the Italian futurists' protofascist visions. The entire town had been conquered, the women raped and children forced into slavery. Smoke rose from what had been the church he had attended as a kid and where he and Helen got married.

His dreams were getting worse. The late-night alcohol wasn't helping, but neither was its occasional absence. A full month of sleep: that was what he needed. A self-induced coma free from his own imagination.

His eardrums pounded hard enough to drive a galley of rowing, half-naked slaves over the horizon of the flat earth. He spent an hour adrift, clinging to the bare mattress for dear life while the coffee burned again.

He woke up around dawn, or he thought he did. From inside a cloudbank it was impossible to guess the time of day. It felt like early morning, but it was just as likely four in the afternoon. Maybe it didn't matter. Ray had no need to go anywhere or do anything and so spent his first morning at Barnhill in bed. The house creaked and moaned around him. Waves of rain splashed against the windows. He fell back to sleep for another hour. His thoughts turned again to that putrefying animal on his doorstep. He pictured it starting to move and squirm back to life. At some point, he pulled himself out of the dirty sheets and padded downstairs. The curtains were open, but the house remained dark. He balled up some newspaper, got a fire going again, and put a pan of tap water on top of the stove.

He filled a big stew pot with water at the kitchen sink and put it on the fireplace. It would take a while. In the meantime, he went upstairs and turned the bathtub faucets all the way on. If he could carry the boiling water from the sitting room to the bathroom fast enough, he might be able to get a decent bath. He slugged back a dram of scotch while the water boiled. Then he drank another one and carried the pot upstairs. The bath was hot enough to set his blisters blazing, but it felt so good to scrape off some of the dry earth.

The rest of the morning or afternoon or whatever was spent drinking whisky and staring out the windows. That woman who had given him a ride on Islay was right: he didn't need his wristwatch anymore. Time operated differently on the Hebrides. It didn't matter what time it was. Every so often the wind would push the clouds aside long enough to offer a view of the sheep that grazed around the house and were impervious to the weather. It felt so . . . so . . . *right* to not be at work. Ray could picture the flocks of businessmen and bicycle messengers and nannies back in Chicago racing in straight lines in adherence to the tight ant-farm grid of those claustrophobic city blocks and reporting their precise whereabouts every five minutes to concentric circles of online friends they had never met. He was free of it now. He had sold his truck and everything else he owned—furniture, flat-screen, turntable, everything. What he couldn't sell, he donated. What he couldn't donate, he hurled into the dumpster behind the dry cleaner's. His smartphone was at that moment leaking persistent, bioaccumulative, and toxic chemicals into Lake Michigan.

A shelf in the kitchen contained a row of guidebooks, histories, pamphlets, and a detailed survey map of Jura. The island looked to be about five miles wide and was shaped like a long, skinny oval of volcanic rock that had been bitten nearly in half by Loch Tarbert, the gaping mouth of which opened into the sound over on the Islay/Colonsay side. A previous tenant had circled Barnhill, but he couldn't reconcile that name on the map with his presence here. It was too good to believe. All Ray wanted to do was curl up under a blanket and read *Nineteen Eighty-Four* yet again, here at the source, to see what new insights revealed themselves. He wanted to think. He wanted to do nothing at all. Other than that, his only goal was to see every square foot of Jura, to find the remaining wild goats and catch a lobster to eat. He wanted to drink gallons of scotch and climb the Paps. He would get to all of it soon, but first he needed to unpack before it got dark.

He placed his water-damaged books on a bedroom shelf and pulled a chair up to a window. The mist obscured the view of the sound and mainland and he couldn't see any farther than the garden. He was so happy to find his copy of *Nineteen Eighty-Four* intact.

Ray checked the bolts on the front and back doors and fixed a bite to eat while he could see. He was still acclimating to life without electricity or gas. It was a hassle, but that was the whole point. He dropped some more peat bricks onto the fire and put a pot on the stove to warm a can of soup. It all felt so *primitive*—and that was wonderful and intimidating at the same time, but if bony and wheezy old Orwell could live this way so could he.

Over the next few days, Ray managed to convince himself
that he was staying out of the rain in order to avoid some
nascent flu symptoms creeping into his musculature. That he
was simply collecting his wits after the awful events of the past
few weeks and months. In reality, however, or in what passed
for reality, he was scared shitless. He heard noises from the
attic crawl space, the chimney, from the bushes surrounding
the house. The floorboards groaned upstairs. Wind growled
at him through the windows. Pacing-the-floorboards boredom became preferable to venturing outside and confronting
the dead animal at the door, which in his imagination had
grown to the size of the red deer that sailed past the kitchen
windows. He tried not to think about what had left it there.

The weather was so dismal that he ended up spending his
entire first week on Jura holed up indoors and drinking as
much whisky as he could pour down his gullet. He did some
reading now and then, but was distracted by the blank wall of
fog and mist out the window. His attention span had shrunk
so much that he couldn't make it through more than a page or
two of Orwell at a time. Unable to focus on anything for more
than a few minutes, he grew restless. Even out in the middle
of nowhere he felt trapped and hemmed in on all sides, but he
did manage to settle into a daily routine.

Every morning, he gathered old newspapers and peat
bricks and built a fire to warm a pan of water up for some
instant coffee. Then he would spend several hours upstairs
in his reading chair, from which he could watch the rain and

allow the day's hangover to withdraw. He stopped shaving because heating the water was such a pain. Sometimes he would attempt to get through a few pages of *Nineteen Eighty-Four* or some selections of Orwell's collected letters or the tedious *Diaries* where he had recorded the minutiae of his farming and gardening, the amount of oil he used every day. None of it offered any insight into Winston Smith or *Nineteen Eighty-Four*.

When, around midday, he finished reading or not reading, Ray would head downstairs to scavenge some organic cookies or, if he was feeling ambitious, a canned good. The days were long. Before the sun could set—not that he ever saw the sun—he arranged some candles and a bottle of scotch so that he could find them in the dark. He longed for a hike, but the rain wouldn't let up. In the evenings, he sat next to the fire and drank whisky again until sleep tugged him down into the cushions. He had neglected to bring pornography. During those late hours, drunk enough to make turning back impossible, his thoughts again began to grow dark and more sinister.

As long as Ray could remember, since he was a little kid running amok in the endless rows of corn, his mind had contained partitioned rooms he knew not to enter; in them were countless self-perceptions better left un-thought about and which generated moods that later in life—particularly after his career at Logos took off—his personal safety required him to avoid. But left by himself for days on end, half-dozing next to a dying fire, with the large amounts of whisky unable to fight off the constant din of the rain, he couldn't help himself from picking open those locks and peering inside.

He thought a lot about his sister Becky, who had taken on the responsibility of caring for their mother. She had it so easy, what with her unquestioned acceptance of the status quo. Becky worked forty hours a week, believed in the literal divinity of Jesus Christ, and took pleasure in the hilarity of network television sitcoms. Unlike his father, Ray didn't care about the failures of a professional sports team or need to insist upon the innate superiority of one soft-drink brand over another. He wished it were otherwise.

Left to his own brooding for too long, Ray came to recognize that nothing in the entire goddamn world meant what it was supposed to. He had just walked away from a high-paying job in order to hide out in a damp house in Scotland. Maybe that was another big fucking mistake. He had been so stupid, but part of him—a big part—no longer cared. Nothing mattered any longer, not really, except for the fact that each gulp of single malt scotch tasted even sweeter than the previous and that remained true down to the very bottom of each bottle.

Every two or three days Ray opened the front door and found another unidentifiable animal carcass on the mudroom stoop. His sightseeing expeditions extended to the edge of the garden, where he hurled the bodies into the bushes with a shovel. Otherwise he stayed indoors. He grew bored and claustrophobic, but some creature was lurking out there waiting for him. His interaction with the locals consisted of peeking out the window when he heard their 4x4s driving past Barnhill. He came to recognize the sounds of five different vehicles that made their way from the Kinuachdrachd settlement down to Craighouse and back again.

Sometimes Ray couldn't remember why he had come to Jura and other times he couldn't imagine living anywhere else. The scotch pooled into a murky, aqueous sense of depression that ebbed and flowed, ebbed and flowed. Some days were better than others. Some days were not.

He was attempting to read the memoir of one of Orwell's contemporaries by the last evening light of the kitchen windows when a scraping noise came from the front door. He remained still, but the words "Loneliness began for me now fierce, desperate, taking on an importance out of all proportion to its quality which was that of a boy in his 'teens who" shook in his hands. There came another sound, and it grew louder. He put the book down.

Something rustled in the bushes outside the kitchen, then a monstrous face appeared in the window: an animal covered in mangy wet fur. It looked at Ray with knowing eyes that in a single glance interrogated him and his intrusive presence in this remote place, trapped in an old farmhouse a mile from the closest neighbors. The creature growled as if to speak and Ray screamed, but the hideous face still stared at him, its eyes shining with some fierce purpose, its crooked teeth glistening sharply from amid the soiled fur, until its so-nearly-human expression changed. In some savage and instinctual way, the thing appeared as startled as he was. It motioned as if to communicate with him through the windowpane: "Is everything okay, Ray?" it asked.

"Farkas? You scared the shit out of me."

"Not literally, I hope. Would you mind letting me in?"

Ray unbolted the front door, where Farkas stood dripping wet. "Come in, come in," he said. "You're absolutely soaked."

"Only on the outside, Ray," Farkas said. "Only on the outside." He sat on the mudroom bench and removed his wellingtons. "I could however use a wee dram if you have some on board."

"I have a bottle I've been saving for a special occasion, in fact. You go sit by the fire."

Farkas pulled a chair up. "I'm terribly sorry to frighten you like that," he said. "And I hope I didn't catch you at a bad time, as I don't mean to interrupt what you're doing up here . . . what *are* you doing up here? I would've telephoned, but that wasn't really an option, now was it?"

Ray dragged another chair next to Farkas's. "I'm grateful for the company. I think I'm going a little stir crazy, in fact. Solitude is a lot less restorative than I thought. It turns out that life off the grid actually kind of sucks."

"You're not the first man to discover that for himself," Farkas said. His voice carried a baritone roundness that in a different life might have lent itself to the opera. He lifted the glass to his nose, which was barely visible through his dense mask of mustache, beard, and eyebrow. "Nor I imagine will you be the last. This would be the eighteen-year-old, if I'm not mistaken."

"You can tell that just from the smell? Slàinte," Ray said. It was without question the most complex and delectable whisky that had ever crossed his tongue. It tasted the way living on Jura felt, like his humanity could reach a greater richness simply by living in such a rough and untamed land. "You certainly know your whisky. I forgot the water—I'll be right back."

"Don't bother, don't bother. I can drink water at home. And I believe that I've had close to enough of the stuff for one day, and, in any account, malt *this* good deserves to be taken neat."

"I didn't hear a vehicle pull up—did you walk all the way up here?"

"Sometimes I forget how big this little island truly is. I left my car at the public road and walked the last five miles. That path has destroyed sturdier cars than my own."

"I believe it. But that's still quite a walk. I have to admit I'm beginning to wonder what Orwell was thinking coming all the way up here. It must have been even more remote back then."

"The whole world's shrinking, Ray, at least in one sense, and that's the truth. As I've heard it, however, our Blair didn't get on very well with the locals. He was liked, as they say, but not *well* liked. There wasn't much use on Jura back then for socialist intellectuals," he said.

"And now?"

"Funny that you mention it. You did manage to upset Gavin. Don't let it worry you, though. It's not entirely your fault. He may be holding you to blame for some past crimes. There are some old stories—and the details are murky—there are old stories that suggest our Mr. Blair got himself into some hot water while here on Jura. Gavin swears that Blair was responsible for some unpardonable offense against his mother."

"Pitcairn's mother?"

"The very same. Blair was unwell even before he arrived. He suffered from tuberculosis where our climate, as perhaps you've noticed, can lean towards the damp. It must have been quite difficult for him, though they say he often took to sleeping outside in an army tent. It wouldn't be a stretch to believe that the man needed someone to look after him. He was incapable of preparing himself a simple cup of tea, so he certainly needed someone to do his cooking and washing up."

"Let me guess. Pitcairn's mother?"

"Aye, Beatrice Pitcairn herself. A saint of a woman, bless her soul. Blair proposed marriage and, ever the practical Englishman, even offered her a considerable dowry in the form of his estate and future royalties to what would become *Nineteen Eighty-Four*. Unfortunately, however, he neglected to take into consideration the fact that she was already married quite happily. Our little Gavin was at that point still little more than a gleam in her eye, yet now he has come to believe that—like our Eric Blair—you're here to split up his family."

"But that's absolutely—"

"Hear me out now," Farkas said. "He knows that Molly plans to leave Jura at her first opportunity and he's none too chuffed about that fact. He believes that exposure to the likes of you and your so-called intellectual ideas is going to hasten her departure."

"I came here to get away from people. Please explain it to him—I don't want to split up anyone's family."

"I know that, Ray. Can I trouble you?" he asked, holding aloft his empty glass.

"Sure," Ray said. "One sec."

The sky had darkened even further. His reflection stared back at him from the same kitchen window in which Farkas had appeared, and Ray yelped again.

He brought the whole bottle. Farkas was adding some peat bricks to the fire and stoking the ashes. The sitting room grew ten degrees warmer. "Now you can't take anything Gavin says personally, Ray. He doesn't care for much of anybody other than himself, but he upholds a special variety of loathing for outsiders—especially the tourists. And although I was born here, he still sees fit to consider me an outsider too, but I do try to get along with him. I can't imagine what you said to the man, but I've never seen him so wound up, and you can trust me when I say that I've seen that man well wound up. You should have heard him the time Molly announced she was going off to art school."

"Art school?"

"Aye, in Glasgow, no less. She didn't even tell him she had applied until the acceptance letter arrived. I would speculate that every living soul on this island other than Gavin Pitcairn knows the importance of an education for Molly. The sheep and deer and seals know it. He called the school and threatened to burn it to the ground."

"What an asshole."

"He's that, aye, but he's also a good man in his way. He wants what he thinks is best for Jura, and it's difficult to find fault with that impulse. That being said, before you go causing him any more trouble, I know for a fact that he would have burnt that school to the ground. Gavin's entirely capable of such a thing, so unless you want to have your guts for garters you might want to stay clear of him, Ray."

"Why, what did he say about me?"

"That at his first opportunity he plans to throw you into the Corryvreckan."

"The whirlpool is real? Orwell mentioned it in his diary, but I thought he made it up."

"I don't know what you consider real or unreal, but right off the north tip of our island there's a whirlpool which has swallowed up more fishing boats than you can count. Every few years the telly producers come out here to shoot yet another daft documentary about how Ulysses himself made it as far as the Hebrides. And some will argue that Corryvreckan is actually the mythical Charybdis, which makes it not so mythical by my reckoning."

"You're telling me that the sea monster from *The Odyssey* actually lives off the coast of Scotland?"

"That's what they say."

"And where do they say Scylla lives? Let me guess—Ireland?"

"As far as you're concerned, she lives in Craighouse and goes by the name Gavin Pitcairn."

Ray took a long drink. From the sound of things, he wouldn't be able to buy supplies at The Stores or collect his mail for fear of being attacked by a crazed Scottish arsonist. "I'll be right back," he said, his tongue thick with whisky. He extracted a hundred quid from his wallet. "Give this to Pitcairn," he told Farkas. "He says I owe him some money. That's why he's so mad. Tell him I'm sorry."

"I'm afraid it may be a bit late for that, Ray, but I'm sure this will help. I'd encourage you to stay out of his way, which you will admit shouldn't be too difficult for you up here. How're you settling in, anyway?"

Good question. How *was* he settling in?

"Being here has definitely been liberating, and the whisky is spectacular. Do I remember correctly that you work at the distillery?" Speaking—or slurring, in this case—to someone other than himself felt great.

"I do, I do. I'm in charge of what you might call quality control." Farkas touched his nose with a hairy finger. "This baby is my meal ticket. Or my drink ticket, I guess you could say. I possess an exceptionally acute sense of smell."

"This house must be torture for you."

"I'll admit I detected a slight plumbing problem when I came in. And you've been burning garbage in the fireplace."

"That's quite a talent."

"A blessing and a curse, Ray. A blessing and a curse, like most things. I will be happy to give you a tour—it's quite an operation. And it's my job, in a way, to keep a record of Jura's history. Now I'm going to pour one more dram and head on back."

"You just got here."

"Aye, but I've quite a long walk ahead of me. I should inquire if given your interest in our Mr. Blair, you happened to take the opportunity to speak with Singer on your way over?"

"The ferryman?"

"The very same. He may be among the last of the locals who knew Blair personally. I'm not saying they were fast friends or anything, but I'll be surprised if he doesn't have some good stories for you—even if they aren't what you might call true." Stupidly, it never occurred to Ray that he should ask the older folks about meeting Orwell. Some of the longtime residents might still remember him. "And Miss Wayward up at Kinu-achdrachd. I understand that her auntie knew Blair, though she's known to be a bit weird even for a Diurach."

"Is there anyone else I should speak to?"

"No one that I can think of off the top of my slightly intoxicated head. Oh . . . Mrs. Campbell."

"I should talk to Mrs. Campbell?"

"No! She is devout in her hatred of everything having to do with Mr. Blair, a fact that might explain why the two of you got off to such an awful start."

"You heard about that?"

"Everybody on Jura and Islay has heard about that," he said.

"That's not why she hates me, though. Or not the only reason. I really was terrible to her."

"Aye, I heard that too."

"What's her problem with Orwell?"

Farkas finished his fifth or sixth glass of scotch. "Well, there's been some speculation . . . and it's no more than that. One story, set somewhere between myth and reality, goes that Mrs. Campbell's dear mother, who lost her husband in the war, took quite a liking to Mr. Blair while he was here for the first time to inspect Barnhill."

"And?"

"What do you mean 'and?' You're going to have to keep your ears open on Jura, Ray. She took quite a liking to our Mr. Blair, if you know what I mean, while everybody else on the island detested the man. She may have even spent a few weeks here at Barnhill."

Comprehension descended more slowly than it should have. "Are you telling me that Mrs. Campbell is Orwell's illegitimate daughter?"

"I'm telling you nothing of the sort. Rather, I'm merely

reporting, for your own edification, about some of the mythologies of the Isle of Jura, like Charybdis or our werewolf."

"Jura has a wolf running loose? I might have seen it!"

"Not a wolf, a werewolf."

"Oh a werewolf. Of course."

"I'm entirely serious and you would do well to hear me out. Have you not noticed anything suspicious hereabouts?"

"Well, I have been finding dead animals on my front step."

"Aye, and who do you think might be responsible for leaving them there, the tax assessor? And if I had to speculate, I'd say the first one appeared the night you arrived. Is that right?"

"I have no problem believing that there's a wolf or bear or something loose on the island. I've scraped the evidence off my stoop, and it has me scared so shitless that I feel trapped in this house, but do you really expect me to believe that at the next full moon a werewolf is going to show up at my door?"

"No, Ray, I don't expect you to believe it, but neither your belief nor doubt changes the reality. I have it on the best possible authority that it is not an ordinary wolf, but a lycanthrope, and we don't only appear during the full moon—that's just Hollywood superstition."

"What do you mean 'we?'"

"Well, if you must know, I have every reason to believe that I am a werewolf."

Ray looked at Farkas. He did not appear to be joking. "Okay, I'll bite. Why do you believe that you're a werewolf?"

"I have my reasons. We'll save that story for another day. I know what you're thinking, but I'm not insane. No more than most people at any rate. That night you first arrived, that was the equinox, if you recall."

"I'll have to trust you on that."

"That's when Gavin and Fuller and the men go out hunting, every solstice and equinox, same as they did when you got here. They don't believe me any more than you do, so they have spent their entire lives trying to find and murder what was in your garden that night."

"Very funny, Farkas."

"There's nothing funny about it, I assure you. I'll take another wee splash after all, thank you. It's not something I can control, and I do worry that someone's going to get hurt, namely me."

"All the same, I think I'd like to see the next hunt. It sounds fascinating."

"Aye, it is most certainly that. But I'll ask you to do me a wee personal favor and refrain from shooting me. You're looking at me like I'm daft, which I suppose I can appreciate, but even if you don't believe me . . . and I don't expect that you do . . . remember that the difference between myth and reality isn't quite as distinct here on Jura as you might believe. Now I should go, it's a long walk. Many thanks for the whisky."

"Any time," Ray said. "I hope you'll come again soon."

"That I will, that I will. I give you my word that the very next time I feel like a five-mile stroll through a snake-infested swamp masquerading as a path, this will be my first stop. I'll see you down at the distillery one of these days and we'll try to sort things out with you and Gavin."

"Should I really be worried about him?"

"I can't say, but it will be best not to risk upsetting him further, just to be on the safe side. This money will help." Farkas slugged back the remaining scotch and sat in the mudroom to put his boots on. From his coat pocket he produced a small stack of envelopes. "I nearly forgot," he said. "I've brought your mail."

Ray watched Farkas splash up the hill until he disappeared into the rainy night. He went to the kitchen and, seeing his own reflection again, drew the curtains closed and filled a mason jar with water from the tap. The mail included a stack of printed-out emails Bud had sent to him care of the hotel. He placed them in the fire without reading them. The papers curled one by one in the heat until whatever bullshit his former friend and boss wanted to regale him with went up the chimney.

He also received a greeting card with his mother's neat cursive on the envelope. He tore it open. Inside, her handwritten salutation "Dearest Raymond" was followed by the printed message:

Thinking of you
and wishing you all
the blessings of our
Lord and Savior.

She had signed it at the bottom, "Mother." Ray put that in the fire too, then regretted it. He would need to send her a letter soon. What to say?

You know what I saw today? That had been his parents' favorite joke. Every day when his father came in from the fields or, later, got home from the plant, he would ask Ray the same question. The habit continued long after he stopped falling for it and after both of them had recognized that the son's humoring of the father signaled a permanent and unmistakable sea change in the relationship. Yet it remained funny even now. *Everything I looked at!*

MOST NIGHTS RAY MANAGED to drag his unexercised body upstairs to sleep off the booze, but every once in a while the dull morning light found him in one of the sitting room chairs, his back and neck howling with pain, at which point he either would or wouldn't bother to heat up a mug of water before stirring scoops of crystalline coffee bits into it and starting a new day all over again. He had grown thinner than usual after two weeks of dieting on scotch and cookies. His eyes sank into their sockets while the bones in his cheeks angled forward. His beard had sprouted in uneven patches of black bristle until he found a pair of scissors and sculpted it to a semblance of evenness. When his clothes started to smell he hung them out an upstairs window and dried them by the sitting-room fire. There was nothing to be done about the sweat stains on the shirts' white collars. He had come to Jura for some peace and quiet, but living alone sucked. He should have remembered that.

Farkas's visit had reminded him how much he needed to get out of the house and talk to someone other than himself. He was so bored that he became willing to risk meeting a wolf out on the moors. The Paps were calling, but that would require a bit of planning and—if at all possible—a clear day. For the time being, he chose a more modest destination.

The remotest reach of civilization on the island was a village a mile or so north called Kinuachdrachd. According to his diaries, Orwell had had friends there, some crofters. That was in the spring of 1946 so it was unfathomable that they were still alive, but Ray wanted to at least see where Orwell took a walk every morning; he would go there for his milk, until he acquired his own moo-cow.

Ray got dressed and headed out. If the sheep could get used to the rain, so could he. What he could not tolerate, however, was another stinking animal carcass. The smell was atrocious. He tossed it into the shrubberies. His socks were already drenched by the time he got up to the road. So much for his expensive boots. The rain was not going to stop him. The weather on Jura was no worse than the storms that rolled in from Lake Michigan—that's what he told himself. The wind churned the surface of the sound. He could make out a small, craggy archipelago that hadn't showed up on the maps. The mainland lurked ever so faintly in the distance.

Kinuachdrachd turned out to be a settlement of a dozen

buildings, some of them in ruins. It looked like a fishing village, or like a fishing village was supposed to look. Smoke rose from the chimney of a little cottage and that was where Ray went. Around the back, a woman was wrestling with a ball of barbed wire. She had a pole through the middle to lift it, but it looked heavy. She was building an enclosure of some sort and having a tough time. A large dog heard Ray approach and it charged at him in a fury of teeth and slobber. The animal looked only semidomesticated, like it had never been indoors a day in its life, and like it was hungry for something other than its owner's table scraps. Ray froze—wasn't that what one was supposed to do? His heart stopped beating as if trying not to call attention to itself. There was nowhere to run, no trees to climb. He could almost feel the teeth sinking into his calf and tearing his pants leg. He tried to figure out where he would need to go for a regimen of rabies shots—Oban, maybe, if not all the way back to Glasgow—when the woman whistled and the dog stopped. It looked disappointed, but trotted back and plopped itself into a puddle in front of its doghouse.

The woman looked to be about seventy. She put the spool down with a grunt and wiped her hands on her overalls. Two of the four sides of the fence were already in place. "I guess you must be Mr. Welter."

"I must be," he said.

"Give me a hand with this, would you?" She nodded toward an extra pair of gloves near the back door of the cottage and held up a length of barbed wire. "Mind the ends—these are quite sharp," she said.

"Don't worry," he said. "I grew up on a farm and know my way around some barbed wire."

She looked at him with some concentration, sizing him up. "Based on what Mr. Pitcairn says, I imagined you were a bit prissier than all that."

"From what I can tell, that man is a borderline sociopath."

"That's where you're wrong, Mr. Welter. There's nothing borderline about him, which is to say he's an utter and complete sociopath, but he's *our* utter and complete sociopath. It takes all sorts and he's exactly as God made him."

The woman's face was leathery and wind beaten and beautiful. She looked like someone comfortable with her own fortitude. She had earned the crow's-feet that led like ancient aqueducts from the sides of her eyes and Ray couldn't help but think of the countless hours he had spent behind desks and in cubicles, staring at computers and watching web videos about animals doing amusing things. He had wasted so much of his life.

One end of the barbed wire had been wrapped and tied around a core post. The two of them lifted the spool together by the pole and let it unwind as they walked the length of the fence. "Go slow now," she said. "That's it." It was a huge job and he couldn't imagine that she had completed the first two sides by herself.

"Well my plan is to stay as far away from Pitcairn as possible."

"Aye, that might be for the best, he's a troubled soul, but in his heart he means well and he wants what's best for Jura, or what he believes to be best."

"And what's that?"

The line got snagged on some debris on the ground. Ray held the entire spool— far heavier than it looked—while she got it loose again. "The sad part of it all is that for all his lip service about maintaining our way of life, as he calls it, and I'm not entirely sure what he means by that, he himself does not feel bound in any way by our traditional Highlands hospitality." She put her side of the spool down again and removed a glove to shake his hand. "Speaking of which, I'm Miriam Wayward. Can I offer you a cup of tea?"

"Nice to meet you, Mrs. Wayward." These people and their tea. Ray would never feel entirely at home in a nation that didn't know how to brew a decent cup of coffee. "I was told to stay clear of you."

"You're welcome to do that if you like, or you can come in for a cup, and it's Miss not Mrs., but by all means call me Miriam. Allow me to guess: Mr. Pitcairn told you I was a witch who cooks the bones of children in a big pot and casts evil spells on my enemies?"

"Something like that. Mrs. Bennett says you're quite friendly, but that I should leave Mr. Harris alone."

"Aye, he prefers his solitude, it's true, and he should thank our Maker every day that solitude isn't a crime even in this ruinous age. No tea, then?"

"Let's finish this first, Miriam. Are you building a pen for your dog?"

"Aye, to keep her in and some intruders out."

"Intruders? Is there much crime on Jura?"

She laughed. "Crime on Jura? Never, not unless you consider driving whilst intoxicated a crime, but then there would be no getting anywhere. We have some sort of predator on the loose these days, not that I can tell you how it got here. Mr. Pitcairn wants to suggest it's a wolf, but I find that difficult to believe."

"I saw it in my garden the night I arrived, and there have been dead animals at my door."

"Well that is peculiar, isn't it?"

"I talked to Farkas about it."

"He wants you to believe he's a werewolf, I suppose?"

"It's the fact that he believes it that interests me."

"He's mad, of course," Miriam said, "but there's little accounting for the beliefs of others." She lifted the spool again and waited for him to do the same. They arrived at the far end and spun the line around the post a few times at the spot she had marked, a few inches off the ground, then continued along the final open side of the enclosure. When they got to the last post, she cut the wire and the end jumped, biting into her sweater. "Almost got me that time," she said. She pulled a hammer from her waistband and used the claw side to pull in the slack, wrapped the loose end around the pole, and then twisted the end around the wire she had already connected.

"There's another one down. If you won't take a cup, how about a wee dram?"

That was not something Ray was about to refuse. "I would love that," he said. "Then we'll finish this off."

The notches on the wooden pole and the two completed sections indicated that they had four more lines to run. It would be an all-day job, and the rain showed no signs of letting up. The dog watched them go into the house.

Pelts and furs and unidentifiable animal skulls decorated the walls and covered the chairs and sofa. A chandelier made from deer antlers hung from the low ceiling. The smell of simmering stew wafted from the kitchen, where Miriam went and then returned with a tray on which she balanced a plate of scones, a bottle of the local whisky, and two empty jelly jars. "Oh do sit down," she said. She poured two large drams. "Welcome to the Isle of Jura," she said.

"Slàinte," Ray said.

"Well, well," she said. She sounded impressed. "Slàinte." She took a long drink and he did the same. It tasted like French kissing a leather-clad supermodel, and felt like someone had turned the thermometer in his stomach back up to a reasonable temperature. He couldn't get a good look at the bottle. "If you don't mind me asking, Mr. Welter, I—"

"Please call me Ray."

"If you don't mind me asking, Ray, what fair wind has cast you upon our humble shore?"

"Excuse me?

"What in the name of our Heavenly Father are you doing on Jura?"

"You're the third person to ask me that and I'm still not sure I have a good answer. I guess I needed to get away from civilization and think."

She laughed a little bit. "You guess? It's quite a drastic step to take based upon a guess. You may find yet that we Diurachs are quite civilized," she said. "Most of us are, at any rate, our Mr. Pitcairn respectfully excluded."

"No, I don't mean it that way. Back in Chicago I felt like Big Brother had come true, and that if I didn't get away from it I was going to lose my mind. I guess . . . I mean, I'm trying to figure out how to live my life in a way that doesn't adversely affect others." He gulped down some more scotch. "I always wondered why Orwell went to the least populated place he could find in order to write about living with an omnipresent government that watches our every move. It seems like a contradiction."

"Yet it's difficult to argue with his results, is it not? One thing you'll need to know is that there was no George Orwell here."

"What do you mean?"

"My auntie knew him quite well, and he visited this very house on many occasions, but he was always Eric Blair on Jura. No one called him George Orwell. It seems a bit daft that a man who took so many others to task for the slightest offense to his rigid sense of British integrity would spend his career hiding behind a pseudonym."

"I never thought of it like that." Ray finished his scotch and felt like a better person because of it.

"Why would you? There was none of that here, I'll tell you: no, he was Eric Blair and when people such as yourself begin poking around looking for George Orwell, I tell them there was no one here by that name."

"Do you know what I'd like to do?" he asked.

"What's that?"

"I'd like to finish that fence. I feel like I've spent the past decade trapped indoors and now I'm dying to be outside. Thank you so much for the whisky."

"Well take a scone with you," Miriam said. She pulled her gloves on again and they got back to work. The rain felt pretty good, actually. "Like this—now pull this bit along, that's it," she said, and showed him how to better manage the unspooling line with his free hand. "You need to remember to give yourself enough slack to work with, but too much and you'll soon find yourself entangled and bleeding."

Ray stopped. That was so true—she was right.

"That's very well put," he said. Over the past few years, had he given himself too much slack or not enough? It was something he would have to think more about.

"I once heard someone say that on the radio."

"To answer your question, what I want to do is leave the earth a slightly better place when I die. In the meantime, I want to be able to sleep at night. That's all. If I can't do that here, away from the world, it may never happen."

"Your problem is, and I hope that you don't mind me saying so, is that our little isle is just as much a part of the world as London or Paris or your Chicago, maybe more so because—and Mr. Pitcairn is right about this point—although we may be remote, and that's by choice, particularly up here in Kinuachdrachd, God bless us, we still like being connected on our own terms."

"And what terms are those?"

"It's true that God's green earth provides us with but one path to Craighouse and beyond, but I might ask you to consider other avenues. The seas also contain roads, there are paths over the water and even highways that sailors have traveled for millennia. If Jura is indeed remote, and I'm not so sure that it is, that's only because the relatively recent invention of the automobile has made us forget our traditional travel routes, and that's the only thing keeping us at arm's length from what you call civilization. You seem like a decent young man, Ray. Troubled, to be sure, and I do hope you find whatever it is you've come looking for, but you don't yet seem to see the full grace and glory of the world that exists before your eyes."

"Maybe not," he said.

Finishing the pen took the rest of the afternoon, until the setting sun turned the westerly sky a pinkish shade of grey. The breeze picked up and the birds in the trees and shrubs sang their plaintive goodnights. Ray's body still thought it was on Central Time and it should be the early afternoon. He stifled a yawn. "It has been very nice to meet you, Miriam, but I suppose I'll be heading back."

"Can I tempt you with one more wee dram?"

"No thanks, I can't keep my eyes open as it is."

"Suit yourself. I suppose I'll be seeing you around now that we're neighbors." She whistled for the dog and let her into the new pen, where she would be safe from the wolf or Farkas or whatever it was that wanted to slice her open and eat her for a late-night snack. Speaking of which—Ray needed to hurry home. What little brightness the clouds contained had all but faded and it wasn't like there were streetlights to guide him back.

He found the path and oriented himself southward before the utter darkness took over. He saw no moonlight, no stars, no boats lit up on the water. He quickened his pace. The wind made noises in the trees. Every wave crashing onto the shore sounded like the breath of the monster out here with him. Ray took off running. He ran all the way to Barnhill and groped his way around the exterior of the house to the front door, and got into the mudroom without being mauled. His heartbeat throbbed in his neck. A knot of pain filled the center of his chest. He didn't have the energy to start a fire and warm up some much-needed bathwater, and he began to snore before he flopped onto the bed.

THE NEXT MORNING, RAY picked up the *Diaries* again and read three pages without absorbing a single goddamn thing. The letters had aligned themselves into words and the words into sentences and paragraphs, but none of them made any sense. It might as well have been in another language. Orwell had written something about shooting rabbits and skinning them. He had liked eggs. Ray put the book down and looked out the window. Nothing had changed. Swirling shapes presented themselves in the mist and then went away. The drizzle spoke to him of mathematical and spiritual concepts. At that moment, he came to understand what infinity was.

Pouring a glass of whisky felt less like the right thing to do and more like the only thing to do. What remained of his supply stood sentry on the kitchen counter. Seven bottles, two of which were still sealed. The five open bottles contained various amounts of liquid, so he pulled the corks from all of them, practiced his embouchure with some kissy faces in the window, then whistled a jug-band rendition of the *Ode to Joy* over the necks of the bottles. When a note didn't sound right, he chugged that scotch—a twelve-year old, a twenty-one—until it did. *Freude, schöner Götterfunken* my ass, he thought.

His boredom had morphed from a meditative state to an emotional liability. He belched up a cloud of single-malt scotch, ate a few crackers from a tin, and put some clothes on. Ray needed to get out of the house again before he hurt himself. The blue jeans and sweater felt cumbersome after so much time spent in sweatpants. He no longer wondered if it was raining or not—the rain was a constant, a given. It wasn't even *rain* any longer, but something immutable and permanent. Something inestimable. The atmosphere of the Inner Hebrides was made not for him but for the sheep and colorful lichens that sprouted from every surface.

The plan for the day was to walk to the source of Loch Tarbert, about halfway down the length of the island. From the map, hiking there looked doable in a few hours. Every place was in walking distance if one had enough time.

He left without locking the door, went a mile, maybe two, before he couldn't ignore the pain in his feet any longer. His boots proved to be useless. No, they were worse than useless—they were harmful. The extent of their utility was to cause pain. After so many miles the leather remained as stiff and unforgiving as the day he bought them. Every step sent waves of battery acid splashing into the blisters on his heels and soles. Each puddle he stepped in—and the path was nothing if not one long puddle—found its way to his bloody socks. He tried to distract himself from the pain tingling up to his knees, to enjoy the scenery and the fresh air, but there were several agonizing miles to go before he reached the road.

He stopped to watch a fleet of dolphins skipping across the surface of the sound. There were said to be seals nearby too, and puffins over on the far side of Islay. He would need to find a better way to get around. All this walking sucked, but he kept going. The blisters felt like hateful marshmallows stuck in his socks. The pain became disorienting. It was inconceivable that such small wounds could inflict so much suffering.

He spotted a cylindrical tower at the top of a hill—a bunker of some sort—and decided to stop there to assess the state of his feet. Even the slight incline caused his Achilles heels to rub harder against the backs of the boots. Up close, the structure resembled a standing stone made of concrete, manmade but more monolithic than Neolithic. It could have been an elaborate marker for a barrow of some sort, but that seemed unlikely. The object served no purpose that he could see—it just *was*. He sat against it and removed his boots to squeeze the water from his socks. It wasn't so terribly cold out; he could walk home barefoot. Whatever it took to avoid putting those boots back on. He tied the laces together to make them easier to carry.

If by some miracle the rains stopped and clouds parted, this spot would have granted a great view of the entire island, but, as usual, Ray had to imagine all that the mists concealed. To the south, Loch Tarbert divided the land in half and, beyond that, the Paps loomed over everything around them. A few long, blistered miles west toward Colonsay would put him on the seaboard. That part of Jura, north of the lake, remained uninhabited and untamed. The coastal cliffs on the western shore were said to be home to a series of caves that he wanted to explore; over the years, they had been occupied by pirates, gypsies, even bootleggers who were said to have produced Jura's first whisky, which they shipped to prohibition-era America.

The attraction of living on a small island—which was not

so small after all, as both Farkas and his own feet attested—
was the belief, mistaken to be sure, that he might get to know
it in its entirety, that there existed one place on the planet that
he could fully understand. So far, however, he had seen so little
and what he had seen made him want to see and learn more.
The natural world was inexhaustible and at the moment he
faced the impossible decision of where to go next. He could
pick any direction, but the number of choices terrified him.
Maybe there was such a thing as too much freedom. Every
decision, big or small, eliminated as many possibilities as it
opened up. He could go anywhere. Or he could make his way
back to Barnhill and stay indoors to drink himself senseless. It
was a tough call, but he preferred the disappointment and self-
hatred he would feel after another solitary bender in the sitting
room over the fiery ache in his feet. He had made it as far as
he could and hadn't reached the public road, much less Loch
Tarbert. The water mocked him in the distance. Hiking to the
Paps would be unthinkable. The day was an abject failure. His
life was an abject failure. He never should have come to Jura.

The rocks and sticks jabbed at his bare feet, just as they had
so long ago back on his parents' farm. He was going to pull his
boots back on when the headlights of a truck came bouncing
up the path from Craighouse. If it was Pitcairn, Ray planned
to ignore him. Let him drive right by. Anyone else, he would
flag him down and beg—down on his knees in the mud like an
animal if he had to—for a ride back to Barnhill.

Then he heard it. The sound of the vehicle was

unmistakable. That roar. That 6.2 liter V8 engine that combusted petroleum by the barrel and farted climate-changing gases. It couldn't be. The truck was still far away, but he made out a few scratches in the paint: O . . . I . . . L . . . H . . .

Ray wiped the rain and sweat from his eyes. When he looked again, the SUV had become a small 4x4 pickup that was getting thrown back and forth by the potholes and puddles. It was the little white truck he heard go past the house from time to time. The revving engine sounded seasick. It stopped and a window rolled down. The driver was a burly man in his fifties. His woolly, fisherman's sweater matched the color and texture of his beard. "Barefoot, is it? You'll be wanting a pair of wellies from Mrs. Bennett."

"I had no idea my feet could hurt this much," Ray said. "Good to meet you, I'm—"

"I know who you are. You'll be wanting to sit in the back."

The passenger seat was empty. The cabin looked so warm, but the driver motioned for Ray to climb into the truck bed. He walked around the side of the vehicle and saw that three inches of black mud lined the back. It squeezed between his toes. The truck started moving again and he had to crouch and hold on to the side to balance. That was when he smelled it. He was squatting in a truckload of fresh fertilizer. The morning's scotch clawed up the back of his throat. Pig shit coated his feet and his clothes and all Ray could do was laugh. When the truck stopped at Barnhill he was still cracking up.

He hopped out and went to invite his savior in for a wee

dram, if only to postpone his own boredom a few more minutes, but the man drove off without as much as a wave. Ray
waited for him to get out of sight, then stripped off all his
clothes and allowed the rain to wash the shit off and then
shoveled the new animal corpse into the overgrowth.

It took no time at all to get a fire raging. Ray's pyroma-
niacal skills had improved in a short amount of time. For the
evening's scotch he chose a lovely ten-year-old the color of
blond wood that had very recently sang bass in his rendition
of Beethoven. He poured a short dram and inhaled the fumes
deep into his nose. If shoe polish could smell delectable, that's
what the ten-year-old smelled like. Shoe polish and salt water.
The first sip felt soothing in his chest, the second in his shoulders. The afternoon faded to evening.

He was skimming through "Such, Such Were the Joys," a
typescript of which Orwell had mailed to his publisher from
Jura around the time he began *Nineteen Eighty-Four*, when
he came to an insight about his own condition. In that essay,
Orwell had written about his days at boarding school, where
the entire hierarchy of the English class system got distilled to
its cruelest possible concentration. The American corporate
world now operated in a similar manner.

The young Blair had suffered at the hands of the headmas-
ters and his wealthy classmates, many of whom had estates in
Scotland. This country had become the place where people
of immense privilege came for shooting parties and to enjoy
all the luxuries of upper crust British life—the kind of life

that Blair was continually reminded he would never experience. Once Orwell attained some small financial success with *Animal Farm* he was able to obtain what had so far been out of reach. Barnhill served as his own privileged estate away from the hullabaloo of London's postwar reconstruction, and in coming here he had achieved the social status denied him as a child. It made perfect sense.

There was a key difference, though, for Orwell. Instead of shooting pheasants and foxes while wearing a tuxedo, he wanted to work the soil with his bare hands. He didn't have servants or host dinner parties—he planted vegetables and plowed the fields and sweated his tubercular ass off, all while continuing his literary correspondence and writing a masterpiece. He came to Jura in order to show up his classmates, even if only in his own mind, as the stuck-up snobs that they were.

The insight inspired a victory dance in the sitting room.

RAY DOZED OFF TO the sound of rain knocking at the windows. The wind eventually woke him and then punctuated eight and a half hours of eyes-wide-open insomnia before it yielded to a series of early morning dreams about every manner of natural and unnatural disaster. He half heard the sitting-room chair shaking and groaning beneath him while he recoiled from the sounds of automobile accidents, plane crashes, and crumbling skyscrapers. From the sickening crunch of metal against metal, the drip drip drop of broken sewer lines erupting into fountains of diarrheal waste. Naked bodies fueled a mile-high bonfire. He awoke disoriented and with the odors of kerosene and burning human flesh still in his nose. The room was strangely bright. It took a minute to figure out where he was. Outside, the sun shined upon Barnhill's back garden.

The sun!

He opened the window to welcome the warm air in, but the smoky smell from his dream didn't dissipate. Something was on fire.

A dozen possibilities ran through his mind: he had forgotten to blow out a candle and it had ignited the spilled whisky on the counter. Or a red ember had flown up the chimney and torched the bushes outside. A milk cow had kicked over a lantern. Whatever had started it, the odor was unmistakable. He was going to be responsible for burning down George Orwell's house.

The smell of burning grease originated in the kitchen. He ran through the dining room with his socked feet sliding on the wooden floor. There were no signs yet of smoke, but the fire crackled and sizzled. Water. He needed a bucket of water. No! Not for a grease fire. For a grease fire, he needed . . . what? Baking soda? The odor grew stronger, more pungent. That pile of charcoaled bodies flickered again through his mind. If he didn't know better he would've sworn that it smelled exactly like—

"Coffee's on," Molly said. She stood at the sink looking out the window and watching the sheep amble around the sunny garden. Their bells usually relaxed Ray, but this morning they sounded like a fleet of screaming fire trucks careening through the yard. The light pounded into his eyes. "Mind you, I can't imagine how you Yanks drink this stuff."

"What are you doing here?"

"What does it look like?" Her voice cracked the tiniest bit. "I'm making breakfast. I hope you don't mind," she said, and turned to face him.

It was called a black eye, but her face appeared more orange and purple: a horrendous masterpiece of secondary colors. A strawberry-sized lump protruded from her forehead.

"Would you mind if I stayed here for a little while?" she asked.

"Sure, definitely. I mean—no. I don't mind."

If he wanted to be honest with himself, Ray would have admitted that his very first thought was about the loss of his solitude. The idea of looking after an abused teenager didn't carry much appeal considering that her murderous dad would be looking for her any minute, but under no circumstances could he turn away a girl who was getting beat up at home. "Does your father know you're here?"

"You're having a laugh, right? He was out drinking all night, so I made a break for it."

"How'd you get all the way up here?"

"On my mountain bike. I brought as much as I could carry."

"I'm not sure this is a great idea, but you can make yourself one hundred percent at home," he said. "Take the room upstairs at—"

"At the end of the hall, aye. My things are already up there. You were still sleeping and, I should add, you snore like a beast. Now have some of this coffee before it gets cold. It's better than that instant shite you've been drinking, and far tastier than Fuller's. I swear he makes it that way on purpose."

She almost smiled.

Sure enough, it was the best coffee Ray had tasted since leaving Chicago. Over his own moans of pleasure, he heard a sound like the release of springs in a metal can. Two pieces of white bread leapt from the toaster and poked their crusty heads out as if to see their shadows and determine how much longer he had to wait for a decent meal. She must have brought some food with her.

"How did you do that?" he asked.

"I pushed this lever down."

"No, how did you turn on the electricity?"

"I switched on the generator out the back, dummy."

"There's a generator?"

"One of those silent ones at that. It's in the stables. Are you telling me you've lived in this house for a month without electricity or gas? You didn't notice the big, white propane tank outside?"

He had noticed it, sure, but it never occurred to him that it might work.

"You haven't had any hot water?"

"I heated some pots and pans up a few times in the fireplace."

"Are you positively deranged?"

He gestured toward her face. "Do you want to talk about it?" he asked.

"About the hot water?"

"About your eye."

She sized him up for a moment. "No, not really. Also, and I don't mean to be insensitive or in any way appear less than grateful for your hospitality, but could I trouble you to put on some trousers?"

Oh hell.

He was wearing only a pair of boxers and black dress socks with gold toes. Cold pinpricks dotted his arms and legs. At least he wasn't completely naked this time.

Ray went upstairs to put on some clean-ish jeans and a black "Oil Hogg" T-shirt. Living with a female again would take some getting used to. Wearing pants. No more pissing out back in the garden. No more drying his naked body by the fire.

Molly had breakfast ready by the time he got downstairs again: full Scottish, minus the haggis. The blazing sunlight illuminated the kitchen but also exposed a layer of grime on the counters and in the sink. He made the decision to ignore it. They sat and without delay Molly tore in to her food. Bacon, eggs, toast, tomatoes. Real coffee. She shoveled it all in with two hands. She slurped at her tea and belched into the crook of her elbow. "Have some tomato," she said, sending bits of egg hurtling onto his shirt. Ray could've gone on eating for days, except that she sucked up everything in sight before he could get his fill. He would need to be quicker. Crumbs stuck to her cheek and wouldn't budge even when she wiped her mouth with the back of her hand, the fingers of which still grasped a triangle of toasted and buttered and jellied bread. She looked like a half-domesticated animal set loose on a feeding trough. Her gluttony was mesmerizing, yet also endearing. It was sweet in a strange and disgusting way. He envied her. She appeared so . . . *healthy*.

After she finished every morsel on her plate and then on his, she leaned back in her chair. "Okay, then," she said. "A few ground rules. In exchange for the use of the room upstairs, I will do the cooking."

She had clearly been rehearsing this conversation. "Ter rific," Ray said.

"Second, I will stay out of your way. I don't want to interfere with your work and I don't want you interfering with mine."

"Fair enough," he told her. Everything was happening so fast: in the span of twenty minutes he had gone from hermit to chaperone for an abused teenager. Also, what work could a seventeen-year-old girl have at a place like Barnhill?

"Most importantly, and I wouldn't be here if I thought this would be an issue, but I want to make it clear that nothing is going to happen between us. Our relationship will be purely, strictly, and chastely platonic. Got it?"

"Got it."

"You promise?"

"You have my solemn oath. Nothing will happen. No thing."

She shook his hand with much ado, leaving a globule of jelly on it. "Now, while you do the washing up, I'm going to unpack my things. We'll reconvene for lunch. Until then, I will appreciate very much having some privacy. Also, you stink—take a bath. Mind you, I do like your beard."

The possibility of a physical relationship with Molly hadn't even occurred to him. It wasn't even within the realm of possibility. "Sure," he said. "You'll have all the privacy your heart desires. Can I help with your bags?"

"No, but you could get rid of the dead fox at the front door. You need to bury it or it will attract carrion and they attack the lambs."

Indeed, another animal sat prostrate and disemboweled at the doorstep, surrounded by a miniature Stonehenge of gooey fur. The stench was unbearable. He squinted at it in the sun. A pair of crows was enjoying a feast and they dared him to chase them away. "Yah!" he said and stomped a foot in their general direction. They looked at him with disdain then continued to peck and pull at their brunch. He went to the garage to fetch the shovel. The generator now powering the house purred almost inaudibly, much unlike the petroleum-spewing models he would see on the neighbors' farms as a kid or powering gigantic TVs and PA systems at Saturday tailgate parties.

Shovel in hand, he scraped the mess into a burlap sack and

carried it to the garden, where he chose a dead tree as a grave marker. The blade of the shovel carved cleanly through the layer of heather and into the soft, peaty soil, but the job would still take half an hour. He got to digging. Molly's uninvited presence got him thinking about Flora and the way his time in Chicago had ended. Flora had asked him once what he feared most and since then he had given the question a great deal of thought. Not rats. Not bad gin. He feared that he would never regain the certainty he had possessed when first reading Orwell.

He brushed the sweat from his forehead and surveyed the new grave. It was a beautiful thing to be in Scotland and to dig a hole on a sunny day. He kicked the sack into the hole and leaned on the handle of the shovel to catch his breath. His fingers grew calloused, but it was strange how easily he could slip off his wedding ring. Without giving it much further thought, he dropped it on top of the burlap sack and threw a pile of black dirt on top until the island itself swallowed the band of gold. That was when he caught Molly watching him from an upstairs window. He smiled at her, but the curtain flittered closed. Ray got down on the ground and reached for the ring. The putrid odor rose to greet him. The burlap squished beneath his fingers. He thought about putting it back on, but allowed the fox to carry it with him into the next world.

He ruled out searching for the other dead animals he had tossed into the bushes and refilled the hole and stowed the shovel back in the garage. The muscles in his shoulders ached and he wanted nothing more than to take a hot bath, but Molly had beaten him to it. She was in the bathroom singing something like a lullaby or children's rhyme, albeit a profane one. He took the opportunity to poke his head into what had become her bedroom. The door creaked open.

Three folding easels stood sentry in a semicircle facing the northern window. A wooden bucket from the garage held a bouquet of paintbrushes and palette knives. White sheets covered the three paintings in progress. The bath was still running, so he tiptoed in and lifted the corner of one.

The painting was a self-portrait, but her hands and feet had yet to be painted. She was completely nude, her belly and big boobs protruding, and looking at the viewer as if to say, *This is who I am. Take it or leave it.* She had laid herself bare and in vivid detail. It was beautiful—she was an *amazing* painter. He couldn't stop staring. Something operating inside his respiratory system came to a halt. His heart was no longer beating. Then the bath water stopped.

Ray covered the painting again and crept back into the hallway. The floorboards whined beneath his feet. Molly surely knew what he was up to. She would be livid. Before she could emerge, he fled to his room and closed the door. The image of Molly had imprinted itself onto his imagination. Her gaze challenged him to look away, but he didn't want to.

In the painting, she had given herself a black eye.

During the days that followed they settled into a pleasant enough routine. Each morning after breakfast they retired to their respective rooms so that Molly could paint and he could read. She asked him a few times about his obsession with *Nineteen Eighty-Four*, and he was unable to come up with a sensible explanation. It had something to do with the fact that Winston Smith had suffered every manner of torture before he surrendered to the system. Big Brother threatened him with starving rats in a cage they placed over his head. The fear got to be too much and by the end he stopped rebelling. Winston came to love his oppressor and in doing so found some semblance of contentment.

Painting was different from reading in that there was only so much Molly could accomplish each day before she needed to stop and let the oils dry. She got restless when cooped up in the house too long. She spent hours sunbathing nude in the rear garden, and he tried not to notice.

Molly had been at Barnhill for over a week when, one afternoon, she barged into Ray's room without knocking and interrupted his reading. "Why are you indoors on a day this lovely?" she asked.

"You can see that I'm reading."

"I'm bored. Let's take a walk. I need to get out."

"So get out!" he said, but was already putting his bookmark in place.

"I'll pack a lunch."

It did look like a perfect day and with the blisters subsiding he was long overdue for some sightseeing. He put on a pair of cargo shorts and tall, burr-resistant socks. Molly was in the mudroom shoving two stained and threadbare mackintoshes into a military surplus backpack. "Raincoats?" he asked. "A little overprotective, aren't we?"

"I'm not going to argue with you," she said. She removed one of the coats and placed it back on its hook. "Mind you, I really don't care if you get drenched."

Ray opened the door to peek outside. Sunlight tickled the endless field of pink rhododendrons. Bees buzzed in the warm afternoon air. The sheep suffered in their winter coats. He looked at Molly, then at the cloudless sky, then at Molly again.

"Who are you going to believe?" she asked. "Me or your own lying eyes? It is going to piss down in, oh, three quarters of an hour."

"Fine," he said. No need to stir up an argument. "Give me that raincoat. Anything else? Maybe some scuba gear?"

She removed the mac from the hook again, crammed it into the backpack, and handed him the whole thing. "The next time you're at The Stores, pick yourself up a decent pair of wellies. I threw away those ugly boots of yours."

Sure enough, his boots were missing from the mudroom. "What do you mean you threw them away? Those were very expensive!"

"I put them in the bin. They're shite at any stupid price. They might be right for the grueling conditions of inner city Chicago, but on Jura they're as useful as nail polish on a snake."

"What am I supposed to wear in the meantime?"

"What am I supposed to wear in the meantime? Jesus, do you listen to yourself? It's not my problem—your plimsolls, I suppose." He looked at her blankly. "Trainers? Sneakers?"

"I have a better idea," Ray said.

The garbage pail at the back of the house overflowed with over a month's worth of refuse. He needed to take it to the dump somehow. He retrieved his boots from the muck.

As much as he wanted to climb the Paps, they were way too far away to reach in one afternoon. They headed in the opposite direction, up toward Kinuachdrach. The air was aromatic with sage and wildflowers and hay. They walked in silence, but it became clear that Molly had something to get off her chest. He didn't push it.

For the first time in months, his muscles seemed to be loosening. Was this what it meant to relax? It had been a long, long time. Every so often he and Helen used to get in the truck and drive up to the woods in northern Illinois or Wisconsin. They could walk for long, tranquil hours. Being on Jura brought back some of that joy, but with Molly there existed a different and tenser variety of shared silence.

After something like forty minutes or an hour, a damp breeze kicked up. He really had gained a new sense of time. His body felt more responsive to the natural environment than to the lumbering journey of an hour hand around the face of a wristwatch. The wind sent the grasses rippling in long waves. The cool air mitigated the heat beating down on his face and the part of his neck not covered by his beard, which had again assumed an unruly life of its own. Molly had remarked that he looked like a second-rate hippie guru capable of mass murder or a millionaire jam-band guitarist trying to resemble his unwashed fan base.

They arrived in Kinuachdrach and he knocked on Miriam's door, but she didn't answer. A cat stirred in the window and the dog growled at them from its barbed-wire cage. "Too bad she's not in," Molly said. "She bakes the best scones in Scotland."

The pickup truck full of pig shit was parked next to another house, one crumbling and half boarded up. "Who lives there?" Ray asked.

"That's Mr. Harris. He keeps to himself."

"He gave me a ride to Barnhill the other day."

"Are you having a laugh?"

"He said he knew who I was."

"He stops by The Stores and even the lounge from time to time, but hasn't spoken more than a sentence to anyone in two years. We're best to leave him alone."

They followed the path up to a summit, from where they could see the mainland and make out several of the neighboring islands. It was Ray's first real view of his surroundings. A lighthouse or bunker of some sort stood vigil on one of the islands. The shadows of clouds spotted the land with fast-moving shapes. He stood at the centermost point of the entire universe and understood, finally, that he was on the Isle of Jura, that his physical experience of the natural surroundings and his mental image of the map were one and the same. He stayed put for a moment while Molly marched ahead; then he jogged to catch up. Beyond the summit, a path plummeted toward a gulf where she pointed to something in the water. "See that?" she asked.

A series of wooden docks housed some small boats, which looked perfect for fishing or even for a short jaunt over to the mainland. "Not really."

"See where the water's a bit darker? That's the Corryvreckan."

They went down to the quay and sat with their legs hanging over the water. Gigantic seabirds screeched at them and broke the surface of the water in perilous dives. Ray wanted to ask Molly a million questions—about Jura, about who might still remember Orwell, about her black eye most of all. They watched the sunlight sparkle on the water until the smell of the air changed and became almost metallic. Molly pulled a raincoat from the backpack. She put it on, but it was several sizes too large so she had to roll up the sleeves. When she stood it hung to her knees like a dress. He pulled the other jacket on. It felt like wearing a second skin of plastic wrap. Sweat poured into his eyes when he sat again.

The rain came at once and from nowhere. Every drop sought his attention. The sky still teased them with sapphirine clarity, but rain fell like it wanted to submerge the island again until the tips of the Paps protruded from the sea to form three smaller and even less populated islands. He thought that the weather would frighten Molly off, that she would turn around and return to Barnhill, but no. She stayed seated, impervious to the weather, watching the sound absorb the deluge until he couldn't stand her silence any longer. "Is there something bothering you, Molly?" he asked. He was full of stupid questions.

"What could possibly bother me about spending my entire life trapped on a medieval island completely devoid of culture?"

He didn't know what to say. He had felt the same way, at her age, about living in the Illinois cornfields, but there was no way to explain that. She would have to figure it all out on her own. "You're only seventeen, and you're probably not as trapped as you think. Your father—and I will grant you he is a raging asshole—in his own messed up way he has your best interests at heart. There's no reason you'll need to stay on Jura forever."

"I knew you would take his side!"

"Here's the thing," Ray said, hoping that something helpful and encouraging would come to mind. He waited. "Thinking in terms of sides is never useful—there really aren't any binary oppositions. Nothing is entirely black-and-white or good-and-bad."

"That sounds to me like lame relativism."

"Let's go back," he said. He needed nothing more than a tall glass of single malt to warm himself up with. They started the return trek to Barnhill. "It's not relativism, it's specificity. Every thing needs to be considered in itself instead of in relation to some false negation of it. Try to think of your situation from your father's point of view. I'm not saying he's right—I mean, look at your eye—but terms like *right* and *wrong* are beside the point sometimes."

Their boots splashed in the mud. Ray's toes grew wet and sent a cascade of prickles up his leg.

"Aye I get all that, but what if he *doesn't* have my best interests at heart? I have every reason to believe he is a selfish arsehole who will do everything he can to satisfy his own needs. This island and our traditions are more important to him than I am, so where does that leave me?"

"It leaves you stuck on Jura, I guess, until you decide you're ready for art school or whatever it is you want to do. As much as you want to moan and complain, I know that a part of you loves it here. A big part of you."

"That doesn't mean I can't hate it too—you said so yourself."

"Right, so tell me what you love about Jura."

"The history, I guess. People have lived on this island since the Stone Age."

"What else?"

"I don't know. In many ways, this may be the strangest place on earth. When I leave—and I am going to leave—I'll miss the eccentricity here. We get all the telly programs from London and America, but we've also managed to maintain a unique way of life. I do love that about this place, but I also hate it. Is that okay?"

"Definitely."

They walked for another hour, long enough for the rain to stop and the sun to dry their hair and clothes. Wet blades of grass stuck to his soggy boots. Back at the house, they stood on the stoop. The stain of animal fluids hadn't washed away in the rain. Molly took off her wellies and socks, but didn't stop there. Just as Ray had done on several occasions, she unbuttoned her pants and climbed out of them. Her legs were pale but looked exercised and uncorrupted by age or high-fructose corn syrup. She removed her shirt and then her undershirt and bra. Ray stood transfixed. Although he did his damnedest not to notice, she had a beautiful body.

Molly raised her arms and stretched with a loud groan in the breeze, soaking the atmospheric conditions into her skin. Her white underpants were the only thing standing between this girl and the full frontal nudity of the painting upstairs. She was so comfortable, so at ease with herself: a living, breathing sheela na-gig. Her nakedness had nothing to do with him. It was like he wasn't there, or like she didn't care that he was. The self-assurance was wondrous. "I'm going to take a long bath," she said, "then I'll see about something to eat. I'm famished."

The water started running upstairs. She was singing a song Ray recognized, but couldn't make out. He poured a large dram—he didn't notice the age—and drank it in one long go. As far as Molly was concerned, he was so old, or now so familiar, so beyond the realm of sexual desirability, that in her mind there was nothing unusual about stripping naked in his presence or sunbathing topless outside his window.

In the weeks that followed, they fell into the habit of picnicking at a different spot every day. He would bounce ideas about Orwell off Molly, and she would fill him in about the history of the island. They visited the sites of Jura's Iron Age settlements and ancient battles. She taught him about the Viking blood feuds that spanned generations, pitted neighbor against neighbor, and still got voiced in the sternly worded letters to the editor of a newsletter over on Islay.

The more he heard about Jura's history —true or not—and the more he saw of its natural splendor, the better he came to appreciate the hardships Orwell had experienced. Molly also got him up to speed on the marital, legal, and pharmaceutical problems besetting the entire population. They found traces of old footpaths on which their stravaigs, as Molly called their walks, grew longer and her stories wilder. One afternoon, they followed a deer trail off into the wild. "I had an interesting conversation with Farkas not too long ago," Ray told her. "He wants me to believe that he's a werewolf."

"Are you suggesting he isn't?" Molly asked.

"So everyone on Jura just plays along, is that it?"

"You still don't understand the ways things are here, do you?"

"I like Farkas, don't get me wrong, but he needs a good psychiatrist."

"As opposed to a bad psychiatrist?"

"As opposed to being surrounded by people willing to play along with his delusions."

"Now I understand that you're the sophisticated advertising executive and we're all a lot of backwards Diurachs, but can't you even consider the possibility that he's not delusional?"

"You want me to believe that Farkas is a werewolf?"

"No, but I do want you to believe that it might be possible."

"Do you think I'd be allowed to join the next hunt?"

"So you can shoot Farkas?"

"It sounds too strange and wonderful to pass up."

"It's also barbaric. Did you know that the preparations begin months in advance? Everyone on the island is supposed to contribute to the feast, but the women aren't even allowed to attend. I sneaked out there once to watch them. Luckily they didn't shoot me."

"What goes on? Is there really a wolf?"

"Mostly the men just let off a little steam. They build a bonfire and go off in small groups to follow each other around in the dark and piss in the bushes. It's not as interesting as you've been led to believe."

"What is interesting is that you think Farkas might really be a werewolf."

"Well he's very hairy."

"I'll grant you that. It's hardly conclusive evidence, however. Do you think he gets hairier when he transforms? Is that even possible?"

"Aye, I see your point," Molly said, "but it is true that when he was a wee baby he was left here by Gypsies."

"Gypsies. Of course."

"It's true. Forty or fifty years ago, however old Farkas is, Mrs. Campbell found him on the front porch of the hotel. There was no note or any indication of where he came from, but back then there used to be a pack of Gypsies that came over from the Continent every seven years and camped out on the western side, where the caves are. I'll take you there sometime. They would catch a ton of fish and lobster, kill some deer, poach a few sheep, then move on."

She spoke with such conviction that Ray wanted to believe her. "You can't be serious," he said. They continued walking.

"They had been migrating back and forth across the Continent since World War II, until one year when Baby Farkas appeared at the hotel. After that, much to the collective relief of our more or less racist and intolerant population, they never returned. Mrs. Campbell says that he was covered in hair even as a wee baby. He looked like a teddy bear. That's how we ended up with a lycanthropic distiller."

"And Mrs. Campbell adopted him?"

"The whole island adopted him. As my da puts it, he was more like a pet than another child. We're not exactly wealthy on Jura, at least no one was back then, so people shared the responsibility of raising him. He lived here and there. The story gets funny peculiar. It was around the time Farkas turned thirteen that sheep and cattle on the island started turning up slaughtered every so often."

That did it. Ray couldn't hide his disbelief any longer. "Now I know you're messing with me."

"It's true, I swear to you. Even now when he drinks too much, which is, oh, every bloody day by my calculation—and you might know something about that yourself—whenever he has too much to drink he boasts that he's responsible for killing all these animals. It's like he's proud of it. He gets quite wound up. That's why he doesn't join the hunting parties. Don't laugh, Ray—I'm absolutely serious."

"You're as crazy as he is."

"I know for a fact that he has been researching laser hair removal systems online."

"How do you know that?"

"There are no secrets on Jura. That's a big reason I can't wait to leave."

They reached the cylindrical tower where he had once stopped to attend to his blisters. It turned out to be a trig point, which, before the advent of global positioning satellites, was used for accurate surveying of the land. It felt reassuring that people had gotten along very well for thousands of years without electronic technology; the earth would continue to spin long after the digital revolution ended and civilization crumbled. They stopped for a bite to eat before turning around.

Molly had so many stories of hidden pirate treasure, arsonist rock stars, visiting authors staying in Craighouse on the government's dime and causing veterinarian-summoning scandals with sheep. It was in those days of long walks out on the heather moors that the morass of his thinking showed the first clear signs of disentangling; those deep, mental knots started to unravel and Ray began to feel like his old, pre-Logos self again. He was able to concentrate on his reading for longer periods of time and some days Molly would have to physically drag him from his chair in order to point out another trail or beachhead or standing stone.

In the evenings, they would retreat to Barnhill tired and sunburned. She would bathe and then return to her painting. He would read until they both grew hungry, at which point she heated up various combinations from the dwindling supply of canned goods. After dinner, Ray would light a fire and sip on some scotch. With more food in his belly those days, the quantities of nighttime whisky didn't affect him quite as badly. Most nights they traded stories about their childhoods or made them up entirely. Ray had been an astronaut and a professional llama wrangler. Molly was actually from Egypt and her real name was Queen Nothinginkhamun. His laughter returned—it sounded strange at first. Only once in a while did he pass out in a sitting-room chair, at which time Molly would help him up the stairs and dump him onto his mattress.

Ray was sound asleep one night when the bed began to shake. It felt like one of the rare earthquakes they would get back on the Illinois prairie. The room rumbled beneath him for four or five seconds and then stopped. A distant voice addressed him. "Would you wake up already?" it asked.

It sounded like Flora. No—it sounded like Molly. The room shook some more. Molly sat in her pajamas at the foot of his bed.

"What's the matter?" he asked. A faint light in another part of the house bled through the door. He hoped he had clothes on under the sheets. "Are you okay?"

"Can I ask you a personal question?" she asked.

Ray sat up. "I don't imagine I could stop you," he said.

"Do you want to have sex with me?"

"What?"

"Do you want to have sex with me?"

"I heard you. Why would you ask me that? No!"

"Why not? Because I'm ugly?"

"No—you're . . . you're very pretty."

"'Pretty' is a pretty vague word. Pretty bad. Pretty ugly. Pretty depressed. Not much of a compliment, is it?"

"You're seventeen years old."

"Almost eighteen. I'm not saying I want to have sex with you either—I don't, I assure you—I'm just curious, you know, if there's some kind of tension going here that I should be made aware of?"

"And you decided to wait until the middle of the night to ask about it?"

"What better time?"

"Don't you worry your, uh, pretty little head. No, I don't want to have sex with you."

"You're not in here at night having impure thoughts about me?"

"No!"

"I'm glad to hear it," she said and lay down next to him on top of the bed. The blankets established a safe, cotton membrane between them. Her hair on the pillow smelled like wet paint. "I saw you bury your wedding ring in the backyard," she said.

"That felt good, but it had nothing to do with you. How do I explain it? Coming to Jura has given me a new perspective. I can't stand the idea of being fenced in anymore. Being trapped in a symmetrical grid of city blocks. That ring just felt constricting, I guess. I'm still technically married, at least for now. I'm waiting for the divorce papers to come through. That is if my wife's lawyers can find me all the way up here."

"Are you still in love with her?"

"What kind of question is that?"

"I want to know."

"Why?"

"I just do."

Wind battered at the windows. The sheep bells were unusually quiet out back. Ray pictured the sheep huddled together to wait out the night, to protect their young from whatever was leaving the dead animals at the door. The weakest and slowest among them wouldn't make it. "I haven't thought about Helen that way recently, no. I'll never not love her, but I respect that she needs to move on and I guess I've realized that I do too."

"Is that why you're here?"

"In bed?"

"On Jura!"

"Can't we talk about this in the morning?"

"Why are you so miserable?"

"I'm not miserable, I'm tired. You want to know? Okay, I don't really blame her for divorcing me. I haven't been a very good husband, and I think I'm in love with one of my former coworkers, or I was."

"So that's why you're so miserable."

"No. Okay, maybe. Yes. But I was miserable before that too."

"You don't have to be the same person here on Jura that you were in America," Molly said. "You can be happy if you want to be."

She kissed him on the side of his head and returned to her room. The lights in the house blinked out. Her paint smell lingered and he couldn't get back to sleep. His mind whirred. He felt somewhat happy, which was really fucking remarkable, but there still existed a source of deep-in-his-bones dread: Molly's father.

Gavin Pitcairn lurked in the back of Ray's thoughts and kept him on constant alert. All the single malt in Scotland wouldn't be enough to make him fully relax. It was only a matter of time before that flatbed came rumbling up the path.

. . .

THE DAY CAME WHEN supplies of food, shampoo, and toilet paper dwindled enough to require an expedition to The Stores. Ray dreaded the thought of running into Pitcairn, but he was also expecting some important mail. There was no getting around it. Molly's aluminum-crafted bike had been engineered with an elaborate suspension system capable of withstanding the special variety of abuse dished out by Jura's infrastructure, and he hoped that his spine would prove equally durable. He also hoped no one would recognize it as Molly's. She had tricked out the frame with a stainless-steel rack on the back and some antique leather panniers liberated from her father's long unused five-speed. The fenders would in theory keep the mud off his clothes.

Molly packed him some lunch and placed it in the wicker basket affixed to the handlebars. He hadn't ridden a bike in years and this one took some getting used to. The machine appeared unnecessarily complex. She taunted him for putting on the motorcycle helmet he found in the garage. "You look like a special needs child," she said. He wore it anyway, which turned out to be fortunate.

He made it all the way to the public road with only minor readjustments to his skeleton, but somewhere beyond Ardlussa the tires slid on an oil slick, probably one left by Pitcairn's truck. Ray squeezed the brakes so hard that the front wheel stopped; the rest of the bicycle however maintained its course and speed and catapulted him from the saddle.

Things grew a bit fuzzy after that.

When Ray arrived at the hotel he was covered in wet peat and had misplaced a sliver of a front tooth. He marched into the deserted lobby. The newly hewn edge of his incisor scraped against his tongue. A dull ache pulsed in his temples and he felt very sleepy. There wasn't a soul in sight. He stood at the reception desk for some amount of time—there was no telling how long—until Mrs. Campbell emerged from the depths of the building.

"We've been expecting you, Mr. Welter. You've received quite a bit of correspondence. My goodness—you're a mess. What happened to your face?"

"I feel a little woozy. May I sit down?"

"By all means," she said. She came around the reception desk and latched her fingers into his arm, leading Ray to a chair next to the dormant fireplace. The remains of a charred log sat on the iron grate like a turd that wouldn't flush. "You're bleeding, Mr. Welter," she said, as if it was news. "Stay put and we'll fetch Mr. Fuller."

Ray attempted to reconstruct the events of his ride, but the headache made linear thought difficult. He had fallen off the bike somewhere between Ardlussa and Craighouse. Images came back to him as if from a slideshow in random order. . .

Wet pavement four feet below him and somehow moving parallel to his body.

Up close eyes of a sheep staring at him as he regained con-sciousness.

A cheese and onion sandwich freed from its wax paper and seasoned with gravel and motor oil.

He had hit his head—that was it. Even with the helmet, he had taken a good knock to the cranium. In his daze he had carried the twisted frame of Molly's bike the rest of the way. He stood to find the washroom and inspect the extent of the damage, but Mrs. Campbell and Mr. Fuller came rushing in.

"We did tell you to stay put, Mr. Welter. Let us have a look at you."

"I fell off my bike," he told them.

"Now why would you go and do that?" Fuller wanted to know.

"I didn't mean to. It was—"

"An accident, aye. One word of advice: try walking next time. This is going to sting a little bit," he said. He held a dirty kitchen rag to the top of a plastic bottle and drenched it in what smelled like bleach. He held Ray's head and patted the rag against his scalp. The electric current carried down to his gut, where it would stay for the remainder of the day.

"If you do that again I am going to punch you," Ray told him. He meant it.

"Do sit still, Mr. Welter," Mrs. Campbell said. "It must have been quite a spill. While we have your attention, and you must forgive us for inquiring, you haven't by any chance seen Molly, have you?"

"Molly? No, why? Is she missing?" he managed to ask. "I do hope she's okay. Have you called the authorities?"

"I wouldn't say missing," Mr. Fuller said.

"No, not missing, just . . . unaccounted for at the moment," Mrs. Campbell said. "She has a habit of disappearing for weeks at a time. Not to worry. At any rate, you should sit here for a few moments. He's a bit concussed," she told Fuller.

"He's just had his bell wrung a wee bit, haven't you, Mr. Welter? Now drink this."

The odor of the tea stung his eyes before he sipped it. It tasted like rotten fish parts. He would've preferred a hot cup of the disinfectant sizzling on his scalp. Mr. Fuller wrapped a large bandage all the way around his head. "This'll stop the bleeding. One word of advice: you might do well to sit still for a moment. If you don't mind, I need to get back to my kitchen. The haggis won't cook itself, will it?"

"Perhaps this isn't the best time, Mr. Welter, but we do have some correspondence for you. From America, from the looks of it. Also, a number of emails addressed to you have arrived via our hotel website. We've taken the liberty of printing them. Normally we don't accept email for guests, but these appeared to have some urgency about them. Now let us see where we put them."

She wandered off.

Mrs. Campbell had read his personal correspondence and then left it lying around the hotel for all to see. These fucking people.

"Here you go, Mr. Welter," she said when she returned, and handed over a stack of papers. She lingered for a moment like she wanted to read over his shoulder, so he held them to his chest until she stomped away.

The printed emails were from Bud. The papers looked like they had been thumbed through. Had there been a fire burning he would've thrown them in it again. The stack also included a large envelope from the Chicago law firm retained by his wife—and Helen was still his wife in some way and would remain so until he tore asunder the envelope.

The words on the top page wiggled in a dialect of Newspeak legalese and amounted to the official and fully expected news that he was no longer married. Pending his signature, the divorce would be final and its financial conditions unfavorable.

Next he found a small pile of greeting-card envelopes. Six of them, each with his mother's secretarial-school handwriting. He opened the first one. The card had a plastic sheath and the cover featured a beach yellowed by a setting sun reflecting in a blue sea. Inside, she had written, "Dearest Raymond." The manufacturers of the card had seen fit to include the familiar sentiment:

Thinking of you
and wishing you all
the blessings of our
Lord and Savior.

His mother had written at the bottom, "—Mother." The other cards were identical, each mailed a week apart from the post office in his hometown.

The last two items in the pile were both postcards. On one, Bud implored Ray to get in touch. The face of the second was completely black apart from the white letters: "Machu Picchu at Night." On the back, a colorful stamp confirmed that it had originated in Peru. The handwritten note read only:

Remain optimistic.

—f.

Ray stared at the postcard in the hope of making some sense of it. Flora had moved to South America as she had planned.

Remain optimistic. He didn't know what that meant or what it was meant to mean.

"Remain optimistic," Farkas read over his shoulder. Ray hadn't heard him come in, which was astounding considering that the man panted like a dog even while sitting still. He took a seat at the fireplace. "What have you done with your head?" he asked.

"I fell off my bike."

"I suppose that accounts for the twisted hunk of metal I saw out on the porch. Maybe you should have worn a helmet."

"I did wear a helmet," Ray said.

"You're lucky to be among the living or at least among the non–brain damaged."

"I'm pretty sure the jury's still out on that one. In fact, I don't feel very lucky at all."

"You wouldn't, now would you? That's some bandage there."

"I have Nurse Fuller to thank."

"Aye, he's a talented man, a talented man. If you'll excuse me a moment, I'll go procure us a couple drams."

"I'm not sure that's such a good idea in my—"

"Well if it isn't the Wolfman and Mummy, together at last," Pitcairn said. Ray slipped the postcards and the emails into the big envelope from Chicago. "Let me guess: you fell off your fancy bicycle and banged up that big brain of yours."

"Just a little spill," he said. "Nothing serious."

"Pour me one too while you're at it, Farkas—especially if Chappie's buying."

"I am not buying."

"It was worth a try. Pour me one anyway, would you?" Pitcairn asked. "You look famished, Chappie. Why don't I go in the kitchen and ask Fuller to prepare you a nice, juicy AIDS sandwich?"

Farkas went to retrieve the whiskies and Pitcairn jumped into the vacant chair. He leaned in close. "I'm going to say this once," he whispered. His breath smelled like gasoline. "As I'm sure you're well aware, my Molly has gone missing." He coughed and then spat something chunky into the fireplace. "I have every reason to believe she's visiting that trollop friend of hers over on Islay. However"—more coughing—"if that's not the case and I find out she's at Barnhill, I give you my promise that I will kill you. Any man here will tell you that I mean it."

Farkas returned carrying a tray on which three large drams sparkled like amber in the sun. Pitcairn slapped Ray on the back, maybe a bit too hard. "Isn't that right, Chappie?"

"I'm glad to see you two have reconciled your differences," Farkas said.

"That we did, that we did," Pitcairn said. "Chappie and me, we've come to an understanding. Haven't we, Chappie? I've even promised—free of charge, mind you—to drive him back to Barnhill when he's feeling better. Slàinte, boys."

"Slàinte," Farkas said.

Ray grabbed his glass, but couldn't bring the whisky to his lips. He needed to warn Molly that her father was on his way. If Pitcairn pulled up to Barnhill and she was sunbathing in the nude there would be real and unmistakable trouble. Ray needed a drink after all. Whisky was a great idea. "Cheers," he said and downed his dram in one gulp. "I'm feeling much better. I need to take care of some paperwork and pick up some supplies from The Stores, then I'll be on my way."

He stood with some dizzy difficulty and went into the lounge, where he could look over the papers from Helen in private. Mr. Fuller busied himself in the kitchen clanking pots and pans together. Ray's signature was all that was missing. He went behind the bar, where he poured another dram and left a tick mark on Pitcairn's tab. Then he used the stubby pencil to add one final and specific clause to the divorce settlement and initialed the margin next to it. He had one modest demand of Helen, then she would be rid of him. He signed the document repeatedly, as required; his scribbled name would stand in for him in his absence.

He sealed the return envelope and carried it back out to the lobby along with three more drams duly charged to Pitcairn. He placed the glasses on the table where the two of them were bickering about a sport he had never heard of, then dropped the envelope on the reception desk, along with more than enough money to cover the postage to America. "I'm a free man," he said. "I just signed my divorce papers."

"Are congratulations in order at such a time?" Farkas asked.

"Hard to believe someone would let a catch like you get away," Pitcairn said. "Anyway, we better get going. Right after this dram."

"Mr. Welter," Fuller yelled from the kitchen. He poked his head through the door. "Seeing as you two are getting along so nicely, perhaps you might like to come back down for our next hunt in a few weeks?" he asked.

"Oh for fuck's sake," Pitcairn said. "I don't imagine Chappie here would have any interest in our old superstitions."

"Why is everybody out to get me?" Farkas asked.

"Actually, I'd love to come along!" Ray said.

"Excellent," Fuller said. "It will be good to have you on board. Maybe you'll hit something. We sure as shite haven't had any luck, have we? We can use all the help we can get. It will be on the evening of the summer solstice. Supper's here at sundown."

Pitcairn groaned.

"I can't wait! What will we be hunting for anyway?"

"A wolf!" Farkas laughed. "Though for the record it's a scientific fact that there hasn't been a wild wolf seen in all of Scotland since the year 1743!"

"It's not funny," Pitcairn snapped. "Something's been killing off our sheep."

"There's still plenty to go around," Farkas said. He wiped the tears from his hairy face.

"That's not the fucking point now, is it? Now finish your drink. I can't wait to see what kind of redecorating you've done at Barnhill."

The remains of Molly's bicycle sat in a heap on the porch. The front wheel had folded in half and the back one was missing altogether. The frame was totaled, but Ray threw it on the back of Pitcairn's truck anyway in case she could salvage the derailleur or other parts for the replacement bike he would soon be purchasing. "I have the very same panniers on my bicycle," Pitcairn said. "Not that I use it much. These roads will do a number on the old nut sack—not that you have that problem, I suppose!" Pitcairn laughed until he choked, then stopped to rest his hands on his knees while some kind of goo rattled around in his chest and freed itself with a loud cough. "Now would you kindly hurry the fuck up?" he asked.

"I need to stop at The Stores," Ray reminded him, hoping to delay the inevitable scene. Pitcairn was going to find his daughter—his underage daughter—running around naked at Barnhill. She would know to run inside and hide when she heard the truck approaching, right? A cell phone, a cell phone! His kingdom for a cell phone!

"For fuck's sake, Chappie. I don't have time to take your sorry, concussed self shopping for your tampons."

"That's fine. You can drop me off and I'll get myself home."

"And how do you propose to do that, then? You going to sprout wings and fly up there? Make it fast now and get me a packet of fags."

Once again Mrs. Bennett charged him an insane sum for the canned goods, fresh bread, and toiletries he required. He put the two boxes on the back of Pitcairn's truck next to the mangled bike. The truck handled the paved part of the road about as well as the bike had. All the bouncing around in the cab made Ray's headache even worse.

Pitcairn didn't say much on the way up the island, which was for the best, and he didn't hit the brakes when he approached Barnhill. He drove right past the house.

"Where are we going?" Ray asked.

"I'm not dropping you back just yet. I have something special planned for you. An outing, you might call it. What do you say we do a little fishing, Chappie? Just me and you."

That was when Ray began to fear for his life. He contemplated opening the door and jumping from the moving truck, but that would have been stupid even in the best of conditions. He already had a concussion—there was no reason to exacerbate it. "I don't really like boats all that much," he said.

"Don't you worry, Chappie. There's nothing to it."

Even at the lowest points of his depressive states, when he had tried with great conviction to do permanent harm to himself, Ray had never felt afraid the way he did now. His lungs were so constricted that he couldn't breathe and he started hyperventilating with a series of sharp inhalations.

Pitcairn drove past Kinuachdrach and to the northernmost tip of Jura and parked next to the wooden dock Ray and Molly had once sat on in the rain. A small boat bobbed in the water. Pitcairn untied it, though it clearly belonged to someone else.

Ray stepped on board and Pitcairn hit the throttle before he could sit. The motor was stronger than it appeared, and he was nearly thrown overboard. He managed to catch his balance and take a seat in the front. There was no life jacket, no seat cushion that in the increasingly likely event of an emergency could be used as a floatation device.

"What you have there," Pitcairn said, "is the Isle of Scarba. That makes this—"

"The Gulf of Corryvreckan."

The Cauldron of the Sparkling Seas. Home of the famous whirlpool—Charybdis herself. The lovechild of Poseidon and Gaia.

"Right you are, Chappie," Pitcairn said. "Right you are!" He killed the engine and gestured toward a patch of water darker than that surrounding it.

Ray looked over Pitcairn's shoulder to see just how far they were from shore. The Paps bounced up and down, up and down behind him.

"This whirlpool has swallowed up bigger fish than you, Chappie, and I can promise that they were never heard from again. Now, I'm going to ask you one simple question."

"There's no—"

"Your ability to tell me the truth will decide if you will be flying back to America in cattle class or in the cargo hold. Is my Molly at Barnhill?" The boat rocked. The whirlpool gurgled at Ray with icy loathing. She longed to suck him down into the murky depths and swallow him whole. She wanted to fill his lungs with her own briny breath, to anoint his sunken body with a thousand barnacles. "One simple question, Chappie. Yes or no?"

Ray's nausea rose and fell with the motion of the water. His headache surged between shades of purple and red behind his eyes. The bandages around his cranium were the only things keeping his head from exploding and sending chunks of his skull and brain matter sailing into the wind. The surface of the sound danced in the evening sun.

He looked Pitcairn in the eye. "No," he said.

"That was foolish, Chappie. You shouldn't lie to me." He sounded calm.

"I didn't—I'm not!"

"Listen to yourself. You're still lying."

Pitcairn knew. Ray didn't know how he knew, but he did and now he would be thrown overboard and into a whirlpool. "Okay," he said. "She showed up a few weeks ago. I would've told her to go home, but she had a black eye. I thought she was in danger. You would have done the same thing."

"So you admit that you lied to me?"

"Don't you understand? I was trying to protect Molly. I would never do anything untoward—"

"Trying to protect your own arse is more like it. You assume that I gave her the black eye?"

"Who's lying now? Who else would've done such a thing?"

"This isn't about me, Chappie, or how I choose to raise my own daughter. It's about some bloody Yank who shows up out of the blue to bless us with his presence and is so fucking smart that he thinks a teenage girl is better off living in his house than at home with her own loving da."

Ray couldn't think straight. He sorted through the rush of ideas overheating his synapses, looking for a kernel of logic or wisdom that might take the form of something meaning-ful to say, something that might help him find some clarity and, if possible, save Molly's skin and his own. He managed to take a deep breath. The sea air tasted bitter with salt. "There is no way," he said, "that I will send her back to you to get physically abused. She doesn't have to stay at Barnhill, but I'll contact the proper authorities and find her someplace safe."

"She's my daughter for fuck's sake! I will discipline the little bitch in whatever manner I, as her father, see fit to do. If anything, she has a smack coming for all the worry she's caused me. Look around you, Chappie. There's not one fuck-ing thing you can do about it."

Ray leapt from the bench with the intention of tossing Pitcairn off the back of the boat, but the moment he stood the motor came to life and sent him toppling into the water. The cold sea filled his nose and mouth. He couldn't tell down from up until the weight of his body tugged him lower. The bubbles of his own breath rushed upward as if to save themselves. The tide pulled at his clothes and dragged him one direction or another. Seaweed and debris gyred around him until he managed to claw to the surface. He pulled a bit of air in and stayed afloat long enough to untie his boots. He kicked them off and they sank like expensive, leathery sacrifices to the gods and their spoiled children.

The sight of the Paps helped Ray regain a sense of direction. He treaded water long enough to watch Pitcairn return to the shore. He swam for it, but the dock never got any closer. Pitcairn lifted the destroyed bicycle from the back of his truck, carefully removed his panniers, and tossed the frame into the water. He threw the boxes from The Stores to the ground and then the truck evaporated into the distance.

The wet bandages around Ray's head made it difficult to see so he ripped them off. The undertow tugged at the legs of his trousers, but he didn't want to remove them because one pocket was stuffed with the cash he had brought to cover the expenses in Craighouse. He grew tired though and soon had no choice. He unbuttoned his pants, their pockets full of sterling, and let them sink.

It took an hour to crawl ashore. He lay on his back—in his

underwear—and caught his breath while the sun approached the horizon. The beach was made out of dull, round stones instead of sand. The tips of the Paps were lit up with the sun's last rays. A cold breeze swept over his skin. It would be dark soon and there were unidentified wild animals prowling the island. Possibly wolves. He was drenched, exhausted, humiliated, and the extreme thirst exacerbated the effects of his concussion.

Molly was probably sporting a new black eye or two already, but all Ray wanted to do was sleep. Find a cozy shrubbery and climb underneath for the night, for the rest of his miserable life. Yes, everyone had been right—he *was* miserable. Sleeping half naked and shivering amid a field of sheep sounded better than going home to an empty house and the knowledge that Molly had been dragged away against her will and beaten up again by her father. Yet he wandered home in the dark, the stacked boxes punishing the muscles of his arms. The shame irritated him as much as the wet underpants. His socked feet ached. The numbness started as a static-like tingle in his toes and fingers, then grew with each step. Something like shock or hypothermia sought to introduce itself to his nervous system. He made it to the back garden more by blind luck than through any understanding of the geography.

Several of the lights were on at Barnhill and Ray saw movement inside, or thought he did. The front door was unlocked. Another vivisected animal sat in a pile at the front door. He ran inside.

"Molly?" he yelled. He marched through the house, still without pants on. "Molly?"

No answer.

He went to the kitchen, poured a big dram of scotch, and carried it upstairs. The door to her room—or what had been her room—was closed. He poked his head in. All of her things were strewn around, including her paintings. He took the opportunity to examine her work up close. The extent of her artistic talent came as a surprise. He lingered over the self-portrait that she had been so careful to keep hidden. The thick brushwork conveyed a kind of aggression, like she couldn't get the paint on the canvas fast enough, but there was nothing haphazard about its application. The subtlety of her color palette—a thousand shades separating grey from blue—insisted upon a slow appraisal. He could look at her facial expression all night and never come to learn its depths. In the portrait, Molly had captured some sad understanding about herself that no teenage kid should have. Ray carried it to his bedroom. He took down a watercolor and hung Molly's bruised and naked image in its place.

IV.

The doors chimed to signal his arrival. Mrs. Kletzski sat on a stool behind the counter staring at her television screen. Through the tinny warble of the built-in speakers, the talk show sounded like a domestic dispute conducted through faulty bullhorns.

"Hello, Mrs. Kletzski." Nothing. "Hello, Mrs. Kletzski!"

"Raymond, where have you been hiding?" She didn't turn the volume down and had to yell over a commercial for a budget airline. The racks behind her, typically full of plastic-sheathed clothes, were all but empty. Only a few suits, dresses, and laundry sacks remained.

"I was here on Saturday, Mrs. Kletzski."

"Do you have your ticket?"

"No, Mrs. Kletzki, I'm sorry. I don't."

"Let me see if I can find your slip!" She kept her receipts in a tall metal box with cardboard tabs for each letter of the alphabet. She flipped through each of them. "Let me see here," she said. "I'm not responsible for garments left over six weeks!"

"It's only been two days, Mrs. Kletzski."

"They drop off their clothes—wedding dresses!—and leave them here like I'm supposed to look after them. What are they saving them for? Their second marriages? So do you know what I did?"

"What's that, Mrs. Kletzski?" He needed coffee.

"When I got back from church yesterday, I rented two dumpsters and took everything that was here for longer than six weeks and threw it out back."

"Did you call the people? Maybe they just forgot."

"I'm not responsible for garments left over six weeks! Here's your ticket. Says so right here! I let the bums come and take it all. Kept the hangers though—I can use those again!"

"Smart thinking. What do I owe you?"

Her show came back on and distracted her. She punched some numbers into the old cash register and the drawer opened with a *cha-ching*. "Twelve dollars and fifty-five cents." She placed his credit card in a plastic tray and slid a bar over it to produce a three-ply impression and he signed the one on top. She handed him a carbon copy and went to retrieve his things. "Welter! What day is today?"

"Monday, Mrs. Kletzski."

"How's Wednesday?"

"Perfect."

"After ten o'clock!"

"After ten, Mrs. Kletzski, got it. Have a nice day," he said, but she didn't hear him.

He spent the morning devising new and unusual ways to separate unwitting people from their paychecks and public-assistance payouts. His job, as he understood it, was to funnel money upward from the masses of consumers and into the already deep pockets of Logos's wealthy clients. He was performing a small, supporting role in a rebranding campaign for two banks that had merged. Nothing interesting.

The shitstorm arrived shortly after lunch. Ray's phone vibrated with a text from Bud:

MR. WELTER—COME HERE—I WANT TO SEE YOU

The TVs in Bud's office were muted, maybe for the first time. "Have a seat," he said. "I just got off the phone with Detroit."

"The entire city?"

"No, just the part that was providing those big paychecks you were enjoying so much. Our friends the SUV makers have sold out."

Was providing? Were enjoying?

"What do you mean sold out?"

"I mean sold-out sold out. Bought-by-another-company sold out. Took-the-money-and-ran sold out. Moving-to-China sold out."

"What does that mean for us?"

"It means there's no 'us' anymore, champ. You're off Oil Hogg."

"What are you talking about? It was my idea."

"Technically speaking, the idea is the property of Logos. The manufacturer will be moving operations to China. Chongqing, to be precise. I'm told it's in the south. Apparently the Chinese are crazy about SUVs—who knew? Looks like your little clusterfuck Oil Hogg idea helped speed along the sale."

"What does that mean for the factories in Detroit? There have to be thousands of people working there."

"What do you think it means? Those grease monkeys better start packing their bags and learning Sichuan or they're shit out of luck."

Ray had never wanted a drink so bad. Thousands of honest, hardworking Americans—people a lot like his father—were going to be out on the streets looking for jobs. He had cost those people their livelihoods.

"Also," Bud said, "you're getting promoted. You're going to take the lead on our next major strategic partnership. It's a doozy. It's the corporate sector and the federal government rolled into one big, spicy meatball of profit. We're talking the big time here and you, my man, are going to run the show."

Ray was afraid to ask. "I'm afraid to ask," he said.

"We are talking horizontal directional drilling for a big dog playa in the emerging geo-thermal solutions sector."

"Are you fucking kidding me?"

"I'm fracking serious. Do you see what I just did there? Fracking, get it? It's short for hydraulic fracturing."

"I know what it is. The answer is no."

"What do you mean no? Don't be a dick."

"Bud, I . . . thank you for the offer . . . but . . ."

"But what?"

"Have you seen what these companies do? They are literally destroying the ground beneath our feet. People have gas flames shooting out of their kitchen faucets."

"Try to look at the big picture. If you can do for these guys what you did for the SUV manufacturers—and the board is convinced that you can—you will own the advertising world. We'll have to call it rayvertising from now on. Think of your career."

"I can't even believe you're serious. Fracking? I wouldn't be able to sleep at night."

"You can't sleep at night anyway. It's also a bit too late for moralizing, don't you think? Whether you're in charge or someone else is, this partnership is going to happen. Your petty hang-ups won't stop anyone from drilling for natural gas. The circus doesn't shut down because an elephant tramples one clown. They paint some other jerk's face and shove him out there."

"Leave me out of this. I've done enough damage. I'd rather go back to rescripting the same three cereal ads and toothpaste commercials."

"No you wouldn't. We really need you on this and I might

be in a position to sweeten the pot. What if just as soon as we're done with these motherfrackers I can convince the board to let you take on an environmental charity, pro boner? Would that make it worth it to you?"

"No, I don't know. I need to think about it."

"Save the trees! Hug the whales! We'll get all of the resources of Logos behind whatever dumbshit charity will help you put your crybaby concerns to rest. We wouldn't want the company to be seen as a horde of savages willing to despoil the planet for a few lousy bucks. We are that, of course—we just don't want to be seen that way. Did I mention the large raise this promotion will entail?"

"How big of a raise?"

"You are going to become wealthy beyond the dreams of mere mortals, I promise you."

Maybe . . . just maybe . . . this was the exact break Ray needed. Making more money would put him in a better position to reconcile with Helen if he could prove once and for all that he was a responsible, levelheaded adult capable of compartmentalizing his work and personal life. He would gladly put any moral qualms aside if it meant patching things up and moving back home. It was time to grow up and be a professional as well as a great husband. It would be a new beginning for both of them. They could start over. "I want to think about it."

"What's this 'think about it' shit? I'm bestowing upon you the creative and financial opportunity of a lifetime."

"I appreciate that—I really do—but after I have my appointment with Helen on Wednesday I'd like to get out of town and clear my head. I'm thinking about going up to Wisconsin, maybe drying out for a few days. I'm hoping to bring her with me. I can use the time to do some research about the benefits of clean, natural gas, and if it turns out I have something useful to say that won't make me want to hurt myself I promise you that I will build the best market-driven solution this company has ever seen."

"That's what I'm talking about, Rey Momo. You'll need to assemble a team and we'll start the initial meet and-greets when you get back."

"I'll consider it, but I'm not saying I would feel good about it."

"No one gives a flying fuck how you feel."

"See you next week," Ray said. He stood to leave. "Thank you."

"You deserve it."

Ray packed his things and shuffled back to his neighborhood with his thought processes trapped in an infinite feedback loop. Logos was going to take on this project no matter what. Maybe he could hold his nose and do the work. He passed an empty lot that a few days ago had been a store or office or apartment building. Someone had stenciled ORWELL WAS AN OPTIMIST in huge letters on the exposed wall.

He stopped. The sight was beautiful—and so true. Things were even worse than what was described in *Nineteen*

Eighty-Four. Not even Orwell could have even predicted the absolute disintegration of privacy. Or the emergence of social media as a means of control. Instead of telescreens, we had smartphones. Instead of thoughtcrimes we had political correctness. What was the Internet if not a way for Big Brother to track our very thoughts?

Could he really help a hydraulic fracturing company repair its public image? To refuse the job would mean letting his father down and letting himself down too. If Ray could pull this one off it would definitively prove his theories about Orwell's usefulness to the advertising sector. Building on what he had done with Oil Hogg, he could revolutionize the entire goddamn industry.

ORWELL WAS AN OPTIMIST. That was what did it. He had to accept Bud's offer. He could suck it up, bide his time, and ride it out. The fracking campaign couldn't go on forever and afterward he would partner with a wind farm or whatever would help him pay down some of his karmic debt. With his tech skills and the company's clout, Ray would be able to create the world's most effective campaign to raise awareness about global warming.

He was going to do it. Of course he was going to do it. Fuck. He would deal with the personal ramifications later. He took out his phone and texted Bud:

I'M IN.

Even if he did hate himself for the rest of his life, there would be plenty of time to deal with that and plenty of scotch to help him do so.

Bud wrote back right away:

I KNOW

Ray powered off his phone and went home. The apartment smelled like old coffee. His face stared back at him from the metal door of the refrigerator. It had a million questions. *What is it you want? Where are you going?* It was insane—he had just received an enormous promotion and yet it was the worst day of his professional career. He filled a rocks glass with ice, covered the cubes with his first scotch of the afternoon, and stirred it with a finger, which he sucked dry.

TUESDAY AFTERNOON ANNOUNCED ITSELF with an excess of sunlight and another bad dream about some hooded figure hammering hot iron nails into his eyelids. An idea had come to him in the night so he texted Bud on his way out the door:

HELP ME COMMIT GRAND LARCENY. COME OVER TMW NIGHT. BRING JUMPER CABLES.

It wasn't really stealing, but Bud was more likely to help

if he thought there was something illegal involved. The response came right away:

HELLZ YES

In the sunlit coffee shop, serenaded by world music so god-damn redemptive it bordered on torture, Ray inched forward in line. Since moving to the neighborhood he had come in every morning on his way to work and had never seen the same barista twice. A gargantuan child strapped into a stroller behind him kicked at him while its mother negotiated on the phone with a series of unwilling nannies and babysitters. By her fifth call, she pleaded and tripled her usual payout, but to no avail. Zithers and harps and a chorus of ethereal female voices conspired in Icelandic or Welsh or Hindi to beat him into more senseless consumption. Steam hissed from a machine behind the counter as if the whole place was about to explode and take a city block with it. It would have felt so good to turn around and kick that little fucker right back. His pre-ordered coffee waited for him to get to the front of the line.

He sat in the front windows, the shop's sunniest spot. The table teetered and threatened to spill his drink. He removed his favorite, disintegrating white oxford and draped it over his chair. His T-shirt said OIL HOGG in dripping letters. He was halfway through his coffee when one of Helen's colleagues from the Department of English walked in. He had met Dr.

Walter Pentode at any number of department functions. He looked out of breath. The man sweated even on the most blustery days of winter, and on a day like this one the stains on his shirt looked like deflated basketballs tucked in his armpits. The sunlight made his freckled head glisten beneath his comb-over. A scholar of Victorian literature, Pentode insisted upon speaking in air quotes in order to maintain a winking distance from the world beyond his fleshy borders and to avoid intellectual commitments of any kind. He came from old money and was said to be worth millions. He was also counted among the nation's foremost experts on operetta librettos. He kept an apartment in Vienna and as a matter of routine flew around the globe for the sake of attending his prissy concerts. He oozed stable mediocrity; academia was a hobby that suited him perfectly. He squeezed past a few tables and joined the end of the line with a huff.

Ray didn't want to be spotted so he ducked his head and turned his chair to face the window, but a shadow fell over the table. Pentode loomed above, holding a grasso-sized iced chocolate-malt coffee and a trio of crumbling selections from the dessert case. Ray's table was one of the few with an unoccupied chair.

"Hello, Raymond. Fancy seeing you here. Do you mind if I sit?"

"I—"

"I'm so sorry I'm late!" Flora said. She maneuvered herself around Pentode, then dropped her messenger bag onto the floor and flopped onto the chair. She had on a red hoodie and matching sweatpants. She had appeared just in time and read the scene perfectly.

Ray smiled at Pentode. "I'm terribly sorry, but this is my colleague Flora. We're holding an important business meeting right now."

"Pleased to meet you," Flora said. She had a habit of wearing multiple men's colognes at once, which she would rub on from magazine samples. Pentode's mouth twitched, sending wave-like ripples through his jowls. "And later, we're going to Ray's apartment to have consensual sex."

Pentode dropped his coffee, splattering the sneakers at the surrounding tables with syrupy goo. People stopped mid-sentence to stare. Ray's white shirt took the brunt of the blast. Pentode stammered something incomprehensible through his bacon-greased lips.

"She's . . . she's only joking, Dr. Pentode, I assure you. Tell him you're only joking."

Pentode stared down at the stains on his boat shoes. His mouth continued to open and close like that of a puffer fish about to be rendered into fugu.

"I'm only joking," Flora said. She raised her arms to high-five Ray over the table. "It won't be consensual at all!" she yelled. "Woo, yeah!"

"That's . . . that's terribly inappropriate," Ray said. He covered his mouth with his fingers, but a small laugh leaked out. It wasn't funny, but he couldn't help it. Pentode turned and left a trail of coffee-colored footprints. Flora, fake pouting, dropped her arms. She had been out of line, but laughter rattled in Ray's lungs. "Holy shit," he said. He couldn't breathe. He laughed because he could, and he kept laughing because he couldn't help it. Pentode's version of events wouldn't go over very well with Helen. "And aren't you supposed to be at work?"

"Aren't you?" Flora asked. "I snuck out to go to the gym."

"I'm glad you're here—I'd actually like to talk to you about your future."

"My future? That sounds serious."

"I'm building a team for a new project, and I want to bring you on full time."

"That's very sweet, but I have other plans. I've decided to quit. As soon as I can save up some money, I'm leaving the country. I want to open a battered women's shelter/art gallery in the slums of Caracas, maybe start a non-profit to hand out reusable feminine hygiene products to impoverished girls. Not to be rude, but I don't want any more part of your corporate death culture."

"I respect that more than you probably realize, but can we at least talk about it?"

"I'll hear you out, but trust me—I'm going to say no. Let's get dinner tonight."

"Dinner?"

"Yes, it's the meal that happens in the nighttime. I'll meet you at your place at seven."

"My place? Are we really going to have consens—?"

"No. You asked me to hear you out and I will. I just want to see what you're like in your native habitat. Text me the address." She stood and when she picked up her backpack Ray caught himself involuntarily looking down the scissored-wide collar of her sweatshirt. She had nothing on underneath. "I need some caffeine," she said. "See you at seven." With the line now gone, she stepped straight up to the counter. A little cloud of cologne lingered behind. The letters on the seat of her sweatpants advertised the sorority Alpha Sigma Sigma. Flora stood at the condiments bar, where she poured half of her coffee into the garbage and refilled it with soymilk and four packets of brown sugar. Ray waved to her on her way out the door, but she looked straight through him. Bovine splotches covered his shirt and they appeared permanent. He wrung some coffee onto the floor and stopped at the dry cleaner's on his way home.

RAY SPENT THE REMAINDER of the day trying to straighten up again. Even though nothing was going to happen between them, the idea of Flora coming over carried with it the fear of transgressing some boundary. He needed to stay on his best behavior. Pentode had likely already told Helen about the scene in the coffee shop and Ray's apparently sexual relationship with a woman over a decade his junior. Thanks to that asshole's flapping gums, she would assume that he was sleeping with Flora.

So that was it.

If Helen was so sure he was screwing Flora, the worst thing Ray could do was to confirm her suspicions. Not fucking Flora was the same thing as fucking Flora as long as his wife believed that he was fucking Flora.

Of course, there was no reason to consider the possibility that Flora was interested in that kind of relationship, and in the morning Ray would get the opportunity to set the record straight with Helen even if it meant lying to her.

Music—Flora would want to listen to music. Ray hadn't purchased a CD in five years and didn't like the idea of downloading songs because he found it difficult to spend money on immaterial products. Helen had maintained possession of all their jazz and soul albums. Another example of poor planning on his part. What little music he owned consisted of rap from his adolescence and college days. Time had relegated it to oldies stations and infomercials. Companies like Logos were now using the edgiest and most radical music from his youth in ads for luxury cars.

The sign above the windowless store said P.M., which served as both the name of the place and its daily hours of operation. Ray had walked past it a hundred times and never seen anyone come or go. Were it not for a tip from one of the interns he would have thought it was an exclusive nightclub or an illegal, happy-ending massage parlor. It looked like no music store he had ever been in. The shelves were arranged to form a maze and their immense height made it impossible to see other parts of the shop.

A series of round blinking lights built into the clear plastic floor tracked his movement. He followed them toward the checkout counter in the center of the shop, zigzagging past every manner of analog and digital recorded media, from vintage video-game cartridges to 8 mm movie reels to computer floppy disks in unrecognizable sizes. A tribal-tattooed fourteen-year-old sat at the counter attaching sticky notes to his knuckles with a stapler. "Yeah?" he asked.

"I need some music," Ray said.

The kid blinked at him. "Good thing you're in a music store. Ow!" On his nametag, beneath HELLO MY NAME IS he had written in "Hello My Name Is." He fingered the buttons of an unseen keyboard built into the glass counter. "Follow the red light. The upload stations have everything you need," he said and dismissed Ray with a wave of his bleeding hand.

The white light at his feet turned red and then the subsequent ones did too, one after the other, directing him deeper into the maze.

"But I don't have anything to upload to."

"Try your phone. Ow!"

"Why would I want to listen to music on my phone?"

The kid put the stapler down and twisted the buds of his nascent dreadlocks. "I'm guessing you're too old to spin vinyl."

"Too old? What? I was spinning vinyl before you were ev—"

"Do you have a CD—excuse me, a compact disc—player at home?"

"Yeah, where do you keep the—?"

"The old-school hip-hop is in zone six. Follow the red light," he said and returned to his stapler.

The bulb at Ray's feet blinked impatiently. He went the opposite direction and browsed the shelves. P.M. was equal parts record shop, museum, and graveyard haunted by the ghosts of technologies past. Not including the clerk, he heard at least three other people brush through other parts of the store, but he didn't see any customers. The sound of the stapler and the yelped obscenities helped him maintain his bearing. The whole place smelled like fruity air freshener. He went back to the checkout counter. A sticky note reading "Ow!" was stuck to the back of the clerk's hand. "How about some new music? What's current?"

"Kimagure."

"Never heard of them."

"I'm Kimagure," said a scrawny bleach-blond Asian kid behind the cash register who Ray hadn't noticed. His skin was so pale that he looked translucent even in his ugly patterned T-shirt. He might have been standing there the entire time. "You need a turntable," he said. "Follow me."

The clerk glided through the shop without the slightest hint of bodily motion. The lights in the floor followed behind him like a trained pet. He stopped at a glass display case containing twenty-four record players of monstrous complexity. "This one," he said, pointing. "Wait here." He left Ray to admire the machines. The model he had pointed to had a $1,200 price tag. It was the cheapest of the bunch.

Kimagure reappeared from the opposite direction and handed over a box with a label printed in a language Ray didn't recognize. "Follow me," he said.

He led Ray through the store, plucking a dozen plastic-wrapped record albums from the sleek shelving units. Ray lost his breath and any sense of direction. His footsteps sounded labored, which made him realize that the place was silent: a music store that didn't play music. Kimagure twisted past miles of reel-to-reel spools and MP3 players and even a small section of player-piano rolls, and then stopped back at the cash register, where Ray charged $1,900 to a credit card he still shared with Helen.

"These will get you started," Kimagure said. "It's all underground shit. Limited pressings. Very collectable."

"Thank you," Ray said.

"I accept tips," Kimagure said.

"Tips?"

"A hundred is standard. From you twenty looks correct."

Ray removed twenty dollars from his wallet and handed it over. "Any advice how to hook this up?" he asked, but Kimagure had already faded soundlessly into the mood-lit gloam of the shop. He followed the blinking white dot back through the maze and, two grand poorer, got birthed onto the crowded sidewalk.

He stepped out of the elevator and turned the corner to find

Flora sprawled out on the floor in front of his door. When she removed her headphones, the violins were broadcast all the way down the hall.

"How did you get in the building?"

"Nice to see you too, Ray."

He put the record player down and unlocked the door.

"New turntable?" she asked.

"I went to buy some new music, but I don't know what you like so I got some help."

"I hope you went to see Kim."

"He shook me down for twenty bucks."

She poked him in the chest. "You got off easy. He supplies every decent deejay in the state. He must have liked you. Nice place—what do you have to drink?" Her tongue stud clacked against her teeth.

"Let's see. Tap water, spring water, mineral water, vitamin-enhanced water, diet cola, milk, beer, and whisky."

"Glass of milk please. Is your apartment always this clean? I had you pegged as a slob."

"I only clean up when guests are coming over."

"Do you entertain often? I bet you're a regular pussy magnet."

"You're the first in a long time. Guest, I mean."

"What is this?"

"It's milk."

"I was joking, dumbass. Get me a whisky. What kind of single malt do you have?"

"What do you know about single malts?"

"Enough."

"Will a twenty-one-year-old suffice?"

She sat down. "That's a loaded question. I'm twenty-one."

"That didn't come out right. It's from the Isle of Jura."

"Isn't that where Orwell wrote *Nineteen Eighty-Four*?"

"I can't believe you know that."

"Make mine neat, please. Have you been there?"

He dumped the milk down the drain and poured Flora a whisky as old as herself. "Not yet."

"What's stopping you?"

"What do you mean what's stopping me? I have other obligations. A job, a wife. I can't just pick up and go."

"Sure you can."

"I thought the exact same way when I was your age. Everything was a lot simpler. I really want to see Jura, but I also worry about being disappointed. I mean, I have this image in my mind of the Scottish Hebrides being a kind of paradise—islands off the grid and away from the world. Everyone says that the Highlands hospitality makes their residents the warmest and most generous people in the world, but what happens if I get there and there's just as much bullshit as everywhere else? Then there would be no place left I could dream of escaping to."

The scotch tasted really good.

"If I ever start making excuses like you do," Flora said, "I want you to hunt me down and slap me."

"Why do I get the feeling that you'd like that?"

"Believe me, I get it. You've got it made. Good job, fancy apartment, a big SUV to cruise around town. They love you at Logos." Her expression made it clear that she didn't share his enthusiasm for the advertising world.

"Apart from being pure, concentrated evil."

"Oh I didn't mean that."

"Yes you did—and you were right. You know, the reason I wanted to catch up with you tonight was I was going to offer you a job and a lot of money, but I've changed my mind. I can't do that to you."

"Are you aware that you're not making much sense? You want me to stay at Logos? Start at the beginning so I can say no."

"I'm putting together a team to work on a pro-fracking campaign."

"You can't be serious."

"I can be and I am. Logos is going to do it whether I'm involved or not, so I decided that having someone with some common sense involved would be the lesser of two evils. I was going to offer you enough money that after a year you could take off for South America or wherever with enough cash to open your art gallery or homeless shelter or whatever it is you want to do."

"It will be for abused women, not necessarily homeless people, and what you're saying is total bullshit. You don't have to choose between two evils. There are always other options. Always always always."

"I want to believe that," Ray said. "I really do. The more I think about it, the more I want you to get away from this bullshit I'm mired in. I want to get away too. I need a change."

He poured another round.

"Yet you're taking on a fracking campaign? You should tell Logos to go fuck itself."

"I know it sounds crazy."

"It's worse than crazy, Ray. What is wrong with you?"

"My wife . . . my estranged wife . . . wants me to quit too."

"So why don't you? What are you afraid of?"

"I'm afraid of what my father would say if he was still alive and I'm afraid of admitting to myself that I've wasted my entire adult life pursuing some stupid career because George Orwell told me to. The truth is that I'm fried. I'm so burnt out I can't even think straight anymore. I'll put it this way: a few days ago, a building right here in the neighborhood got torn down. They must have had a wrecking ball, bulldozer, the whole scorched-earth deal. It took no time at all. The entire lot got cleared as if the building had never even existed. Now here's the thing. Looking at the empty space, I couldn't even remember what had been there. I could not remember. What kind of shops? Were there apartments upstairs? Were the tenants evicted? Where did they go? So I'm walking past the site and someone had graffitied the next building over. Big letters: 'Orwell was an optimist.' I couldn't believe it—but it's absolutely true. Orwell *was* an optimist compared to what we have now."

"That was me," Flora said.

"What was you?"

She took a drink of her scotch. "The spray paint. My friends and I did that. I finally read that copy of *Nineteen Eighty-Four* you gave me, and I see why you're always raving about it."

"I love that! I mean . . . As your boss, I can't condone the wanton defacement of public property—"

"That's the thing," she said. "It's not public property. It's just a private business owned by some rich asshole who probably doesn't even live in Chicago, and you're not going to be my boss much longer. I appreciate the job offer, if that's what this was, but I'll be arriving in Quito two weeks from tomorrow."

"That makes me very happy. I mean, I hate to see you go, of course, but it's the right thing to do."

"I'm super excited, obviously, but I'll admit and I haven't told anyone this—that I'm also scared. Before I leave I need to go spend some serious quality time with my dads. They're going to store my stuff in their basement, not that I have much." She helped herself to the bottle and poured them each large measures. It was going down way too easy.

"Let me ask you a question," Ray said. "Why are you here?"

"Chicago?"

"My apartment!"

"You asked me to meet you, remember? I wanted to see where you live—don't read any more into it than that. It doesn't have to be weird. As much as I hate Logos, you personally aren't without one or two redeeming qualities. I bet that buried deep inside your miserable-ass self there's a joyful and charming and funny human waiting to get released. Too bad I never really got to see it."

"What if that's not true? What if this miserable-ass me is who I really am?"

"I've wondered about that, but you're one of the few men I know who has treated me like a person instead of as an object."

"I'm sure I've done that too a little bit." His phone rang in his pocket. "Sorry," he said. "It's Bud."

"Speak of the devil—he's a pig. Ignore it."

"Sorry," Ray said. "I really need his help with something tomorrow." He took the call. "Hey, Bud . . . What do you mean you're here? Here where?"

A loud knock came at the door. He got up and let Bud in. "What the hell are you doing here?"

"Ray-dicchio. I thought we were going to steal your truck."

"That's tomorrow!"

"Hello, Bud," Flora said.

"Holy shit. How long has this been going on?"

"This is not going on."

"She just got here."

"Sorry to break up the party," Bud said. He took a beer from the fridge and twisted it open. "Place looks great. You already got her cleaning up? Nice."

"Fuck you."

"Relax, missy. I'm just teasing you. If my daughter turns out half as smart as Raypunzel tells me you are, I'll be very happy. Now I smell whisky. Pour me one and let's go steal this truck of yours."

"You just opened a beer."

"We're stealing a truck?"

"It's in the garage at my wife's place and I need to pick it up. On second thought, maybe it would be better if you stayed here."

"No way."

In the time it took to pour another round, Flora had hooked up the turntable and put on an LP that sounded like a series of vintage soul songs sampled down to incoherent syllables, their tempos warped and mashed, and then reconstituted again into songs that weren't really songs, but weren't really not songs either. It was a revelation. It made all the sense in the world.

"The fuck is this?" Bud asked. "It sounds like someone changing the radio dial."

"What's a radio dial?"

"It's perfect," Ray said.

"It's terrible. Don't you have any old-school hip-hop?" Ray gave Bud a glass, which he sniffed. "Islay?"

"Very close—Isle of Jura," Ray said. "It's right next door."

"Nice," Bud said.

"We talked about it and Ray's going there," Flora said.

"Really? Where?"

"Jura."

"No I'm not."

"That's a great idea. I like this girl."

"Woman."

"Woman, sorry."

"I never said that. It's not—"

"He's going to see where Orwell wrote *Nineteen Eighty-Four* and then quit the advertising business because he's—what did you say?—burnt out?"

"That's where you're spending your week off?"

"I'm not really . . . I don't know. I haven't thought about it until now. I'd like to go, but I'm not sure it's feasible."

"Not feasible? That's a shitty excuse."

"Unlike your decade-old plan to visit Asia?"

"This isn't about me."

"I can't go to Scotland now. I'm paying for two apartments, remember? Money's tight as it is."

"Don't play that—I know how much you make. What do you mean you're burnt out?"

"Why are you two trying to get rid of me?"

"We're not trying to get rid of you, we're—"

"Because you've turned into a miserable fuckface, Ray. Because you need to get away and refocus on your career. We did great with your Oil Hogg thing, don't get me wrong, but I have to be honest with you: that play clock has expired and we need to come up with the best next thing for these fracturing people if we want to keep shitting in the tall cotton, but all you do is talk about it and make excuses. I need more time. Wah! I need more money. Wah! So go get your head right and then we'll get started on this sweet new deal."

"Does it bother you," Flora asked, "that you're a raging asshole?"

"Not one bit," Bud said.

Ray took a large gulp from his whisky and poured another round, emptying the bottle. The spinning record sounded like it was changing speeds all on its own.

Ray broke the seal on a ten-year-old. The three of them drank steadily and with conviction. Flora sat on the floor next to the turntable and spun a few minutes of every record in the pile, then went through them all again. The music, for lack of a more precise term, lacked structure or even recognizable time signatures. It was glorious: without boundary—other than that of duration—and liberated from the narrow conceits of the pop-music vernacular. One of the LPs had two grooves on each side so that depending on where she dropped the needle it would play entirely different tracks. She placed the whisky cork on the center of the record to watch it rotate.

The whisky flowed downhill and they soon stopped with the pretense of using glasses, opting to pass the bottle until, good and liquored up, they went for a joyride in Bud's vandalized SUV. Nothing about the trip was a good idea. The vehicle smelled like wet dog. Bud was the proud parent of an untrained Jindo named Curly, whose red fur clung to every interior surface of the truck and, now, to Ray's clothes. The ride downtown was a blur of streetlights and sirens.

His former home was wedged on the eleventh floor of a neo-gothic high rise. The mortgage was unrealistic—if he didn't move back in soon he and Helen would need to sell it. She would have to recognize that she couldn't maintain it herself on an educator's salary. He still possessed the keycard that allowed Bud to navigate a subterraneous network of parking facilities. They found his assigned spot, and he was glad that his truck remained where he had left it. Helen's boxy station wagon sat in the next spot, which meant she was at home upstairs at that moment. He didn't relish the thought of meeting her now, all drunk and in the company of Bud, who she had always despised, much less with the sexy coworker into whom—his reconciliation with Helen notwithstanding—he was pretty sure he wanted to insert his penis.

Ray looked at his truck, unsure of his next step. "What do you think?"

"I don't know," Bud said. "You're fucking this monkey, I'm just holding it down."

"Lovely."

"Will it start?"

"I still don't know."

"Did you bring the jumper cables?"

"No."

"Then it better."

He got out. The paint of the truck was very dusty, except for the Ten Commandments–shaped spot on the windshield that attested to the range of the wipers. That was strange. Some jokester had written "Warsh me" in the grime of the driver's side door. He unlocked the vehicle and climbed up

inside. The interior smelled funny. He switched on the over-
head lights. A sports coat laid neatly folded on the backseat.
He got out again and opened the back door. A tweed coat
with professorial elbow patches. Definitely not his—it was
way too big.

"What's that?" Flora asked out the window. She had moved
up to the front seat of Bud's truck.

Ray held the jacket away from his body like it was radio-
active. In the glow of Bud's brake lights it looked like a
bullfighter's cape. Based on its size, it clearly belonged to Dr.
Pentode.

Pentode had been driving his SUV? That meant that . . .
Ray didn't even want to consider the possibility. It also meant
that Helen was . . . ? It was impossible, yet here was the evidence.

Dr. Pentode was fucking his wife.

That fat piece of shit was probably upstairs in Ray's con-
dominium at that very moment with his pork-chop fingers all
over Helen.

Ray tossed the coat back into his truck. Goddamn it. He
got behind the wheel and it started up. He would check the
GPS later to see where Pentode had driven. "What now?" he
wanted to know, unsure whom he was speaking to.

"Let's go get some grub," Bud yelled. "Meet us at
McCrotchety's."

"I'm not going to that yuppie hellhole," Flora said. "I know
a better place. Follow us, Ray."

Bud took off with a squeal of his tires and Ray did the same. Pentode of all people. Goddamn it. He stayed on Bud's tail until they got to the bridge, at which point Bud ran a red light and dared Ray to follow him, but he chickened out. By the time the light changed, Bud was out of sight. Ray reached for his cell phone but instead of calling Flora for directions he powered it off, plunging the interior of the vehicle into darkness. He drove home and threw up in the elevator.

The apartment reeked of scotch and he felt sick from the booze and the thought of Helen's affair and the realization of just how drunk he was and that he had driven in this condition. The turntable's needle spun in the inner groove of an LP, kicking up an ambient, low-level static from the speakers. He ran to the bathroom and vomited until he cried, and then vomited some more.

HE BINOCULARED HIS EYES against the glass, but couldn't see anyone inside. The shop was empty, the hanging labyrinth of clothes gone. Only a local realtor's FOR SALE sign remained. He knocked a few times and then banged on the door with the butt of his fist. The counter and shelves and racks had been stripped bare. He took a step back. In addition to carrying his coffee-stained shirt, he had that fat asshole Pentode's sports coat draped over his arm like a blanket. He planned to return it, though he would've preferred to tear it to ribbons and tie them to the nearest maypole.

The appointment with Helen was in a little bit. They had a

lot to discuss. He would give her every opportunity to explain why Pentode's coat was in his truck. He walked around the corner, pushing through the morning crowd. Scores of plastic trash cans, each with a street number painted in sloppy white letters, had spilled their garbage all over the narrow alley that ran behind the row of shops. The names of the stores appeared on the back doors, but he didn't need the signs to find Kletzski's Kleaners. Two dumpsters halfway down the block overflowed with clean clothes. Hundreds of the bags inhaled and exhaled in the wind. The bins seethed with plastic. Mrs. Kletzski had thrown everything away, the entire contents of her store. His beloved shirt was somewhere in there.

He turned his cell phone on to check the time. Bud had left four messages, but Ray would catch up with them when he returned to work. Other things occupied his mind. Despite everything that had happened—and everything that hadn't happened—Ray still wanted Helen to let him move back in. He had made enough mistakes of his own and couldn't hold her adultery against her. Still, the word sounded acidic and vile in his mind: *adultery*. In forty-five minutes he would make one final attempt at reconciliation. She had to let him come home.

Late commuters and early loiterers filled the sidewalk while the automobile traffic wore him down with a circus-orchestra repertoire of horns and sirens. It was sickening—physically sickening—that he needed an appointment to see his own wife. The weather, however, remained perfect, as if the clear sky above existed to spite the congestion around him. A half dozen new construction sites had appeared in the neighborhood since the weekend. The skyscraping windowpanes reflected a false, second sky adorned with video cameras that perched above every intersection. The authorities made no effort to conceal them. If anything, their ubiquity served as a threat, and a reminder that he lived within the confines of Total Empire, as horizon-to-horizon vast as language itself. Ray's every step, every phone call, and every keystroke was recorded, his spending habits, downloads, and library rentals entered into electronic databases housed somewhere in vast server farms. The commercial entities, like Logos, headquartered in these buildings predicted his ideas before he even thought them. It was too much. He felt *this* close to losing his shit. The whole city conspired against him. Chicago had become a police state with no need for policemen. On the grid, under constant surveillance, every individual was Big Brother incarnate. That was true of him too—he was made to feel corrupted just by living his life. He had built his career by exploiting all these poor proles, and he couldn't stop dwelling on those out-of-work assembly-liners up in Detroit. They were real people with real lives and families, and they were unemployed because of him. He couldn't take it anymore.

The pedestrian sea parted, and from it a homeless man appeared wearing a full bridal gown and a frilly white veil. He carried a pile of plastic-wrapped designer clothes. Ray stopped to take a photo. "What, you never seen a dude in a dress before?" the man asked. He paraded past, the long train of his gown dragging coffee cups and debris behind him down the sidewalk.

The humanities building enjoyed a temporary stillness reminiscent of the atmospheric conditions that preceded a tornado siren. Classes were in session so the hallways were deserted save the stray bathroom-bound slacker. Fluorescent tube lights glared against the fishbowl exterior of the English office and the wall-mounted display cases half-empty with faculty publications. Ray stopped to use the men's room and collect his thoughts.

The time had come for him to straighten himself out. The most wonderful moments of his life had been spent in Helen's company, and he could be that person again. They both deserved to be happy, and he would commit every effort to making it happen, maybe even quitting his job. He was washing his hands when in the mirror Pentode emerged from a toilet stall.

"Hello, Dr. Pentode," Ray said. He dried his hands on the sports coat and handed it over. "I found this in my truck," he said.

"Raymond, oh, I—"

"Which is kind of strange, isn't it?"

"Listen, Raymond."

"If the next words out of your mouth are not 'I apologize for fucking your wife,' I will flush you down the toilet one fat body part at a time," Ray said, but didn't stick around long enough to hear what Pentode had to say. The temptation for violence was too great. Pentode of all people. It made no sense. It made no goddamn sense at all.

The hallway lights buzzed like a swarm of locusts presaging some half-assed apocalypse. The class bells rang, and faster than he could say Ivan Petrovich Pavlov the corridor teemed with rival tribes differentiated by the number of beats per minute throbbing around their precious heads and the corporate logos advertised on their too-tightly clothed chests. A hundred cell phones chirped all at once, a collaborative ringtone technique destined to put Schoenberg and Webern out to pasture.

Nan, the departmental secretary stationed next to the door, glowered at Ray without looking up from her video game. She had the restless look of someone standing in the rain waiting for her cocker spaniel to finish taking a steaming dump. Helen's office sat next to the mail room. He entered without knocking—she was on the phone.

The esteemed Dr. Maas, the departmental chair whose job Helen presently occupied, was recuperating from chemo; she kept a webcam next to her sickbed and every week she and her partner emailed updates to the entire faculty about the progress of her deterioration. Helen was scheduled to fill in for her through the summer and fall term, when either Maas would return from the living dead or the provost would appoint a permanent replacement. Helen had the inside track on the job, the financial rewards of which might have tempted less compassionate souls to cheer on the cancer.

More grey hairs had sprouted since he last saw Helen. She looked tired, but also—he had to admit—beautiful. Her hair was longer and it accentuated the shapely bones of her face. "Can you hold on a moment? . . . Thanks. Raymond, you can see that I'm on the phone."

"Do you find it strange that I need an appointment to see my own wife?"

"Sorry, I'm going to have to call you back." She hung up. "Listen, Raymond, don't make this any more difficult than it has to be." She got up and closed her office door. A framed photo of Dr. Maas, completely and defiantly bald, hung on the wall.

"Why do people keep telling me to listen?"

"Everyone's trying to help you, but you won't let us."

"I want to come home," Ray said. "I know I was impossible to live with. I got a promotion and I'm learning to take on more responsibility, just like you wanted. I'll get some help."

"That's . . . that's not going to happen."

"Just for one month. If it doesn't work out, fine. I'll never bother you again. I'll go get a job somewhere else. Another state. One month—that's all I ask."

"Please, Raymond. This is difficult enough as it is." She wiped at her eyes with a wrinkled tissue. "I think we've had a breakdown in communication. You've put me in a very difficult position."

"I've put *you* in a difficult position? I'm not the one fucking somebody else."

"Oh no?"

"No! Though I freely admit that I wanted to."

"See this is what I'm talking about. Some things are serious, Raymond. You come strolling in here and try to make my life as miserable as your own. You think you're so clever that you can just explain away your rotten behavior with some kind of clever mumbo jumbo, but you can't. This isn't some fictional Oceania or Eurasia, this is real. Your actions have real consequences in the real world. I'm sorry."

"You don't even know what *real* means. It means nothing. You think reality is something objective and external, but that's delusional. Nothing is real, Helen, not my career or this university or that fat fuck Pentode. Not you or me, not our marriage. These are just constructs."

"I filed for divorce," Helen said.

"You did what?"

"We're getting divorced. I called Jacobson and started the process."

"Why would you do that?"

"What do you mean why? You're a mess, Raymond."

Through the window behind Helen's head, a large metal dumpster was being borne aloft into the heavens by hundreds of inflated plastic bags. Ray rubbed at his eyes. When he looked again it had floated upward and out of view.

He needed to leave. He needed to leave this office and he needed to leave this entire rotting, putrid city and this entire corrupt system that he had contributed to all these years. If he was to stay, Ray would spend the next year working for Big Brother and espousing the benefits of fracking and then hate himself for the remainder of his life. He didn't want to be part of the problem any longer. He had been so wrong. There was no goddamn way he could fix it by himself, not from the inside and not with a thousand pro bono environmentalist campaigns. He stood and walked out.

"Where are you going?" Helen called after him.

"I don't know," Ray said, but in fact he did. For the first time in his life, he knew exactly where he was going. Instead of heading straight home, he went to the front desk at Logos and handed in his company ID card. A week later, he was on the Isle of Jura.

V.

Without Molly at Barnhill the bottles emptied at their previous, brisk pace. Ray woke up most mornings in a sitting-room
chair. Days rolled by without direction or purpose. He spent
more time in his boxers. He would wake up late, sometimes
in Molly's bed or, once, on the staircase with a puddle of six-
teen-year-old slinkied down the steps below him. After a week
alone, another swan dive into the Corryvreckan whirlpool
began to sound less awful. The irony did not go unnoticed:
he had gotten off the grid for the purpose of eliminating all
distraction from his life and to find some kind of inner focus.
The email and social networking sites, the text messages,
microblogs, and forgotten passwords. Yet now that he was
alone again he found it impossible to concentrate.

Hours passed him by while he sat in the garden or hiked
until his feet bled into the sneakers that weren't designed
for long distances. The sheep grew accustomed to him and
no longer regarded him suspiciously or drifted away when

he approached—they ignored him and the bells around their necks stayed quiet. He carried books with him and would stop in a shepherd's abandoned enclosure to try to read and sometimes snooze. He wouldn't return to Barnhill until it had grown dark, and, because he always neglected to leave the lights on, he arrived home to invisible, shin-bruising furniture and, every few days, another animal carcass on the doorstep.

He was spending another quiet evening at home with the whisky when he heard someone or something approach the house. In the absence of mechanical or digital noise, every footstep could be heard in the bed of mud and stone outside. He roused himself from the easy chair and grabbed the shotgun, which he had taken to keeping handy and as fully loaded as himself. Pitcairn was certain to seek revenge for whatever indignities he imagined Ray had perpetrated upon his daughter. Ray crept upstairs with the shotgun in one hand and a bottle of twelve-year-old in the other. The bedroom window afforded the best view of the front door. He wasn't going to shoot Pitcairn, obviously, but he wasn't going to let him in the house either. They had no further business to discuss.

The footsteps outside came slowly. Ray took a long gulp and put the bottle down. Something was approaching the house. He would fire a warning shot into the air if he had to. He went to slide open the window when—blam!—the gun went off. The glass crashed onto the intruder below. "Holy shit!" Ray yelled.

"Holy shite!" Farkas yelled.

It had only been a matter of time: firing the gun was something he could now check off his list of things to do. He knocked away the loose glass and stuck his head through the window frame. "Are you okay?"

"Right as rain, Ray. Only in this instance the raindrops are made of broken glass. I do appear to be bleeding the tiniest bit. Might I come in?"

Ray ran downstairs. Farkas stood panting in the mudroom. A thin line of blood had found a path through the forest of his eyebrows and came to a rest at the tip of his nose. Nestled in his arms he carried a fresh case of scotch, duly delivered as ordered.

"Come in, sit down. I'm so sorry!"

Farkas took a seat next to the fireplace. "I did ask you not to shoot me, but try not to let it worry you. I would, however, appreciate a little sip of something to calm the old nerves."

Ray poured two healthy drams from the best bottle in the house. The glass shook in his hands. He could've easily killed Farkas—or himself. He took a big sip and topped his whisky up, then carried the drinks to the sitting room. Farkas mopped at his face with a handkerchief. His nose twitched. "Now this is a treat."

"Only the best for my attempted homicide victims. Can I get you a towel or something?"

"I'm fine. Do you suppose this is the first time I've been shot at?" Farkas asked. His laugh sounded like a sea lion mating with a dump truck.

"No, I can't imagine it is."

"I've brought you your case of malt, though the truth is, Ray, that I came to see if you were still alive, if you know what I mean."

"I'm not sure that I do."

"Well, our dear friend Gavin, as you've discovered, suffers from certain, shall we say, sociopathic tendencies. And I thought he might have paid you a visit with the intention of causing some not insubstantial physical harm."

"He did throw me into the whirlpool."

"Aye, he mentioned something about that. I'm pleased to see you on this side of the ground."

"I thought you were him. That's why I had the shotgun out."

"I imagine it does have a safety mechanism. And a wee bit more caution might carry you a long way."

"Are you saying I don't have to be worried?"

"About your marksmanship? Most definitely. About our Gavin? It's hard to say, hard to say." He took a sip of whisky and groaned with delight. "It's true that he's liable to get a bellyful one night and come knocking. He believes that you behaved inappropriately towards Molly and feels honor bound to respond."

"That's not true. I only gave her a place to stay after he hit her. Did you see her black eye?"

"Aye, but he's worried about more than that. A girl of her age."

Now Ray understood. "I need to make this perfectly clear: I swear to you that my relationship with Molly is . . . was . . . totally innocent. I never laid a hand on her. If Pitcairn doesn't believe me there's not a thing I can do about it, but that's the truth."

Farkas appeared relieved. "I am glad to hear that," he said. "However, you of all people should appreciate the distinction between perception and reality. I'll talk to him. Sometimes he listens to me, although most of the time he doesn't."

"What should I do?" Ray asked.

"If you decide to reload that shotgun of yours, please do mind the safety. Many thanks for the whisky. I should be getting back."

"But you just got here. How about a refill?"

"I'd love to, Ray. Next time, next time."

Something didn't feel right. Farkas had come a long way just to stop in for a quick drink. He had something up his sleeve beyond lugging a case of whisky through the mud. Maybe it was an espionage mission. That was it. Farkas was serving as a spy for the rest of the island. He had infiltrated the foreign enemy's compound in order to collect intelligence. The locals were no doubt sitting around at the hotel lounge waiting for him to report back. "Farkas, did you come all the way up here to find out if I fucked Molly?"

"Not precisely, no," he said, but he looked guilty. "I've come to deliver your whisky and your mail. Some of it looked important." He stood and handed over a large paper bag full of envelopes.

Maybe that was all there was to his visit after all—the mail. Farkas seemed like a good guy, even if he was delusional. "Thank you, I appreciate this a lot," Ray said. "It's difficult being so out of touch. I came here with all kinds of romantic notions of communing with nature or whatever, and for a while I felt like I was getting close, but it ultimately hasn't really worked out."

"Give it time, Ray. Give it time. Thanks again for the whisky. I suppose I'll see you in Craighouse next Friday evening. You'll be joining in the carnage, is that right?"

"The hunt—yes. I wouldn't miss the chance to practice my aim."

"I wouldn't think so. I'll come meet you at the end of the public road, save you a bit of a walk."

"You're obviously a very good sport about all of this, so let me ask you something. How do you know you're a werewolf? You have to admit that it sounds a bit far-fetched. What evidence do you have?"

Farkas took a deep breath. "To tell you the honest truth, I don't think in terms of evidence. I have memories of doing things—atrocious, horrible things beyond the ken of mankind. They're more like visions or dreams than memories, but they're as real as you or me. There comes a time every so often, usually around the time of the new moon, when I cannot control my actions, when my body operates at odds with my best rational thoughts. I hate it. I hate it more than I could possibly convey to you. I'm not an educated man, but

I know what I know, and I know that I'm capable of terrible things."

"Aren't we all."

"Aye, but until you've awoken with the taste of blood so strong on your lips, and tufts of some pelt beneath your nails, you cannot hope to understand the things I've done."

"Have you considered the possibility—and I hope you'll forgive me for this—have you ever wondered if you're delusional?"

"Ray, I pray that I'm delusional because that would be preferable to the waking nightmares I've had all these years. And now I should be off. Good night."

From the doorway, Ray watched Farkas's progress into the utter darkness of Jura. A biblical swarm of insects sought the light of the sitting room, so he went in and poured another drink, and then another. Farkas didn't sound crazy, except that he kind of did.

It was a good hour before Ray felt ready to read his mail. A black, imageless postcard read "Rio de Janeiro At Night" on one side. On the other:

Ray, I hope you still
feel as optimistic as
I do. With love —f.

He was overjoyed to learn that Flora was still thinking about him. He read her haiku again and again looking for clues about the true nature of their relationship. "With love," it said. He then opened the three identical greeting cards:

Thinking of you
and wishing you all
the blessings of our
Lord and Savior.

Next he tore into the large envelope from Helen. She had used her personal stationery, not her lawyer's, and had had it reprinted to redact his name from her own. He scanned the cover letter for the only news that really mattered . . . and . . . there it was. Molly would be ecstatic.

Helen had agreed to his final and somewhat awkward stipulation of the divorce settlement, perhaps in violation of her own precious ethical standards: upon the successful completion of the minimum requirements of admission, Molly Pitcairn was to receive a full, four-year scholarship to attend the university where Helen taught. The offer included a generous housing stipend and a work-study job in the college of fine arts to cover additional expenses. Ray had it in writing. He had secured Molly's ticket off Jura and couldn't wait to tell her. Her father would be furious, perhaps murderously so, but there was nothing that could be done about that. Ray had acted in Molly's best interests and anyone who didn't like it would be cordially invited to go fuck himself.

In exchange for the scholarship, Ray had surrendered all

rights to his share of the condo and agreed not to pursue additional monies from Helen. He was now broke. It felt liberating.

HE FOUND A PEWTER flask under the sink and filled it with a young and lightly peated scotch, tucked the legs of his trousers into his socks, and without locking the door behind him trekked out to meet Farkas, who simultaneously was and was not a werewolf. The shotgun he left behind. Ray had nearly killed himself and, besides, a real weapon would never work against an imaginary beast.

Hiking to the public road would be some of his greatest physical exertion since Molly's abduction. Jura's terrain had all but destroyed his canvas sneakers. The blisters under his socks begged to come out for an encore; he would need to finally pick up a pair of wellingtons from Mrs. Bennett if she was still open. Whisky formed a warm kiddie pool in his belly. He drank half the flask before he got up the hill and past sight of Barnhill.

The evening grew colder and worked its way through his sweater, his feet ached, and although he wasn't much closer to piecing together the bits of his fractured mind he felt something like happiness about the night ready to unfold, about participating in a werewolf hunt on the Isle of Jura on the night of the summer solstice.

Farkas stood waiting for him next to his compact car, an Eastern European model that had gone out of production shortly after the fall of the Berlin Wall. "Sorry about the mess," he said. "You can throw that shite on the seat into the back."

"Good to see you, Farkas. What can I expect from this affair tonight?"

"I don't fully participate, for reasons you can appreciate, so I can't rightly say. But if these goings-on are at all consistent with every other aspect of life on Jura, it's fair to warn you to keep your expectations to a minimum."

"A salient point. I've brought some scotch—care for a blast?"

"Wouldn't say no to a wee sip, would I?" Farkas took Ray's flask in his hairy hand and, steering with the other, drank what appeared to be the entire contents. He looked disgusted and rolled down his window to spit it out. "Have I insulted you in some way, Ray?"

"Insulted me? No!"

"Then why in heaven's name are you giving me this new malt? That shite is best left to the tourists, and that flask of yours might have done with a good washing up as well, I might add."

"I'm sorry, I didn't—"

Farkas handed the empty vessel back and reached into his own pocket. "Try on this tasty little fellow for size," he said. He passed over a flask that contained a whisky so delicious it might have come from the Virgin Mary's own tender nipples and been used to suckle the baby Jesus in his downy crib as mother and child were serenaded by a host of angels.

"What on earth is this?" Ray needed to know.

"I told you that we—" he hit the brakes to let a family of red deer pass. They scampered off unaware of their near collision and of the fictional wolf in its make-believe den waiting for darkness to come in order to find the most vulnerable among them. "I told you that we Diurachs save the best of the whiskies for ourselves. Well I personally keep a small collection, an archive if you will. And what you have here was aged for twenty-eight years and will never again see the light of day. When this final bottle is gone it will be gone for good. Try it again while you can."

Ray took another sip. It tasted entirely different the second time down, and even better. More nuanced. It tasted like caramel and wood smoke and moonlight glowing on a winning lottery ticket. It tasted like drinking joy itself. "I didn't know whisky could be this good."

"It can't. Not anymore, at any rate."

"Nevermore. Right around here is where I did that face plant off the bike."

"Aye, nevermore. That would be a nice name for a whisky. Things are different nowadays—maybe that's Gavin's point. No going back, as they say."

"I don't mean any offense, but just how different are things? It feels to me like the island is stuck in time."

"Only everything is different, Ray, and that's the truth. It's a matter of perspective. The water's different now. The air we breathe. The whole climate. All of it affects the whisky."

Darkness settled in and the beginnings of Ray's reflection appeared in the passenger-side window. He hadn't trimmed his beard in a few weeks; the locals were liable to mistake him for the wolf. "Maybe change isn't always bad, though?"

"When I say that malt whisky is the lifeblood of this little island, I want you to understand that literally," Farkas said. "This new RAF flight plan changes the amount of the jet fuel in our atmosphere, and our atmosphere is not only what we breathe, but what the whisky breathes. Do you mind if we make a quick stop? There's something I'd like you to see. I know you're expected at the hotel, so we'll do this with some haste."

Farkas pulled into the grounds of the distillery, which sat on a hill and took up a large chunk of downtown Craighouse. Not that Craighouse had much in the way of a downtown. The distillery compound contained two white plaster structures that stood three or four stories tall. They had been built on top of some old, painted-over ruins and were big enough to be seen all the way from the mainland. A warehouse of blue sheet metal loomed above them and the height of the smokestack dwarfed that. The hotel across the street was even larger. People were already gathering over there and Ray was eager to join them, but not before a free tour of a working distillery.

They got out and Farkas conjured a key ring the size of a basketball hoop and festooned with more keys than there were cars and houses on Jura. For decorative purposes, three oak barrels stood in a pyramid next to the entrance. "I thought you didn't lock your doors here," Ray said.

"Aye, I know you're teasing me, Ray, but you understand that our distillery, she's a different story—she must be locked or casks would be drained dry before you could blink."

"By who, Mr. Fuller and those guys? They do seem like troublemakers."

"By me. I can't even count the number of times I've awoken here after one of my new-moon escapades, my hands in the cookie jar, as it were. I cannot always control my own actions, Ray, and that's the sad truth. Besides, seeing as I'm still considered an outsider on Jura, I don't feel quite as obliged as some of the others to obey every little superstition." Farkas found the light switches and revealed a reception area. "Now follow me," he said. "We'll do the short tour now, and I'll show you around the whole works another time."

Rooms were filled with a network of tanks and tubs and tubes: the equipment that produced all that delicious single-malt scotch. The distillery turned out to be a highly technical operation; this was no backyard still, but rather a modern facility that used computers and specialized, carefully calibrated machinery for maximal yield and quality. Farkas led him to a grimy room containing two huge wooden vats suspended up high on a catwalk. Their shoes clanked against the metal steps. The pungent stink reminded Ray of one of those extinct, old-timey bars in Chicago and Ray saw why: the tanks looked like swimming pools full of stale beer.

"Here put these on," Farkas said and handed him a pair of sweaty rubber gloves and an oar from a rowboat. "I use only Scottish barley, though much of it comes in by ship. We let it germinate in one of the buildings out back for two or three weeks until it's ready to get dried in the kiln, which is where it picks up that peat flavor. After that, we grind it to a fine grist that we brew with hot water in the mash tun. What you're seeing here is the fermentation. We take the wort and add the yeast until we have what might in lesser hands form the basis of beer. We have machines to stir it during the wash, these blades that rotate automatically, but I prefer to do it by hand when I can. Watch me now. Skim the paddle across the top of it, like so."

Farkas moved with more precision than his frame and usual level of intoxication led Ray to believe possible. He stretched over the railing and stirred the very top of the broth.

Ray followed his lead, but the sweeping motion was more challenging than it looked. "Is this the wort—is that what you called it?—that gets distilled?"

"Right you are! Now don't chop at it, Ray. Gently now, that's it. Once I have this where it needs to be, it follows through there to the stills." He pointed to the pipes leading through the wall to another room. The door sat beneath the smaller of the two tanks. They climbed back down. A sign affixed to the low catwalk said MIND YOUR HEAD. Good advice.

Ray didn't grasp the nuances of the entire process, but Farkas appeared to be in a rush to get upstairs. He had come fully to life inside the distillery and moved like a man half his age. The whisky-to-be flowed from the vats, through the walls and into the actual stills, eight containers shaped like big butt plugs that stretched to the ceiling. That was what they looked like. More tubes led at right angles from the tops of the stills to some holding tanks in another room.

"When the whisky's good and ready, and not a moment before, I store it in oak casks to put some years on it. And it might just interest you to know that some of those casks come from none other than your America. We buy them from the bourbon manufacturers as a matter of fact, so however much our Gavin wants to cry about outside influences—that's what he calls anything that didn't originate on Jura—the malt he's drinking relies on your people for its flavor. Try to keep up," Farkas said.

Ray followed him downstairs and outside, through a courtyard and to a barn topped with a pagoda-shaped cupola. A bank of clouds approached from the seaside.

"We have one more stop. Once the malt has been casked, we store it in here. Three years is the absolute minimum, and even that is a disgrace. A good whisky doesn't even know its own name before the age of twelve, and that's the problem with that cack you're carrying around in your pocket tonight, I might add. It has no years on it yet. Again, like your America. Now feast your eyes upon this."

He pulled open the doors and Ray beheld the kingdom of heaven. The warehouse contained hundreds of casks of single-malt scotch stacked to the rafters. A row of open-air windows near the top welcomed in the evening mist. "It's beautiful," he said.

"Aye, that it is. We house the whisky here for decades in many cases, and you'll notice that the casks get exposed to the elements, to the rain and the sea air. See those wee little ones? Those are called pins and contain four and a half gallons. The next one up, a firkin, holds twice that. Most of these are barrels, which hold thirty-six gallons of liquid gold. While I'm sad to report that we don't have one on the premises, the biggest cask of all is called a butt and it contains one hundred and eight gallons. The size of the cask and the location, that's how every malt gets its distinct flavors. And from the geographical location of the distillery and the tiniest variations of coastline and altitude too. Is it made inland, as in the Highlands? Or perhaps near the water in a small bight such as we are in Craighouse. Over on Islay, you have Bowmore sheltered in a deep bay, but also Ardbeg or Lagavulin smack on the quay and exposed to the full teeth of the sea. Over there they will rotate their casks for consistency—for uniformity—until the entire bottling tastes the same. Bah! With my malt, I can tell you from appearance how long it has aged and, from the taste, where in my warehouse it slept. So if you ask me if the change in our atmosphere is all bad, if the pollution and the rising temperature of the globe and the deforestation is all bad, I say aye. Aye! Because it means the end not just of this bottle"—he took a small pull from his own flask, closed his eyes—"but the end of an era. I'm a historian, if you will. The bottle of single malt is a time capsule. A record of the natural life of Jura."

"You're making me very thirsty," Ray said.

"To tell you the truth, all this talking has given me quite a thirst too. Now, technically, I'm not supposed to do this, but we have some experimental batches over here. What the marketing people call our boutique barrels. These don't often travel far beyond Craighouse." Farkas extracted the cork from a cask. "Sometimes I'll fill a barrel with madeira or dessert wine or whatever comes to mind, simply to see how the malt takes to the treated wood. That's a fairly common practice these days, but I've had the idea of setting the insides of a cask on fire and aging some malt in the charred remains. Let's see how she looks!" Ray followed him over to another cask. "Here we are," Farkas said. He used a thin hose to extract two drams of black, opaque whisky. "Now that's something! Slàinte!"

"Thank you, cheers!"

The scotch tasted like a forest fire, all smoky and ashy. It made Ray thirsty and quenched the thirst at the same time. It was unique, and kind of gross.

"Not quite ready yet, is it?"

"It's pretty interesting."

"Aye, that it is. We'll try her again another day and see if she behaves a bit better. Now let's get you to the hotel. I imagine you've already missed supper."

"That's all right, I'm not very hungry." Not for Fuller's

stew, anyway. "I really appreciate your showing me around. You're like a mad scientist."

"You're wrong on both counts. I'm neither mad, contrary to what everybody believes, and I'm certainly no scientist, just a humble man charged with recording Jura's natural history one bottle at a time. Now I know what you're thinking, Ray," Farkas said. They stopped at the road to take in the sights. The fog had swallowed the water and was coming for the hotel next. Cars, trucks, motorbikes, and the odd horse or two filled the parking lot. People had gathered together from all over the island to hunt down a wild animal and far more importantly, Ray now surmised, to maintain the vestiges of Jura's traditions. They were here out of a sense of shared responsibility, but also to celebrate themselves. "You're a smart man. A man who can see beyond the trappings of his present circumstances. And that's why I'm so glad you've come to stay with us. You're a man of vision. You're thinking that the natural life of the present is equally worthy of recording, am I right? Certainly it is. Here you go. Slàinte."

He handed Ray his flask one last time. The whisky tasted different yet again, as if Farkas had been secretly switching them. The flavors—licorice, sour cherry, honey—came one after the other and were followed by a burst of laughter and the squawk of bagpipes. The party was in full swing. There were maybe fifty people in all, with more stragglers pulling in every few minutes.

"And here's what I want you to try to understand," Farkas

said. "You have already affected the natural life of Jura, we all have, and I would not want for it to be any other way. Unlike our Gavin here"—Pitcairn had appeared, coughing into a handkerchief, on the hotel's porch—"I recognize that change is unavoidable and I appreciate the likes of you who try to affect things for the better. Even your visit today will have an effect." He took his flask back and drained the final, precious drops.

"I find it tragic," Ray said, "that that scotch is gone now and it'll never exist again."

"Now I'm not prone to excessive philosophizing, not even about such important topics as malt whisky, but that particular batch was made to be drunk and enjoyed, and it was. It's gone, aye, but that's the way of all things. And that's one reason we'll continue to make more this year and next year and the year after that and every year until the seas rise and reclaim our little island. The batch you had a small hand in today will tell some lucky sod in the future a great deal about who we were and where we lived, just like this one has done. Even your three minutes of stirring will make a difference down the road in one bottle or another."

Ray looked around. It was a glorious night: damp and so misty that he couldn't see more than a few feet in front of him. The fog demanded a certain presence of mind, a being here that did not come easily otherwise, like everything that mattered in the entire world was contained in his immediate vicinity. The party was raging, and he couldn't wait to join in.

He had watched enough overblown PBS costume dramas with Helen to expect the full foxhunting circus. Buglers and beagles, tweed waistcoats and whinnying steeds snorting their oat-breath into the mist. The reality wasn't all that far off. Cigarette smoke and the salty stench of whisky hung in the air. A pack of braying dogs was tied up someplace behind the hotel. The assembled men ranged in age from young teenagers to the antiquated ferryman, Singer, and taken together they resembled a good, old-fashioned mob. Many wore kilts in the tartans of their proud, if dwindling, clans. They sang crude songs and told familiar jokes and spat in the dirt. They carried hunting rifles, pitchforks, torches that fought off the encroaching night. Bagpipers wheezed out nationalistic hymns and drunken-sailor ditties. The mist made it difficult to see from one side of the parking lot to the other, but he recognized a few faces from his first night on the island. Was that already three months ago? Even the dour Mr. Harris was sulking around. Pitcairn's phlegmatic chortle rose above the commotion. The periodic discharge of a rifle cracked through the conversations and songs and they silenced the men and hounds alike for an instant, only to have them resume their boasts and oaths and threats and wagers. Bottles of scotch better than what Ray had brought got passed around freely and he availed himself of a swig from each and every last one. A ten-year-old and then another, and another. A sixteen came by—rich caramel and brine and seaweed and cotton candy—and another ten or maybe one he had already sampled. He felt loose, and ready for the evening's spectacle. He was going to shoot a werewolf! Only he hadn't brought a gun; maybe that was okay.

The ferryman ambled over. He brandished a rifle even older than himself. It might as well have been a musket and should have been in a museum.

"Hello, Mr. Singer," Ray said.

"If it isn't our Orwell aficionado!" He was so far along in his booze that he couldn't stand straight. He held the rifle by its iron barrel and leaned on it like a cane.

"Farkas tells me that you knew him?"

"Who's that?" Singer asked. "Farkas?"

"Orwell."

"George Orwell?" He took a long swig from a bottle of whisky and made faces like he was chewing it without teeth. Some of it dribbled down his white-bristled chin and glistened in the lamplight.

"The very same."

"I spoke to him on several occasions, aye." He looked around to be sure no one was eavesdropping and lowered his voice to a whisper. "I can let you in on a little-known fact about our George Orwell."

"What is it?" Ray asked.

"I don't suppose there's any harm in telling you this," Singer said.

"Yes?"

"I mean, the man is dead and gone, as they say, so I don't really see the harm."

"Yes?"

"Enough time has passed and we need to let bygones be bygones."

"Yes? Yes?"

Singer took another long drink. "You will be surprised to learn, young man, that George Orwell was not his real, God given name."

That was it? That was Singer's big secret? "You don't say," he said.

"No, no." Singer looked around again. "His real name—and you should write this down—his real name was Eric Blair. E-R-I-C."

"Eric Blair. Got it. Thank you, Mr. Singer."

"Not at all, not at all." Singer took another gulp and examined the barrel of his gun as if looking through a peephole, and found it clogged with mud. Ray took the opportunity to slip into the hotel. He had important matters to discuss with Molly, as far from her father's earshot as possible. Mrs. Campbell stood waiting for him behind the desk. Damn. "Good evening, Mrs. Campbell," he said. "You're looking well."

"Mr. Welter, some correspondence has arrived for you."

She handed him a small stack—more cards from his mother and something in a green envelope—and he was surprised that they hadn't been torn open and pored over. He shoved them into a pants pocket. "Thank you, Mrs. Campbell. Is Molly here, by any chance?"

"What would you want with her, then?"

"Frankly, I'm not sure how that's any of your concern."

"Being equally frank, Mr. Welter, we can't imagine the sort of sordid business a grown man such as yourself might have with a young girl like Molly."

"Mrs. Campbell, does it please you to single-handedly destroy the Highlanders' otherwise deserved reputation as the most hospitable and friendly people in the world?"

"You leave that girl alone and get out of this hotel this instant."

"Leave her alone?" he asked, walking away. "I've done nothing wrong, you old bat. In fact, where were you when her father was beating her up? You weren't so protective then, were you?"

"Mr. Welter!" she called after him. "Mr. Welter!"

Molly sat perched behind the bar in the lounge, a book open on her lap. "That was awesome," she said. "Mind you, you won't be seeing any more of your mail."

"Doesn't matter. There's no one I want to hear from anyway," he said and then realized that it wasn't entirely true.

"I suppose you're here to murder some animals tonight?"

"Yeah—I mean, no. I'm not even sure there's a wolf, much less a werewolf. It's absurd."

"Of course it's absurd, but if you want to get by on Jura you need to embrace the absurdity, not run from it."

"If Farkas thinks he's a werewolf, and if I simultaneously think I see him turn into one, then he is a werewolf?"

"Exactly," Molly said. "All happenings are in the mind. Whatever happens in all minds, truly happens."

"Clever girl."

"Why *can't* two plus two equal five?"

"Because they just can't."

"You're a lost cause, Ray."

"So how do you explain the dead animals at my door?"

"I can't help you with that one. Some things can't be explained, not with all the logic in the world."

"Maybe you're right. Either way, I have some good news for you." He lowered his voice so the old bat wouldn't hear. "My divorce went through and—"

"Hold on, Ray," Molly said. "Are you asking me to marry you? Because if so, I don't think—"

"No! My wife—my ex-wife—teaches at a very prestigious university in Chicago. It took some finagling, but as part of my divorce settlement I insisted on a full scholarship for you. You will have four years, all expenses paid. Housing, room and board, an allowance for books and living expenses. It's not entir—"

Molly screamed. She held her hands to her face and belted out a scream than would've made Edvard Munch proud. The iron chandelier swayed. The candles flickered. The men outside probably heard her above their gunfire and revelry.

"The offer doesn't include airfare," he said, "but I can try to help you with that. The university has an excellent art program and the best art museum in the nation is a couple of stops away on the L."

Mrs. Campbell rushed in to investigate the noise. In her mind, Ray had probably torn the poor helpless child's skirt off and started raping her behind the bar. She was surprised to see them both clothed and laughing. "You leave that girl alone! What is the meaning of this?"

"I'm going to Chicago!" Molly yelled. She jumped up and down. Her shoes hammered against the floor. The bottles rattled behind her.

"Chicago?" Mrs. Campbell asked. "We'll just see what your father says about this! You are a wicked man, Mr. Welter. Shame on you."

"All the information you'll need is here," he said and handed Molly a large envelope stuffed with paperwork. It also included enough cash for a replacement bicycle. "Now I'm going outside to murder a defenseless animal that both is and isn't there."

"Just one minute, Mr. Welter!"

He didn't stop to discuss it. "Good evening, Mrs. Campbell," he said and tracked his muddy sneakers back across her floor.

She followed behind. "Mr. Welter!" she said.

Ray ignored her until, outside, she pushed past him and found Pitcairn behind the wheel of his flatbed. Farkas stood on the porch taking in the excitement. The caravan had already started to pull away and Pitcairn's truck sat idling, last in line at the hotel entrance. The area on the western side where Loch Tarbert emptied into the Sound of Islay was said to be prime wolf territory. Engines roared. The headlights of the pickup trucks carved at the fog. Innumerable dogs barked and howled like a Greek chorus foretelling some poor sucker's fate. Peat smoke and diesel exhaust fought off the fresh sea air. All the men and boys filled the backs of the trucks to form a drunken parade of the deluded and kick up mud behind them. *There's no fucking wolf*, Ray wanted to holler after them. It wouldn't have done any good. Mrs. Campbell leaned in the open window of Pitcairn's truck. Standing with Farkas on the porch, he couldn't hear them, but it was clear that she was telling him about Molly's scholarship. Pitcairn looked at Ray and leaned on his horn. On her way back inside Mrs. Campbell refused to as much as look at him. His comeuppance had been long, long overdue.

Pitcairn stepped out of the truck with a groan. Sponge and Pete sat fidgeting in the cab like bored children. Pitcairn stretched his shoulders and cracked something in his back. He looked calm, which was unnerving. Outright hostility, even violence, might have been preferable. He had already tried once to kill him. That was no joke—the man was capable of murder. "Care to join us, Farkas?" Pitcairn asked.

Farkas was already smashed out of his gourd. Whisky and drool glistened in his immense beard. He held to the railing of the porch for balance. "Not this time, Gavin," he said.

"How about you, Chappie? You ready?"

"With all due respect," Ray said, "I think I'll stay here with Farkas."

"Respect now, is it? Well there's a lovely fucking change of scenery. Oh no—you're coming with us. I'm not supposing you have a gun, now do you, Chappie?"

"No, unfortunately I don't."

"You're not much of an American, are you? I thought all of you Yanks had guns."

"Here's where I'll say my goodbyes," Farkas said on his way back in to the lounge. "Catch me if you can!"

Farkas clearly didn't want to know about whatever it was Pitcairn had in mind for Ray. He wasn't going to stick his neck out for a foreigner. On Jura, as back in the advertising world, remaining noncommittal on all things was the key to self-preservation. It was a shame, but Ray couldn't count on Farkas's help, not even with someone as dangerous as Pitcairn.

The last of the other trucks rumbled off into the fog. The engine noise tapered to oblivion, leaving a pocket of silence. Behind the hotel, the water slapped against the docks and seawall. A slight wind sounded in the palm trees, the tops of which were rendered invisible by the mist. There were no lights to be seen beyond the hotel grounds. The mainland— and all of civilized, gridlocked Europe—was so close that Ray could feel its magnetism, but with no direct route of escape it seemed so distant. Jura was another planet unto itself. "I have an idea," he said. "I'll stay here at the hotel until you guys are done. At that point we can discuss anything that's on your mind."

"You're full of bad ideas tonight, Chappie. I have half a mind to go over to the rescue and rehoming center and adopt a cute little puppy just so I can name it Welter and have the pleasure of kicking it every night."

"Would you hurry along, eh?" Pete shouted. "They'll have shot that wolf before we've even left the car park."

"You heard what the man said," Pitcairn said. He lifted the front of his soiled soccer sweatshirt to show Ray the wooden handle of a small, antique pistol. "Now be a good lad and get in, Chappie. It wouldn't do to make a scene here."

Pete and Sponge squeezed over to let him in. Sponge, who was pressed against the door, swigged from a bottle of whisky, but Pitcairn let go of the clutch and nearly cost him his front teeth. The bagpipe cassette provoked the same sensation in Ray's skull that a hacksaw might have. They pulled from the relative safety of the parking lot and turned south into the foggy night. The headlights couldn't penetrate more than a few feet in front of the truck, so Pitcairn turned them off. He plunged the truck, at full speed, into total darkness.

"What are you doing, eh?" Pete asked.

"I know this island like the back of my wanking hand."

Ray closed his eyes and sat sandwiched by sweaty, half-drunken Scotsmen in a truck with no lights on. Pitcairn didn't slow down. The cabin of the truck vibrated like a motel room bed. The road turned and climbed and twisted and every so often the tires ran off the road. Pitcairn somehow corrected his course in the dark and only turned the headlights on again in time to swing the wheel onto a trail even worse than the path to Barnhill.

Several pairs of eyes appeared in the headlights, froze for a moment, and then disappeared. The afterimage remained glued onto Ray's vision and imposed itself on everything he looked at. "Where are we going anyway?" he asked.

"Why to the Paps of course," Pitcairn said.

THE TRUCK SLID TO a stop in the cleavage between two of the island's three mountains, a mossy patch of land the locals called the bealach. Three men were playing bagpipes that sounded out of tune even by the lax standards of that instrument's repertoire. A bonfire blazed in the center of the clearing and, yes, several grown men were shimmying around it naked, including Singer, who at his advanced and flaccid age looked like a dancing skeleton celebrating the Day of the Dead. Ray got out of the truck. The whisky had hit him hard, but that didn't deter him from partaking again from every bottle that passed by. The alchemical process that had produced their contents utilized little more than earth and air and water and time. Single-malt scotches, he had come to understand, were as individual as people and, like people, became toxic in large doses.

The rest of the caravan had already arrived and the celebration carried over from the hotel, but the laughter had taken a turn; the men still made jokes, told stories, but the voices were quieter, if only marginally. A subtle seriousness had overtaken the proceedings, maybe a greater sense of purpose. Wagers were made, liters of whisky consumed. The flames curled to the sky as if to chase off the fog and Fuller toiled around it in preparation for a feast. A goat rotated slowly on a spit. At dawn, at the conclusion of the hunt, two cauldrons full of seawater would be set to boil; they awaited the dozens of lobsters, caught nearby, that tangled and jousted in their ice chests. There was fresh cheese and bread and an entire cask of single malt, all of it local. That the food was organic went without saying. Jura had its own ecosystem, its own cycle of consumption and replenishment. Ray thought about what Farkas had said. Had his own presence contributed to the isle's natural life or disrupted it?

Men unpacked rifles from truck-bed lockers and loaded them with lead shot. The younger participants had the responsibility of lighting torches from the bonfire, which they would soon carry off into the shortest night of the year.

Ray watched as Pete took a long, three-Mississippi swallow from his bottle and handed it to Pitcairn, who with noisy deliberation hacked up a butter pat of green phlegm and drooled it into the remaining whisky. It bobbed in the beam of his flashlight like a bloated worm. "I'm supposing the rest of this belongs to me now," he said.

"You're an arsehole," Pete said. He took the bottle from

Pitcairn and, undeterred, drank another long swallow. Sponge looked on in disgust that verged on awed respect and then opened his hunting bag, from which he produced a bottle labeled ISLAY. He peeled off the foil, pulled the cork, and enjoyed a long taste.

Pitcairn climbed onto the bed of his truck. The crowd grew quiet, the bagpipes wheezed their last breaths. Even with everyone's attention, he didn't speak right away. He surveyed the assembled party with approval, then took a drooling gulp from a bottle handed up to him. He lit a cigarette while his congregation awaited his gospel. "I thought I might say a few words," he said, and took another gulp. He swayed on his feet. "The problem we face, gentlemen, is one that is within our power to fix so long as we can come together on a night like this under the moonless sky to fix it."

A few voices spoke out in assent from the crowd.

"I'm talking about an invasive species that has come to savage our lambs in the night and to ruin our very livelihoods and those things most precious to us."

"Aye," a few more men said.

"We're talking not only about this wolf we are going to skin this night"—a cheer went up — "but about the parasites bleeding us dry."

"Aye!" said the crowd.

"I'm talking about the men who come from Glasgow to harvest our peat and sell the very soil out from beneath our fucking feet!"

"Aye!"

"I'm talking about the bloody fucking tourists who leave their bottled water on our beaches and pollute our seas."

"Aye!"

As the token American, Ray could see where things were headed and slinked out of Pitcairn's line of vision.

"Here we go," Farkas whispered. He had appeared out of the fog.

"I didn't think you'd be here," Ray said.

"I'm not."

"I'm talking about the scholars," Pitcairn continued. "The intellectuals like old Eric Blair who deem fit to grace us with their presence and treat our Jura like their own private museum, who turn our proud heritage and our way of life into some kind of tourist attraction. Have they forgotten that we actually live here?"

"Yeah!" Ray shouted from the back of the crowd. He was enjoying himself despite the hatemongering now directed fully at him. "Those fucking intellectuals!" he yelled. "Let's string 'em up!"

Laughter rippled through the men. "Good on you," someone said behind him. Pitcairn tried to continue, but his audience had turned—not against him necessarily, but the mood had shifted with the sea breeze. "The danger is worse than you think," he warned them all, but a dozen other conversations had begun. More wagers got placed. People were eager to get the hunt started and then, no doubt, climb into their warm beds. "You ungrateful bastards will wish you listened to me one day."

"Not today!" someone answered, inciting a good deal of amusement. It sounded a bit like Fuller, but who could tell?

"Shut your gobs one more minute, you fuckers," he shouted, but it was too late. The bagpipes squawked back to life. Pitcairn stumbled while climbing back down and landed in a heap on the ground. A hunting dog licked at the whisky on his lips and it yelped when he punched it in the face.

The men congealed into parties of five or six. Each group had one torchbearer, who was armed with either a flashlight or a real fiery torch and who was also responsible for carrying the bottles of whisky. Every man kept his voice low now. They peeled off into the darkness. Some headed straight up the inclines of the Paps, others toward the shore or along some unseen paths leading into the fog that seemed to extinguish the torches like so many birthday candles. Only a few people remained. Fuller tended the fire in preparation for what looked like a lavish feast.

"You're coming with me, Chappie," Pitcairn said. He stood at a trailhead that Ray hadn't noticed and shined a flashlight in his eyes. Ray squinted in time to see Sponge and Pete go on ahead and get swallowed whole by the encroaching fog.

"I think I'll stay here and help Mr. Fuller," Ray said.

"Oh so you're now a gourmet chef, are you? I think Mr. Fuller can manage without the benefit of your expertise."

"But . . ."

"You go ahead, Mr. Welter," Fuller said. "I can take care of this. One word of advice: it's easy to get lost on the moors at midday, not to mention on a night such as this one. Keep an eye on where you're going."

"He's right, Chappie. We wouldn't want you wandering off, now would we?"

"I don't have a flashlight."

"I don't have a flashlight."

There was no point in arguing. Resistance was futile. Anyway, Pitcairn wouldn't dare hurt him, not with Sponge and Pete as witnesses.

"Not to worry. You just stay close to Mr. Pitcairn," Fuller said. "Bring us back some fresh meat to add to our feast."

"You heard the man, Chappie, you stay close." Pitcairn turned and went off into the night. He took four paces before his flashlight blinked out of view.

Ray followed after him, but the bonfire behind him soon evaporated and the darkness hit his body like a sudden fever. He couldn't see a goddamn thing. "Pitcairn?" No answer. The soles of his sneakers sucked at the muddy ground, and just like that he was lost. Nothing existed except nothingness itself. The entire universe consisted of the absence of light. Panic swelled in Ray's windpipe like a chunk of unchewed beef. Sweat tickled him from beneath his beard. The fog seemed to distort the sounds of the wind in the bushes. Somewhere there were waves lapping against the stony shore, but he couldn't tell which direction they came from. He stumbled over unseen rocks and roots and divots, but walked in what he hoped was a straight line. Then he felt the terrain change and found himself on an incline. A hill, maybe the base of one of the Paps. If the peak jutted above the fog, maybe he could gain his bearings from there. Even if the lights in Craighouse and at the ferry port and over on Islay only illuminated small patches of fog, that would be enough to figure out which direction the hotel was in.

The mountain was too steep to climb straight up, so he circled it in progressively higher rings the way the groove of a record album eventually terminates in the middle. His sneakers were worse than useless and his intense intoxica tion didn't help. The flask was empty. His ankles twisted back and forth. His progress—if he was making progress at all—was slow and laborious. His eyes had not adjusted to the light because there was so little light for his eyes to adjust to. The worst part was that Pitcairn had done this to him. Getting him lost out here, that had been totally intentional. It had to be. That asshole purposely led him out here into the black night with the purpose of getting him lost. That had been his agenda all along.

Ray climbed, blind, for twenty minutes, maybe more, and the higher he went the better he came to appreciate the reality of his circumstances. The seas would eventually rise again, as Farkas said, and that was thanks in some part to global warming and the thousands of SUVs he had unleashed. Ray had come to Jura in order to escape the consequences of his actions, but that was impossible. For the time being, however, here he was on one of the Paps of Jura, high above the cares of the mundane and overcrowded world.

He had to be nearing the top and so he hiked faster, his treads skidding on the rock surfaces, until a horrible sound reached his ears. It was a disgusting, retching howl that came from above him and echoed between the Paps then returned to its maker. There was something out here with him. The noise came again, closer, but this time it sounded like someone coughing up the boozy contents of his stomach. A halo of light bobbing in the fog guided Ray to the peak of the mountain, where he was actually glad to see Pitcairn. "I want you to take a deep breath, Chappie," he said, wiping his mouth on his sleeve.

Ray did so. He stopped and tasted the sea on his tongue. The Scottish night felt so clean, so good and pure; it was unpolluted and sweet in his lungs. "Mr. Pitcairn, I'm so—"

"What you have a hold of there is fresh air. Something you won't bloody well find in your Chicago." He pronounced it *She-cah-go*. "Do you know why I wanted you to come up here with me tonight?"

"To shoot me?"

"That's a very good guess, but I haven't decided yet if I'm going to shoot you or not. I wanted you to come with me so that you might understand why it is that I don't want you filling my Molly's head with ideas."

"If you ask me, her head's already full of ideas," Ray said. His heartbeat made its presence felt now in his neck. "Nothing you or I do is going to change that."

"That's what I'm talking about, Chappie." Pitcairn spoke quietly. A bird *peep-peeped* at them from some nearby overgrowth. "I'm not asking you. No one is asking you any such fucking thing. No one has come pleading for your almighty opinion. Understand that. Right now, we are standing on Beinn a' Chaolais. While you can't see her at the moment you can believe me when I tell you that to our left is Beinn an Òir and on her other side is Beinn Shiantaidh."

The three Paps. Translated from the Gaelic, they were called Mountain of the Kyle and Mountain of Gold. The easternmost one—hidden behind Beinn an Òir—was Holy Mountain. On a clear day they could be seen in all their glory from as far away as Northern Ireland.

The buzz Ray had going alleviated most of the pain in his feet and his fear of Pitcairn. He felt at home in the natural splendor of the Inner Hebrides. The wind pockmarked the cloudbank and exposed a pair of stars above. The swatches of night sky were remembered and forgotten like good intentions.

"I guess you heard about Molly's scholarship?" Ray asked.

"And what scholarship is that, Chappie?"

"I know that Mrs. Campbell told you about it."

"Told me what, then?"

"That's how you want to do this? Fine. As part of my divorce settlement I got—at tremendous personal expense, I might add—a full-paid scholarship for Molly to attend a university back in Chicago. I'm talking about a world-class education for her, and it's absolutely free."

Pitcairn started walking again, following the crest of the mountain, and this time Ray stayed close to the light. It would be easy—way too easy—to get lost again. "I'll need you to keep your voice down, Chappie," he whispered, "if we're planning to kill this wolf."

"There's no goddamn wolf, Gavin. You know that. Why the charade?"

"I said to keep your fucking voice down. If there's no wolf, what's slaughtering our sheep? I know what you're thinking here, Chappie. Maybe in the vast recesses of that sophisticated brain of yours you really do believe that you, above everybody else on God's green earth, know what's best for us bampots out here on Jura. Free education? There's a free education from Beinn a' Chaolais. Under the stars. Even if you can't see them, Chappie, they're still twinkling all the same. I also suppose it's equally possible that you think you're helping Molly by getting away from her big, bad da. For all your books and your advertising awards and your prissy clothing you don't understand the first thing about what this world is really like."

"Yes, but—"

Pitcairn stopped again and turned to face him. He had in his hand the old-fashioned six-shooter. Maybe it was loaded with silver bullets. "Now just keep your gob shut for once in your entire bloody life. Do you smell that, Chappie? That's the sea air in your lungs, not smog or fast food grease or petrol exhaust from all your sport utility vehicles. What makes you believe for one instant that I would allow you or any man to deprive Molly of this? I would rather be dead than live in Chicago, because they're pretty much the same thing. Do you even know how it feels to be alive?"

"Don't you think that it's up to her? I understand that—"

"Here's what it feels like," Pitcairn said.

The loud crack hit Ray's ears first, echoed four or five times off the Paps, and then came back to rest in his stomach. He had been shot.

The pain arrived as a new sensation. It wasn't like anything. Not the sharp sting of an insect or like being hit with a hammer. It didn't feel like anything except what it felt like to get shot. He knew now. It fucking hurt. His own fluids glued his clothing to his body. The wound wasn't a small toothless mouth or a reproduction of *A Sunday on La Grande Jatte* done the size of an Indian Head nickel; it was a bullet hole in his stomach. The metaphors arrived slowly. His belly now contained a tiny baby of lead who sucked the nutrients from his body. Then it was a fisherman's sinker plugging a hole in the ocean. A .44-inch paperclip fastening his mortality to his immortality.

He had been shot. Pitcairn had shot him. The smoke danced from the barrel of the pistol and was lost amid the fog. The pain was mesmerizing. Ray fell to the ground and remained there. Pitcairn looked down at him and spat into the cold heather in which Ray now wanted to sleep. Just a short nap. The ground was comfy. The fog blanketed him.

Pitcairn's boots grew smaller, quieter. Ray closed his eyes.

The earth itself grabbed wetly at his clothes; it found his skin, pulled him closer, held him tight. *Shhhhhh*, the wind said. Every so often a gust blew away some of the fog and the stars would poke through the shifting windows of starry sky. All the tensions and tightnesses inside him gave way and his body deflated even further to the ground.

Another breeze brought with it a sharp odor of putrefaction, something animalic and rotten.

A live wolf stood not three feet away. It smelled of iron, of decaying earth. Its luxurious coat glimmered like polished silver even in the little light afforded by the stars. The creature looked him in the eye and growled ever so quietly, a low sonic rumble Ray felt in his chest. His body purred along involuntarily with the wolf's breath. He felt the weight of the creature's heartbeat, heard the blood sluicing through its taut musculature. He became aware of his own pulse beating at the base of his neck, and the enormous wolf sensed his quickened pulse too; it wanted to find the source of Ray's remaining warmth with its teeth, to drill its hungry muzzle into the too-small bullet hole.

"It hurts," he told the wolf. He showed it the blood on his sweater. "Do you see what happened to me?"

The wolf moved a step closer. Ray read its yellow eyes. The growl grew louder, more specific to him and his last moments on earth. Louder than the agony in his belly. The wolf understood him; it was here to lift him from his pain.

With this creature breathing its moist breath onto his face, the only choice now was between acceptance and resistance. That had been his only choice all along. All of his previous ideals about freedom and independent thought, all the marketing strategies in the world, every advertising campaign, those were meaningless in the face of a lunatic with a gun or a carnivorous monster. His life all along had followed a circumambulating path between free will and fate, but had always returned to the fate side.

Ray chose acceptance: there would be no more fighting it. No more challenging the collective wisdom of his grand and enlightened civilization. He would neither fight any longer nor flee. Not to the most distant corner of the most remote island on the planet or into the darkest recesses of his own miserable and troubled mind. He would accept with all his heart what the wolf had come to tell him; he would take responsibility only for those things within his power to control. The plundering of the rain forests was not his sole doing. Neither was the destruction of the last orangutan's native habitat or the mercurial toxicity of seafood or the fact that Moby-Dick could no longer communicate with other whales over long distances because of the human race's vehicular noise. Even the immense pollution caused by fossil fuels—that wasn't entirely his fault. "Do you know what I saw today?" Ray asked the wolf.

A flicker passed through the creature's eyes, and it flinched an instant before the beam of a flashlight captured it.

"Everything I looked at," he said.

The blast from a shotgun kicked up the dirt next to him and lodged a few hot pellets in his skin. The wolf, unharmed, was gone as if it had never been there.

The rest of the night was a blur. He remembered lying next to the bonfire in the clearing between the Paps. He watched Fuller tap a barrel of whisky and rub some of it on the wound in his side. That pain was even worse than the initial gunshot. He seemed to remember Sponge and Pete carrying him from under his shoulders across the lobby of the hotel, his feet dragging across the floor, where thanks to Mrs. Campbell's bitterness he went the entire night without food or water or even clean bandages.

A DOCTOR CAME OVER on the first ferry of the morning and tended to Ray's wounds, which were neither superficial nor life threatening. The prognosis was better than the pain led him to believe. The doctor, out in the hallway, gave Mrs. Campbell the tongue-lashing of her long and nosy life. "Is this how you treat your guests on Jura?" she asked. "You should be ashamed of yourself!"

Ray restrained his laughter, but only because it hurt so goddamn much. The bickering was interrupted by the sound of someone coming up the stairs whistling. His next visitor was Mrs. Bennett, who had very thoughtfully brought him some expensive supplies from The Stores. "How are you feeling, Mr. Welter?"

"Like hell."

"Well that'th to be expected—you *have* been thot. I've brought you thome thingth." The box she carried contained bandages, ointment, cotton balls, medical tape. Everything he would require to keep the gunshot clean. "When you're feeling up to it, I'd like to talk to you about your planth for Barnhill."

"My plans for Barnhill?"

"Yeth. Our letting agenthy hath a young couple in London who ith quite eager to athume the leathe on the houthe."

"You're kicking me out?"

"Oh heaventh no, Mr. Welter. We had jutht thought that you would be leaving, given your condition. They are offering to pay conthiderably more each month than yourself, tho I'm confident we could work out a mutually beneficial arrangement. There are many other beautiful and more convenient hometh available should you with to thtay on Jura."

"I'll give it some thought, Mrs. Bennett. Thank you for the bandageth . . . I mean, bandages."

He got out of bed. Every step hurt. The envelopes and pewter flask weighted down his pants. He had forgotten about that. In the movies, a man's flask was supposed to deflect the bullet and save him from this kind of agony. Reality was infinitely more subtle, and more painful.

Still in his bloody clothes, he made it downstairs with Mrs. Bennett's help and without running into Mrs. Campbell.

"Pleathe think about what I've thaid, Mr. Welter."

"I will, thank you. I'll drop by for some boots as soon as I'm feeling better."

Ray sat on the porch of the hotel, unsure of his next move, until Farkas pulled up. He looked like he hadn't slept. There were sticks and twigs in his hair and beard, mud on his nose. "As I understand it," he said, "you're lucky to be alive."

"What's so lucky about attempted homicide?"

"There is the attempted part."

"Pitcairn tried to kill me," Ray said. He had to bend over to climb into the car and pain filled his lungs. "He should be in jail."

"He says it was an accident. And if he did go to jail, who would look after Molly? You?"

"What are you trying to say?"

"That you and I both know that no one here—and I mean no one—will take the word of a stranger over Gavin's, even though we know you're right."

The surface of the road jostled the tiny car, sending pain squirting through his entire system until it settled into one all-encompassing ache that stretched from his groin to his teeth. "That doesn't bother you?"

"A lot of things bother me, Ray. But that is simply how it is here."

"We're talking about attempted murder."

"You have to let it go, as there are bigger and more impor-tant issues at stake."

"More important than my death?"

"I've come to a bit of an insight, if you will. Gavin believes he's the only one who understands how to maintain our traditional ways, but he may be trying to preserve something that never existed. The best bottle of malt ever produced is worthless if it stays in the bottle. And I've spent too many years trying to be accepted as something I already am. I know what you've done for Molly, and I want to help. I told her I would smuggle her off the island and help her get to Chicago."

"Really? What if Pitcairn finds out?"

"In that event, he will most certainly have another attempted homicide under his belt. And even if he lacks the wisdom to understand as much, having Molly get an education is what's best for her and what's best for this island in the long run. The big picture here is the only picture worth attending to. I'm a historian, I'll have you remember. That girl doesn't belong here right now any more than you do. You're not cut out for life on Jura—this isn't exactly a theme park."

"So I've learned," he said. "What about you—do you belong here?"

"Aye, of course I do, even if not everybody appreciates that fact just yet. And if it's my lot to be treated as an outsider on the only home I've ever known, so be it. And speaking of home—Mrs. Bennett tells me that a young couple keeps ringing up from London hoping to hire Barnhill."

"She told me the same thing just now. It sounds like she wants to get rid of me."

"No, we hate Londoners as much as Americans, but it does sound like they'd be willing to take over the lease. They're apparently very keen on it. You might even make a profit on the deal."

"Is that what you think this is about—making a profit?"

"Not really, that's just something one says to Americans. She also sent along some wellies. They're in the back. You can pay her whenever it's convenient. Here we are."

Farkas stopped at the end of the road. Ray climbed out and leaned on the open door to collect his strength for the walk ahead of him. "I appreciate your advice, Farkas. You're right. Maybe it is time to go home."

"I brought you a little get-well gift," he said. He reached into a bag on the seat behind him and produced a bottle. The handwritten label said 1984.

"1984?" he asked.

"That's when it was distilled. It's an extremely rare whisky. I put a small batch aside because of that year's significance to our merry little island. May it treat you well."

"I don't know what to say."

"How about, slàinte?"

"Slàinte, Farkas."

"You get yourself better now. I'll stop by in a few days, see how you're holding up."

The little car puttered away, back toward Ardlussa and Craighouse. Ray fingered the shape of the bandages under his clothes, the strips of cotton and medical tape holding his insides inside. It hurt so much. If he opened the bottle and drank a gulp, would whisky trickle out his wound and further stain his sweater? For the first time in months, years maybe, he had no desire for a drink.

The hike homeward took forever and each step hurt more than the previous. He clutched the bottle of scotch and his new boots—they looked comfy and dry, but he couldn't bend over to put them on. The sky blazed in a spectrum of blues and watched over its own reflection in the sound. By the time he arrived at the crest and Barnhill came into view, it had ceased to be George Orwell's house and had become his own. He had never felt more up to the challenge of being himself.

He was tempted to take a long nap, but lying down and getting up again would be way too painful. He made it to the kitchen for a glass of water and found a sunny spot in the sitting room to read his mail. With some reluctance he opened the strangely shaped envelope made of green paper reminiscent of the papyrus an intern once brought him from Egypt. The return address was printed with soy ink in a curling font designed to appear earthy and earnest and it came from an organization called the Ethos Co-Op of Chicago, Illinois. Before he opened it he knew that it contained a job offer from Bud.

He had not, however, expected the check made out in his name for $50,000.

Bud's letter began "Dear Raytard" and detailed how his former friend had been so inspired by Ray's bold decision to move to Scotland that he had arrived at an epiphany concerning the inherent evil of the business model at Logos. Bud had quit his job and opened his own agency, one organized around the principles of ethical responsibility and environmental awareness. Ethos Co-Op dedicated itself to working for progressive companies that focused on issues of local and global sustainability. He wanted Ray to sign on as executive vice president.

The case for returning to Chicago had become more persuasive, though it didn't pass his notice that the word "nonprofit" was nowhere to be found in the letter.

"I traded in my SUV," Bud had written. "Can you picture me driving a hybrid! Reuse recycle and all that shit. Please accept this offer. Ethos needs you."

Ray sipped from his glass and remembered that it contained only water. The scotch had been such a constant in his life that it felt odd to drink anything else. He tucked Bud's letter back into its envelope and placed it on the mantel instead of in the pile of kindling. There was another greeting card from his mother. The airmail stamp had been cancelled with a brown splotch of his own blood.

He spent the day drinking tea, of all things, and rereading the end of *Nineteen Eighty-Four*. Something felt different about the text this time. Something was different. It seemed too convenient to attribute the change to his near-death experience, but it was clear now that he had been so wrong about that book. He saw it now. The appendix to *Nineteen Eighty-Four*, the infamous and thorny essay "The Principles of

Newspeak," was in past tense. That meant it was set after the demise of the entire Oceania empire. The appendix hinted at a world after Big Brother.

Orwell was an optimist after all.

Flora was right.

The end of *Nineteen Eighty-Four* suggested that all the degraded conditions and noise pollution and invasions of privacy people put up with every single day—it could all eventually end. Even after the builders whitewashed over Flora's graffiti, her message would remain there, hidden yet waiting to get read again some distant day after the current and all-too-real version of Big Brother disappeared.

He put Orwell down and reread the letter from Bud. The physical sensation of holding the check in his hand was not enough to convince Ray of its existence. He stayed up half the night considering his options.

When Molly showed up a few days later, his belongings were packed and Barnhill's floors mopped clean. She had carried a picnic basket on her new bike, freshly arrived from a mail-order company in Oban, and let herself in without knocking. Ray was fully clothed this time. He sat in the kitchen sipping a cup of black tea.

"What happened to your face?"

He was clean-shaven, with a constellation of bloody toilet paper pieces orbiting his chin. His skin felt raw and taut. Exposed. "Your father is right about at least one thing," he said. "You really are a little bitch."

"I see now why he shot you. Anyway, I heard you were leaving."

She knew where he was going. He hadn't told anyone yet.

"Who else knows?"

"Everybody. Mind you, it wasn't that difficult to figure out."

"It's funny how an attempted homicide can make you rethink your life."

"Aren't we being a bit melodramatic today?"

"Am I the only one who thinks getting shot is kind of a big deal?"

"I heard that the bullet only grazed you."

"It was worse than that. Anyway, it's more the intent that bothers me."

Molly sat and helped herself to his plate of food. "How are you feeling otherwise?"

"The fever's gone. But look." He held his arm out and the coffee cup rattled in its saucer. "I have the shakes. It won't stop."

"Too much whisky last night?"

"Not enough. I haven't had a drop since I got home. I've been shaking the entire time."

"I hope you're up for a walk. I've packed a picnic."

"No way. I'm going to catch the ferry tomorrow and need to get some rest."

"You are not going to spend your last day on Jura moping around this dreary house. There's one more place I want you to see."

"What is it?"

"I said I want you to see it, not hear about it. Jesus." She ran upstairs to check on her easels and collect the few clothes she had left behind, which she carried back down in a bundle and stacked in the sitting room. "It appears that something is missing."

"I should've asked. Is that going to be a problem?"

"Pack your raincoat and a blanket so we can sit without being eaten alive."

Another unidentifiable dead animal lay prostrate on the steps. It was enormous—the size of a deer. They stepped over it. The sky was bright and the air sharp in his lungs. A bank of clouds in the distance promised a shower. The two of them walked westward or maybe northwestward at half their usual pace in deference to his wound. It felt more like a leisurely stroll than their typical forced march. The clouds moved in and an advance party of raindrops persuaded them to put their coats on and quicken the pace. It fell in sheets by the time they got to the cliff that overlooked the water and the island of Colonsay. "We never get to see the sunset from here," Molly said with some disappointment. The storm sat swollen in the sky between them and the sun. "Mind you, I have another idea. Follow me," she yelled over the sound of the rain and the surf.

Molly found a switchbacking path that led down the cliff and to the beach below. The descent was treacherous with mud and slick rocks. She moved as gracefully as a mountain lion and waited for him at the bottom, then took his hand and led him on farther. A lamb had spilled from the cliff and lay mangled on the ground, where it fed a murder undaunted by their presence. A crow popped out one of the animal's white eyes and flew off pursued by his friends.

"Here we are," Molly said. She pointed to the opening of a cave and ran inside. He shuffled after her. The cave smelled of rain and freshly mown hay. Spray-painted graffiti covered the walls and the small fire pit contained some charred beer cans. Molly pulled the blanket from his pack and spread it on the ground at the opening, just beyond the range of the dripping water. He sat with some difficulty. Molly curled up next to him for warmth and pulled one end of the blanket over the two of them.

Even with the ache in his side, Ray felt satisfied now: neither sad to leave Jura nor eager to return to Illinois. He enjoyed the quiet moment in Molly's company and looked forward with equal parts anticipation and dread to whatever his life would present him with next. "It has occurred to me," he said, "that I no longer have an email address or even a phone number, but once I get settled I'll send you my contact info. I can look around for apartments, unless you want to live in the campus housing, which I don't recommend. You're going to love Chicago. I mean, it'll be a little overwhelming at first, but you'll—"

"I'm not going."

"—find that. What?"

"Don't be mad."

"What do you mean you're not going?"

"I've decided to stay on Jura."

"Because of your father? You can't listen to him! You need to decide for yourself."

"Aye, he was against it, but this is my decision and mine only."

"What are you going to do? Spend the rest of your life here?" He didn't like the tone of his voice but didn't know how to modulate it without sounding like even more of an asshole.

"Maybe I will, mind you. This is my home after all. I want to be a painter . . . no, I'm already a painter. No fancy university can make me get better at my art the way the sunlight and the sounds and the Paps will. I appreciate everything, Ray, I really do! But I belong here, at least for now."

Ray felt like he had been shot all over again. Pitcairn had brainwashed this poor girl. There was no other explanation. The scholarship had cost him a fortune in the divorce settlement. Didn't she understand the opportunity she was throwing away? "Don't you understand the opportunity you're throwing away?"

"I think I do. I'll always be grateful to you, but there's an opportunity here too." The rain formed a wall in the mouth of the cave, but it appeared to be letting up. "To be honest, I'm a bit tired of every man I know telling me what I should be doing with my life."

He closed his eyes and inhaled the musk of the cave and the sweat of Molly's hair. Here he was, even further off the grid than ever before and outside of time, returned for a moment to a state of bucolic perfection. The rain slowed to a steady drip. Molly exhaled a wheezy snore. He slid her hair off her face and tucked the blanket under her chin. "I'm sorry," he said. "You're absolutely right."

It was dark when they awoke. Neither of them had moved. "Oh hell," she said. "I need to get home. My dad's going to kill me."

"You and me both."

Ray stood and the soreness in his back and neck obscured the pain in his side. He helped Molly up. She kept the blanket wrapped around herself.

"I'll come visit you in Chicago," she said.

"I'd like that. I'll need to find a place to live first, though. Speaking of which, my lease of Barnhill isn't up for a few more months. If you have any more trouble at home you're welcome to stay there."

"What about the people from London?"

"If they offer you enough money for the place, take it."

"I may just do that, thank you. It looks like I need some new art supplies."

"Yeah, about that."

Back at Barnhill, he had removed her self-portrait from the bedroom wall and, without asking, rolled it up and packed it with his things to bring to Chicago. It remained unfinished—she never got around to painting her hands or feet.

"I would've given it to you if you'd asked, you know. I do want you to have it."

"Thank you—that means a lot to me. You can finish painting it when you come visit."

"It is finished, Ray, or at least as finished as I want it to be. Portraits are unlucky here. They say that the woman who gets her portrait painted will never enjoy a day of health ever again."

"Do you believe that?"

"It doesn't matter what I believe. I'm glad that at least my image, if nothing else, will get off of Jura. Now I really have to get home. You can find your own way back. Leave my bike in the garage. I'll get it another time. Look!"

A falling star dripped into view, a hunk of rock that had come too close and got sucked into the earth's atmosphere to die a fiery death. They watched it burn with its own innate sense of purpose, but it didn't flicker out. It kept moving, steadily, perhaps in too straight of a line.

"They're watching us," Molly said.

"Who?"

"That's a satellite."

She was right—the flight path was too perfect to be natural. Only the manmade achieved such pristine linearity. Ray's precise location at that moment, and at every other moment of his gleefully inconsequential life, could be found and plotted on some celestial map of the cosmos. That had always been true. There had only been the grid the entire time.

"I need to go," he told her. "Goodbye, Molly."

She hugged him and headed in the opposite direction, back to her father.

The next day, he awoke with the dawn and set out for a final errand. All of his affairs were in order except for one thing. Wind stirred in the trees. The sheep *bah bah*-ed at him with contentment, their bells tickling his ears. He smiled into the morning sunlight, and it smiled back at him. His new boots made all the difference in the world, and he regretted not buying them sooner. They were sure to keep his feet dry during even Chicago's slushiest winter days. He didn't look forward to those, but he also did. Some wool socks would be essential. Maybe he could score some from a local spinster before he left.

Smoke rose from Miriam's chimney, so he knocked. "Miriam?" he called. No answer. He knocked again. "Miriam, it's Ray." Her dog growled at him from her new prison of barbed wire. It looked like she had grown even fatter. A curtain fluttered open at the next house over, where Mr. Harris's truck was parked. Ray understood his desire to be left alone and had once shared it, but he gave Mr. Harris a regal wave all the same and the curtains shot closed with grumpy finality. Some people really did want to be by themselves.

Miriam opened the door a crack and blocked Ray's view of

the interior. Her face was covered in sweat, her hair matted to her forehead. "Hello, Ray, this is quite a surprise."

"Did I catch you at a bad time?"

"No, I'm just dismembering some children so they'll fit into my cauldron."

"I'd be glad to help."

"With all this proper nourishment these days, these vitamins and whatnot, their little bones aren't as quite brittle as they used to be." She smiled and wiped at her forehead with a paper napkin. A loud scraping noise came from the direction of the kitchen. "If I might have a moment to straighten up I would be glad to offer you a scone."

"No, no, that's not necessary—thank you. I just wanted to say goodbye."

"Aye, I understand you're taking your leave, and I hope you didn't find we Diurachs too unaccommodating."

"Well I did get shot and thrown into a whirlpool."

"Aye, I can see how that might be frustrating. Speaking of which, before you go, do stop at the strand facing the Corryvreckan."

"I know it all too well. In fact, I'm on my way there now."

"Good, good. Some people will tell you that if you take a stone from that particular strand and bring it home with you, it means that you will come back to Jura one day."

"I'll do that. Thank you, Miriam."

"God bless you, Ray," she said and shut the door. She appeared to be in some hurry.

"Bye," he said and there was so much more he wanted to say. He continued on to the island's northern tip, where he had a date with a whirlpool.

On days like this one, even with the lingering discomfort, out in the sun on the planet's last unspoiled corner, the amount left to learn felt more like a privilege than a chore. Jura still contained so many things beyond his experience or understanding—but so did Chicago.

The boat Pitcairn had commandeered still bobbed next to the creaking dock. Ray went down to the shore and chose a flat, grey stone to bring home then sat at the end of the pier with his feet dangling over the water. The Corryvreckan gurgled her farewells in the distance.

He pulled the first edition of *Nineteen Eighty-Four* from his pocket and tore out the first page, crumpled it up, and tossed it like a basketball free throw into the water. He had done the same thing in Chicago with his cell phone. It felt even better this time. Perhaps there was a trend in his behavior. The paper sat for a moment on the surface as if surprised to find itself getting wet, then caught a prosperous current and moved slowly away from the shore. With calm and joyous deliberation, Ray ripped all the other pages out, one after the other, for what had to be an hour or maybe two or three. He watched each page of the appendix float on the surface and drift, ever so slowly, in single file, toward the whirlpool: a fleet of rudderless paper boats carrying the sum of everything he had learned and wished to forget.

. . .

THE BELLS TIED TO the doorknob jingled, and Bud walked in. It had only been a matter of time. Ray muted the TV on the wall behind the counter. The White Sox were playing the Tigers. The game had gone on for hours. The Sox had been his father's favorite team and Ray was praying for them to win. "Hello, Bud," he said.

"The fuck are you doing, Ray?"

"What does it look like? I'm the proud owner of a dry-cleaning business. How did you find me?"

"I knew you were back in town when that check cleared. Then I saw your ads on TV. Fifty thousand dollars, Ray."

"Yeah, thanks for that. It was the only way I could get the mortgage on this place. Do you like what I've done with it?"

He hadn't changed all that much other than upgrading the television and having new signs and plastic sacks made. A photo of a young Mrs. Kletzski hung next to the board listing all the prices. The bells tied to the door were new—they had been liberated from the necks of Barnhill's ovine population.

"That check was an advance against your salary at Ethos. It wasn't your money yet."

"That's strange. It had my name on it. I assumed it was a bonus for the millions of dollars Logos made from my Oil Hogg campaign."

"You knew perfectly well what that money was for."

"I wasn't trying to steal your money. You're now a twenty-five percent owner of Welter's Warsh House. I have the paperwork around here somewhere. Our accountant says we may not see a profit for five or ten years. Dry cleaning just isn't as popular as it once was. People are apparently content these days to throw away their clothes when they get dirty. I'm bringing in just enough business to pay the bills and get those TV spots made. Catchy, aren't they? The apartment upstairs is mine, though. I'll show you around sometime."

"I don't care about the money, Ray. My problem is with friends quitting on me. You left me hanging."

"I left you hanging? Tell me this—did you fuck Flora?"

"Is that what this is about? It wasn't for a lack of trying. She just wasn't interested."

"Hard to believe."

"She said to tell you that she plans to stay in South America more or less forever, but if something changes she'll look you up. You're right, though, that I would not have thought twice about selling you down the river just for the chance to sniff her panties."

"There are plenty here in the back if that's what you're into."

"Dry cleaning? You can't even keep your own clothes clean."

"It's tough to explain, but this is exactly what I want. Real, honest work. These clothes are either clean or they're dirty. There's no middle ground, no ambiguity."

"The fuck happened to you over there?"

"Among other things, I got shot."

"Did you deserve it?"

"No! I don't know. Maybe."

"What the fuck, Ray?"

"I need to finish up here. Come back at seven when I close, and we'll talk then. I have a bottle of scotch I'd like you to try."

"Is it worth fifty thousand dollars?"

"No, but it's a very special single malt distilled in 1984. Even you will be impressed."

"We'll start with that and then hit the town. We'll go see Miss Ukraine. Oh, wait . . . let me guess. You've quit drinking too."

"No, I've definitely dialed it back a bit, but I'd love to go get shitfaced. In fact, that would do me a world of good."

"That's a relief. On the way, we should visit Lily at McCrotchety's. She's been asking about you."

"Sounds perfect," Ray said. The cleanup hitter for the Sox struck out with men on base, sending the game into extra innings. "Damn. Meet me later and we'll talk."

"You're a strange man, Ray-son d'être," Bud said. "Now are you going to clean this for me or what?" He handed Ray his overcoat, which felt soft and outrageously expensive. The inner pocket had a stain that looked like the result of an unsecured whisky flask.

"I'm not responsible for garments left over six weeks," Ray said.

The bells rang again when Bud pulled the door closed

behind him. He got erased by the crowds of shoppers on the sidewalk, by the nannies and beat cops and the homeless men whistling happy songs through missing teeth. Summer sent its final breath of old newspapers and fast food bags flying past the windows. A cold, lake-effected winter was on its way, and then spring. Ray un-muted the ballgame, which was still away at a commercial. One of the teams would eventually win and the other would lose, even if it took all night. He busied himself pressing strangers' clothes and waiting for the jingle of his next customer.

055828108

The Isles of
ILLAY JURA &c
being Part of
ARGILE SHIRE
By T. Kitchin

4°

40′

20′

English Miles

2 4 6 8 10 12 14

.56

40′

Don hyrtac

4°

Ron

4°

40′